Totally Bound Publishing books by Deana Birch and Amelia Foster

Single Books
Luca's Lessons

Totally Bound Publishing books by Deana Birch

Single Books
Love Repaired

I0680750

LUCA'S LESSONS

DEANA BIRCH & AMELIA FOSTER

Luca's Lessons
ISBN # 978-1-83943-853-0
©Copyright Deana Birch and Amelia Foster 2019
Cover Art by Erin Dameron-Hill ©Copyright June 2019
Interior text design by Claire Siemaszkiewicz
Totally Bound Publishing

LUCA'S LESSONS

Dedication

For Meka, our cherished friend and fellow author who has held our hand every step of the way with *her* Luca.

To the amazing group of readers who encouraged and supported us — Evie, Maureen, Hannah and Cora. None of this would be possible without you ladies.

Chapter One

Luca

A silver foil wrapper tumbled down the stone walkway along the Limmat River, and Luca stepped to the side, his arms crossed. A giggling young couple with too many piercings for his personal preference hurried by, unaware of the menacing, forgotten paper. In his dark suit, crisp white shirt and matching silk navy tie, he waited.

The improperly disposed-of litter flopped one more time, trapped itself at the edge of the stone wall and, away from the light breeze, rested. Satisfied by his small conquest — surely it was his will that had brought its journey to an end — Luca smirked. He walked over, picked it up and secured its fate in a wire bin. A pestering thought of germs poked at his side, but he brushed his hands together at a job well done and continued on his path to the private bank.

While the inconvenience had been a distraction, it had been welcomed. Early and eager were two qualities he admired, but not in himself. He reached for the door of the gray, historic building at exactly seven minutes past his scheduled appointment. *Perfetto.*

After a brief check through security, including a confirmation of his identity, he climbed the two flights of stairs to the private bank of Steinmetz and Favre.

The heavy wooden doors of the suite opened to sleek metal-and-cream marble that created a stark contrast to the building's dated exterior. But the interior did not surprise Luca. He'd already seen the clean, powerful reception in the magazine article about the youngest woman entrepreneur in the history of private banking.

And it was no mistake he'd sought out Claire Favre. Young, driven and on-the-rise was exactly the kind of mind he wanted handling his soon-to-be-acquired secret business. The piece about her and her partner in the weekly publication inserted into the Sunday paper had done more than pique his interest. Fortunately, Luca's reputation and family history had provided enough of a motivation that he'd obtained an appointment without too much delay.

He gave his name to the young, just-above-cheap-suited man behind the massive desk and took a seat in the black leather club chair. Magazines in four different languages were fanned on the iron table next to him. He aligned the one on top to sync with the others and the rhythmed echo of high heels ricocheting off the hallowed walls made him look up.

Madonna mia.

The picture had done her no justice. Claire Favre's sharp hip bones pointed behind the fabric of her tight black skirt and they swayed in a hypnotizing motion as she drew nearer. The formfitting blazer matched the skirt, and a pink silk blouse formed a deep V below.

Different from the photo, where her blonde locks had been loose and casual as she'd smiled, her hair was now pulled back into a low, tight bun and her lips remained firmly locked together.

Luca stood, happy his height put him at an advantage, and buttoned his jacket at the waist. The momentary shock of her in-person beauty sank into his gut. It had no business in his throat or chest.

"Herr Bernardi." She extended her small, manicured hand but barely smiled.

"English, please." Luca ignored the slight jump in his heart rate as they touched.

"As you wish." Her light shrug remained formal.

Surely a coincidence.

He narrowed his eyes.

Ms. Favre's smile grew tighter and she spun around. "My office is just down the hall."

Luca followed the banker and stared at the back of her exposed neck. He would not check out her ass, not in a professional setting where the woman deserved respect. He would not.

He did. He most certainly did. And damn it all to hell and back if his palm didn't twitch with desire.

When the penance of being a gentleman and walking behind a woman to whom he owed respect — not ogling — had finished, he squared his shoulders at the threshold of her office and renewed his purpose — business.

Ms. Favre ushered him to a cubed leather chair opposite her desk and he reached for the button of his jacket while she floated to the other side of the impressive oak plank.

A quick glance of her surroundings revealed nothing — no framed photos of her and the late husband the article had referred to or children it had not hinted at. Truly nothing. This woman was clean, uncomplicated and professional—everything Luca desired in a banker...and perhaps other things.

"Please," she said and motioned to the seat behind him. With a quick brush on the back of her skirt—*is hand jealousy a thing?*—she gracefully sat. "Tell me what brings you here, Mr. Bernardi."

Where to begin? The long and challenging path of fully respecting and refining one's own needs? The obvious motivation of a man-made success? Best to start with the not-so-shocking. One never knows.

In the warmest, most casual tone he could muster he said, "I am in negotiations to buy a business. A private club, actually. And I was hoping to keep said investment separate from my others."

Her blue-gray gaze pierced him and she drew her light, thin eyebrows together. "You have a business you'd like to hide, and you want to use my bank to do so?"

"No." Convincing her was going to take some massaging, especially since the bulk of his wealth would not be coming along for the ride. "I have a business I'd like to keep to myself, but I'd like you to handle investing and growing the worth of the account."

Claire crossed her fingers on the desk and circled a thumb slowly into the opposite palm.

"Is it an illegal business?" she asked.

"No, but it is private, much like your bank." Luca flattened his lips and fought a smile. The woman calmed herself with touch. He admired and recognized the gesture. In a cold room full of stark decorations, her softness slammed into him.

He blinked. Business. And the need to hide his new project.

"And what is this soon-to-be-acquired opportunity?" She creased her pink lips.

There was the catch. The hitch. The hard-sell.

He stared into her eyes. "A private club."

She stilled her hands and cocked an eyebrow. "A misogynistic group of racist old men smoking cigars and plotting world domination?"

Interesting choice of words.

"No." This time he allowed the smile to shine. Her spunk and terseness must have helped her along the way.

But what way? According to the magazine article, she was barely thirty years old, and her private schooling, with winters in Gstaad and springs outside of Geneva, had assured her enough wealthy contacts for life. Her path and its perks had been easy — a silver spoon and a glass slipper.

"Are women welcome in your club, Mr. Bernardi?"

Her chest rose then fell slowly.

"Very much so." He dipped his chin.

She'd mentioned it twice now. Maybe empowering women was her motive.

Luca continued, "I welcome all to my club, Ms. Favre. The members and I pride ourselves on acceptance."

This brought a slight tilt to her head and what Luca hoped was a glimmer in her hazy eyes.

"All? That doesn't sound too private."

Her objection was welcomed with fervor, the familiar heat Luca longed for in a challenge. That, and her 'As you wish' comment from reception, braided into a perfect rope of feisty and submissive — not that the powerful woman before him would ever admit to wanting to surrender herself to the will of another.

But, contrary to what were probably her beliefs, she had all the signs. Her manners were impeccable. Her attention to detail...perfection. And that softness... The gentle side of her that Luca would bet his portfolio she didn't think people saw — but he did. He knew exactly the kind of woman who sat in front of him.

"I assure you that the membership fee secures the privacy," he said with a quick nod.

"And what is the membership fee? If I may ask?"

You may. Such lovely manners.

"Fifty thousand euros initially, plus another fifty thousand a year. On top of that, there are certain benefits that members may or may not choose to acquire. But, essentially, ten million would be my earnings in the first year."

She smiled curtly. The minimum balance to open most private banks in Switzerland was usually around a million francs. With a promise of more, maybe the risk of taking on what appeared to be a seedy client would dissolve.

"What exactly transpires at your club, Mr. Bernardi?" Her business etiquette remained flawless.

Well, that would depend entirely on which room one would peep into. But there was no reason to beat around the bush.

"Exploration of one's boundaries, Ms. Favre." Luca met her stare with heavy eyes.

"Sex. You plan to run a high society sex club." Her tone was flat, almost bored.

How could she hold his gaze? He was certain she was more a bottom than a top.

"I'm interested in continuing the initial goal of the founder, who provides a safe environment for all genders to escape without worries or hassles. It has been a tradition for years that every member sign a confidentiality agreement. It covers everything done and witnessed behind the closed, or sometimes open" — he tilted his head — "doors of the club."

Claire Favre appeared to remain unfazed. *Is she?*

She looked past Luca and he studied the pale, sweet skin exposed from her neck to her chest. From the lack of freckles and spots, it hadn't seen much sun over the summer. He knew its shade well, the perfect cream that would flush pink with proper stimulation.

Luca lifted his gaze. He would not be caught dreaming about bunching up her skirt and examining the most sensitive areas of her body. *Business*, he reminded himself.

"Might I ask why you thought *I* would be the right banker for your secret investment?"

Luca was still very much denying the answer himself. The woman had intrigued more than his financial affairs when he'd seen her in the photo.

"Empowerment, Ms. Favre. We're in the same business. You want to empower — "

She raised a hand and scoffed. He'd finally rattled her.

"I fail to see how tying up women and spanking them with riding crops is empowering." Her expression must have been attempting to scold him.

Hilarious.

Ah, the misconceptions. The fantasized, glorified, utter wrongness in the perception of the lifestyle… Luca had hoped a woman of Claire's status would have been better read than what popular opinion had painted as the BDSM culture. But alas, stereotypes were indeed festering wounds.

Luca curled his index finger around his mouth and tucked the opposite hand under his elbow.

She sat behind her desk, eyes slightly narrowed and waiting, oh so patiently with her hint of challenge, for his response. The blend was intoxicating.

Before the stirrings of his under-thoughts could bubble to the surface, he said, "I'd like to prove you wrong. The best way to do that I think would be to show you."

Her eyelids fluttered and the rosy flush he'd been trying to deny he craved crept up her neck. Claire swallowed hard.

Sorry, Ms. Favre. Flexing my mental muscle is an unbreakable yet delicious habit.

"Excuse me?" she managed.

Luca cleared his throat. "There are, perhaps, images you have about what goes on in a private setting such as my future club — images that, while they may scratch at the surface of truth, do only that…scratch."

Her skin returned to its cream natural state and Luca grieved the departure of the pink.

He continued, "Why don't you visit? Take a tour. I'm sure you'll find that it's just as much a legitimate business as the pesticides that kill millions of bees every year. Hopefully, more. I assure you that no one gets hurt unless they want to." Another man might have winked, but Luca only shifted his jaw instead.

She stiffened her posture. "You want me to come to a club and watch people get spanked and have sex?"

He grinned. "You seem rather fixated on the spanking part."

She rolled her eyes.

That would never do.

"I'm not fixated on anything. I'm just wondering… If your business is so much on the up and up, why would you want to hide it in my bank, because it doesn't seem like any of your other sources of income are shifting into my vaults with it? And secondly, why then, would I take a risk on you, a stranger to me, for a venture that you would like to brush under the rug?"

Luca crossed his foot over the opposite knee and adjusted in his chair.

"To answer your questions…" He twisted the platinum watch below his starched cuff. "For starters, perhaps I am interested in having some privacy on this matter and wish to not mix it with the accounts that have been in my family for decades. I am well aware of the labels that accompany my lifestyle. I still have a sweet, aging grandmother, and I have no intention of killing her with rumors of my sex life."

Claire's hands folded once again, but this time she rolled her shoulders back and shivered.

"And secondly, I read about you. I know you are a perfect balance of risk-taker and security. Much like anyone, I'd like to see my money grow. As I have no friends who are clients of yours, I feel the risk is mutual."

She sat back and tapped her delicate thumbs together three times.

Stalemate.

Her gaze ran the length of Luca and when it met his, she gave a slight purse of her mouth. "When?"

He wet his lips.

"Friday or Saturday night. You'll need to sign a non-disclosure agreement and you won't be able to visit the higher floors. But you will get a sense that the members are as normal as you and me." He paused at the brief fantasy of her in his private suite. "And you will see the respect and consent of a tight community."

Her eyes raked over him again. *A good sign?* He couldn't tell.

"I'll think about it."

She rose, as did he, and he followed her to the door.

"I'll see myself out." Luca nodded. There was no way he could follow that ass down the hall after he'd discovered how her skin could blush with just a few words.

"As you wish," she said.

Despite the brakes halting in his mind, Luca exited her office.

How had she known? How could she have possibly known the symphony of music those words were to his ears?

Chapter Two

Claire

Claire took a quick inventory of the rainbow of clothes hanging before her. Even something as simple as choosing an outfit held so much weight. What she wouldn't give for someone else to make the decisions. Someone she trusted. Someone she...

Bah.

She scanned the various items again and chewed the inside of her cheek. A man could don a suit with little-to-no thought and receive the same respect and admiration from the coffee shop to the boardroom.

But Claire was a woman — and barely thirty. Every day she had to choose her attire based on what statement she wanted to make, not what she wished to wear. She had to toe a fine line in the banking world, appearing capable enough to make transactions of millions of euros and appease the staid, older clientele while still looking trendy enough to entice the fresh-faced young businessmen taking the tech world by storm. Even her nail polish had been chosen for its subtle pink hue, adding a little shine without appearing too garish.

Some days the mountains of decisions and expectations were overwhelming.

She landed on the chiffon sleeve of her favorite sapphire blue blouse. She tugged gingerly, trying to free the garment from the overly stuffed row. The hook of the hanger tangled with the one behind it and, with a final pull, both items fell out.

The lump that hadn't seemed to have ever fully disappear in the ten months since Liam had died clogged her throat as his black button-down shirt fluttered to the floor. She picked it up and held it close to her nose. The spicy scent of his aftershave was long gone.

But a hint of bergamot and lime tickled her nostrils. She groaned and laid Liam's shirt on the bed. That blasted Luca Bernardi. She huffed as she slid her blouse over her shoulders. The smell of his cologne had lingered on her hand far too long after she'd shaken his, distracting her during several conference calls.

Claire pulled the black pencil skirt up over her hips and slid the zipper into place. But it was more than the undeniably addictive scent that had wreaked havoc long after his departure. It was the deep, rumbling invitation that echoed in her mind.

"I would like to prove you wrong. And the best way to do that I think would be to show you."

She tucked her black heels into her bag and slid on the ballet flats she'd kicked off in the living room the previous night, much more practical for hurrying on and off the train. A flick of her wrist to consult the thin silver watch she always wore confirmed her suspicion.

Late.

Again.

She swiped a banana off the table, grabbed her briefcase from the floor and ran out of the front door. At this rate, she'd be lucky to catch the next train.

A grin tugged at the corners of her mouth. Liam had found her perpetual tardiness charming and endearing, even when it had resulted in an hour delay for their wedding. Mr. Luca Bernardi would probably never approve.

The eight o'clock train disappeared around the corner just as Claire reached the platform, and her shoulders sagged. She sent her partner a quick text message to let him know she'd be late then dropped her case to the ground and leaned against a post as she peeled her banana, taking a large bite with much more gusto than the soft fruit required.

As if filling her mind with the unapologetically commanding — not to mention insanely attractive — Mr. Luca Bernardi for hours yesterday hadn't been enough, now he was seeping into her morning. And why in the world would she compare him to Liam?

His offer played on repeat as she boarded the next train and throughout the entire ride. When she disembarked, she squared her shoulders and shook her head. She couldn't allow Mr. Luca Bernardi any more space in her brain — not even if his eyes spoke of secret promises, not even if his deep voice caused a vibration all the way to her toes, not even if she'd had an instant stirring at the sight of him that she hadn't felt in far too long.

What was that American saying Helen quoted all the time? It was from some old movie... Claire grinned as she marched up the incline. *"I'll think about it tomorrow. After all, tomorrow is another day."* She rolled her eyes.

"Or at least I'll think about it after lunch, since he needs an answer today."

Her self-satisfied smile turned to pure joy when she crested the steep sidewalk and spied her favorite vendor nestled between two local farmers. The quintessential elderly Swiss woman sat behind the square table with small trinkets spread out before her. Claire was still several feet away when her gaze landed on a teacup and saucer she knew were meant to be hers.

"*Guete tag!*" She leaned down to kiss the silver-haired woman on each plump cheek. They exchanged a few pleasantries before Claire slid the money across the table, several francs more than the woman was asking.

She could easily afford new — and perfect. But the cream porcelain with the intricate plum-colored designs reminded her of Helen, especially the tiny crack running down the side of the cup and the small divot on the saucer. Those meant more to her than any level of ideal.

Gingerly, she stowed her latest purchase in her bag and lifted a hand. "*Tschüss.*"

The new addition to her eclectic little collection kept her small smile in place as she walked the rest of the way to her office. As soon as the aged stone building came into view, however, her back instinctively straightened. She paused at the corner to exchange her practical flats for the heels she loved and loathed at the same time. Her smile disappeared, her mouth settling into a firm line as she crossed through the wrought-iron gate and into the lobby of the office space.

She offered a brisk nod of her head to the security guard on the first floor. "*Guten morgen.*"

Too many stairs and tight smiles later she plopped behind her desk—and groaned when Julien burst through the door. "*Sie haben einen Anruf von—*"

Claire shook her head. "Please, English. I didn't get even half enough sleep last night for anything else."

Julien snorted and sat in the chair across from her with a little wiggle of his shoulders. "Honey, with that gorgeous hunk that was in your office for far too little time yesterday, I'm surprised you managed any sleep."

She dipped her chin and held a hand out. "Messages? Appointments? Schedule? Any of the millions of things you are responsible for that don't include my bedroom habits?"

He rolled his eyes with an overly dramatic sigh. Although, really, everything about Julien was exaggerated and provided Claire with exactly the dash of levity needed to get her through the day.

"You have three conference calls, the final meeting regarding the inn's grand opening, a three o'clock check-in with David and"—he laid the last piece of paper in her outstretched palm—"a reminder from a certain hot Italian that he is looking forward to your response."

The officious, presumptuous, domineering… The very last thing she wanted was to witness some privileged debutante in black latex getting recreational spankies, but she couldn't really alienate someone as powerful as Mr. Luca Bernardi without at least humoring him first. His connections had the ability to cement her position in the banking world. And playing nice was second nature for her.

She pursed her lips and slid her smartphone across the desk. "Fine. Program reminders for the calls and the meeting in my phone."

Julien's eyebrows rose as he grabbed her phone and his fingers flew across the screen. "And the heartthrob with the sexy-as-hell voice?"

"I'll handle him." Her declaration was voiced with far more confidence than she possessed. It was probably naive to think her breeding had prepared her to manage anything the corporate investors could throw at her. A seedy sex club run by a pushy Italian certainly hadn't appeared at any point in her Diploma programs and certainly hadn't been on the Oxford course list.

A knowing smirk settled on Julien's face as he handed back her device. "Oh, sweetheart, I don't think *that* is the kind of man who is handled, even by you."

Claire glared at his retreating back and the closed oak door for several minutes after he'd left. More often than not Julien had proven to be not simply a competent assistant but also a trusted confidant and a surprisingly dear friend—especially after Liam had died.

Lately, he'd also become quite the pusher of men. She rolled her eyes and pulled up her email on the slim laptop she preferred to use over the hulking PC her partner clung to. Line by line she answered inquiries, directed personnel concerns to HR and scheduled several initial consultations.

By four o'clock she was chewing her lower lip and wondering if she'd given the all-powerful Mr. Luca Bernardi enough of a silent treatment that he'd understand she wasn't about to be ordered about by him. She picked up the receiver of her office phone and held it dangling from her fingers for a moment before dialing the number Julien had written on the yellow slip of paper—the number she certainly hadn't memorized after looking at it repeatedly throughout the course of the day.

"Luca Bernardi." The voice practically purred across the line after only two rings, not nearly long enough for Claire to prepare herself for the sound.

She fought the urge to clear her throat. No need to let that man have any inkling that she found him intriguing far beyond his business acumen. "Mr. Bernardi, this is Claire Favre. We spoke yesterday."

"Yes, Ms. Favre, I do recall. I also believe I called you nearly nine hours ago." His short-clipped tones were drenched in disapproval.

Heat crept up Claire's neck and she was grateful he wasn't there. His all-too-knowing gaze had zeroed in on her discomforted blush yesterday with far more interest than she'd liked — or not enough.

"My deepest apologies, Mr. Bernardi. I've been incredibly busy today. However, I would like to revisit your invitation…"

"Yes, I assumed so. Please be ready by eight. I'll send a car."

Claire's mouth fell open and moved fruitlessly several times before a sound finally came out. "Now, Mr. Bernardi, with all due respect, I was calling to tell you I wouldn't be available until tomorrow evening."

Silence. She chewed on her lower lip to halt the flood of apologies and pleas for him to take her tonight. *Why does his pleasure matter to me so much?*

A heavy sigh broke the dead air. "Tonight would be far more convenient for me, but I suppose I am to blame for giving you the option. Very well, I shall send a car tomorrow evening. Same time."

Claire's mind raced. She wanted to tell him that she could drive herself. She wanted to tell him he should meet her at her office. More than anything she wanted to ask how he even knew where she lived. Just as had happened yesterday, her words were stolen, manipulated and spoken without any input from her brain. "As you wish, Mr. Bernardi."

A deep rumble sounded as he cleared his throat. "Good evening, Ms. Favre. I look forward to seeing you tomorrow."

She cradled the phone and let her head hit her desk with a thud. "What have I just done?"

"Please tell me that Tall, Dark and Bossy is the reason for this."

Claire lifted her head far enough to pin Julien with a glare. "Close the door." She sat back and stared silently at Julien for several minutes. "Not one word of this leaves these four walls, understand?"

The humor disappeared from his face as he sank into the chair across from her. "I… don't like the sound of that, but you know you can trust me with anything. I've never brought up that one summer at boarding school when you—"

"Julien!" She didn't want to tell even him, but she needed help from someone open-minded, experienced, younger and… Hell, sharing the truth with Julien was all she had anymore. "Mr. Bernardi wants us to manage the investment and growth of a new business he is acquiring." She dropped her voice to a whisper. "A sex club!"

Julien's steely gaze widened. "Just when I thought hot couldn't possibly get hotter." He sat back in his chair and fanned himself. "I don't get it. Why does this matter? His business will undoubtedly be discreet."

Claire fidgeted with the hem of her skirt. "The problem is that when I questioned him, he invited me to come…experience the club personally." She ran her hands down her face. "And I agreed. Tomorrow night."

A slow smile spread across Julien's face. "Oh, my darling Ms. Favre, this requires a shopping trip."

She groaned and covered her eyes. "Fuck, I didn't even think about that. What does one wear to a human meat market? They never covered that at my cotillion classes."

Julien tilted his head back and crowed with laughter. "Sweetheart, bars are human meat markets. This is an elite dining experience." His gaze washed over her. "Oh, I am going to enjoy dressing you up."

Chapter Three

Luca

Forty-three. She was forty-three minutes late. Fifteen—maybe twenty—would have been annoying but forty-three was downright punishable. Who was he kidding? One minute would have been too much for any other woman he'd sent a car for to meet him at Bruno's club, soon to be his.

Located right inside the city, within plain view for all to see, was the five-story pre-war, massive building Luca had been renting to Bruno for over a decade. Once his friend had opted for a calmer life and the top floor residence had become vacant, it had been natural for Luca to take up occupancy—after a remodel, to be sure.

Another town car drove by on the well-lit street and Luca checked his thick watch. *Forty-four.* For a brief moment, his heart sank. *Is she not coming? Preposterous.*

He straightened his cuffed sleeves and perked his pointed, tieless collar as the familiar dark Audi hugged the curb in front of him. *Finally.*

No longer able to wait, Luca moved to the back door and leaned down to open it. Two bare, pale legs attached to black patent-leather Italian heels swung out to the sidewalk. He extended his hand and the firm pressure that was returned when Claire stood almost made him forget her tardiness.

Her black dress, while short and tight, had long sleeves and a neckline that revealed nothing. *Pity.* He would miss the flush of her chest. *Another time. Another woman.* This was business.

She smiled up to him. Even in those shoes she could not compete with his height.

"You're late, Ms. Favre. How exactly does one do that when a car is sent to fetch you at a specific time?"

Her blue-gray eyes glanced to the ground. "I..." She twisted her jaw and her cheek caved in as if it was being sucked in from the other side. "I wasn't sure what to wear..." She stepped to the side to allow Luca to close the car door and she held her small clutch with both hands below her waist.

Unsure. The little lamb hadn't known how to dress. And why would she? She'd never been to a club like this before. It was evident from her opinion at the office about what transpired behind the thick stone walls. Proving her wrong was twofold — one for his money and two for his curiosity. Had her magical words meant more?

Luca tilted his head and gave her a rare, warm smile. "I'd say you look perfect. A successful partnership of class and sleek."

He reached his arm around her back to guide her toward the entrance, only to be met with soft, cool skin. A calculated breath calmed his racing heart as the contact blanketed his insides with heat.

Madonna mia.

There was no back to her dress. In fact, after a glance for further inspection, the entire C curve of her lower spine was revealed — and it was heavenly.

They walked in silence to the broad double doors and Luca reached inside his jacket for his key card. After a scan at the discreet pad to the left, both doors quietly popped open and gave way to a massive marble foyer.

He nodded to the flanked security guards and led the lovely banker down the hall toward the bar. Perhaps his hand didn't need to return to her skin, but surely chivalry mattered in business as well.

They passed the closed doors of the offices and surveillance rooms and arrived at the archway of the bar. Boring — in their current state, anyway — faces chatted in tiny groups that filled the dimly lit den. But, like the smell of fresh meat in the cage of a panther, all eyes shifted to Claire Favre, especially those of that young blond bastard Noah Paulick.

But unworried, due to status and knowing that the mere fact of being seen with him had laid his claim to the beautiful banker, he led her past the leather couches and low tables to the bar. She sat on the stool and crossed her lovely legs. Luca chose to remain standing and admired her back again as she swiveled around to the bartender.

Wedging himself between the empty stool and Ms. Favre, he said, "Red wine? Let me guess… Pinot Noir?"

She narrowed her eyes but smiled. "Am I that obvious?"

Before he could answer, Max, the bartender and occasional security guard, asked, "You drinking tonight, boss?"

Never one to blur his thoughts while being trusted to control another's desires, Luca Bernardi did not mix playtime with alcohol. And after the skin-to-skin contact with his preciously brave guest on his mind, he would not be playing with another. This, he knew.

"Two glasses of my Barolo please."

Claire cocked an eyebrow. "I thought you said Pinot Noir."

Max smiled his acknowledgment of the order and went to find the bottle.

"This is wine from my family's estate in Italy. It's better than a Pinot Noir." He winked.

I winked? Caro Dio, am I attempting to flirt?

Claire spun back to the crowd as Luca leaned on the clean counter of the bar. Without turning around, and just above the soft music playing overhead, she said, "I admit that this is not at all what I expected."

He raked his gaze over her spine and met her light, loose hair just below her shoulders. He contemplated the idea of actually bending forward and tasting her skin. Worshiping her...

Max cleared his throat and the wine glasses chittered behind him. Luca turned around, accepted the drinks and handed one to Claire.

Tipping it up, he said, "To a new partnership?"

She rolled her eyes. A grave error for any other woman of non-Domme status in the club. He regretfully let it slide. *Business.*

"I haven't made up my mind yet, Mr. Bernardi."

He inhaled the faint hint of rose from his glass then sipped. Indeed, this was better than any Pinot Noir. He replaced the drink where he'd found it and turned his attention back to the bewitching banker in front of him.

Claire Favre was too tempting. Like a moth to a flame, he leaned in close to her ear, probably too close — definitely closer than he'd ever been to any financial advisor that he could recall.

With a low hum in his voice that he begged would meet her skin, he asked, "And what is holding you back, Ms. Favre?"

If she thought he didn't notice the small quiver in her lips and the stuttered exhale, she was mistaken.

She stayed facing forward. "You've shown me a bar. Everyone here is dressed as normally as you and me. I have a hard time imagining they pay fifty thousand euros to chat it up."

No, no. They most certainly do not.

Giggles, too loud for his liking but nonetheless pleasing, grabbed their attention at the entrance. Three subs were dressed in short but tasteful attire. One had been recently trained by Luca himself and the other two had been begging their Doms for a scene involving them all together and they must have finally gotten their wish. The three locked hands and exchanged smiles.

Gwendelyn, who'd been collared years prior, shot a look back to her Master. He nodded once, and Luca admired the beauty of their unspoken, sacred communication.

Flashing her dark hair and darker eyes, Gwendelyn reached for Luca's recent graduate. The girl had been an exemplary student, so eager to please. *Too eager.* He'd had to end her lessons abruptly when it had become clear her feelings had come into playtime.

The women locked eyes for a moment while the third sub brushed her fingers up and down Gwendelyn's snow-white arms. Then the two women kissed. First simply, like testing the waters, then more intensified, as if realizing their luck and freedom to act.

But the real show for Luca was the transfixed Claire Favre. She stared — no, gawked — at the scene unfolding in front of her. She wet her lips and swallowed as small moans reached his ears from across the room. The three subs must have kicked it up a notch. Perhaps he should have reminded them of their manners. *Perhaps not.*

"All right, you three." Elias, the wealthiest member of the club and Gwendelyn's Dom, popped up from the dark couch and clapped once. It stopped all action and commanded the attention of the entire bar. "Up to my suite before I change my mind."

With their eyes fixed on the ground, the trio of beauties filed out of the bar. Elias shot a wink to Luca and followed the women with a spring in his step. Gwendelyn's partners would definitely pay for their public display of affection. The tricky little vixen would not, however, as she'd acted with the full-on authority and probable encouragement of her Dom.

With the haze of arousal obviously still humming around her, Claire swiveled in the stool and placed her wine glass next to Luca's. She blinked a few times before turning her cloudy gaze to Luca, who tilted his head and waited for her to speak.

He itched to touch her inner thigh and confirm her desire. Watching a scene, any scene, was erotic, but watching a scene live, for the first time, could be downright explosive. And she'd seen practically nothing, the bare minimum.

"Where are they going?" she asked in a quiet, urge-filled voice.

Why is this woman my banker? He needed to touch her, explain, teach—turn her skin pink and praise her bravery, comfort her courage, show her how free she could be by letting go.

To hell with propriety. He reached out and brushed her soft cheek with the back of his hand. A delicate sigh escaped her chest as she closed her eyes.

"Are you okay?" He drew back his hand.

"I... Uh..."

"Didn't expect that to evoke a *physical* reaction?" He rubbed his lips together.

Her eyes shot open, as if that could erase the previous ten minutes. Luca relaxed into the bar stool he'd been avoiding with a mild grin.

Her pout was undoubtedly the best he'd ever seen, and the Italian Dom had seen many.

The smile on his face was unstoppable and he arched a thick eyebrow. "What? Really? You're going to tell me that didn't make the mighty Claire Favre of Steinmetz and Favre just a little hot and bothered?"

No reason to push. The battle had been won the second she'd practically whimpered at his breath on her neck. So easy and yet so challenging at the same time. Why had he done this to himself?

With the hour drawing late, the once-full bar was emptying around them. Those without a pairing for the evening were headed to witness what they could or put themselves in a free room to participate.

"You never answered my question. Where did they go? Where did everyone go?"

Luca refilled their glasses with the remains of the bottle Max had set in front of him.

"Ms. Favre. As you well know, this is a sex club. They've gone to have sex, my dear."

She scooted closer to the bar. "But I thought you brought me here to show me?"

"I believe that's what I just did. I proved to you that the members are the same as you and me, that it's a well taken care of and private establishment."

Claire circled the rim of her wine glass with meticulously well-manicured fingers.

"And that's all you intended on showing me? The *bar*?"

"Ah… The spanking." He lifted a finger. "Right. You did mention that part."

She rolled her eyes.

Speaking of spanking.

"Well, for that I'm afraid you are out of luck. Only members can get upstairs. Members come with one hundred thousand euros and a signed doctor's note of clean health. I'd love to make an exception. Truly, I would."

More than he cared to confess. "Unfortunately, I'm waiting on a beautiful banker to help me buy this place. Until that happens, I'm subject to following the rules just like everyone else." If Luca had been the type to shrug, he would have added it to sell his case.

She folded her hands and focused on the glass in front of her. She repeated the same pattern with her thumb from days before in her office, making what Luca now recognized as a deliberate path around the opposite palm. Delicate, he decided. Not weak, but internally frail.

With her eyes still fixed down, she asked, "What if I want to become a member?"

He couldn't tolerate her self-soothing any longer. He cupped his hand over both of hers and pressed gently. She stilled, and her obedience sang to the needs of his soul.

In a low, quiet voice, he said, "Claire— May I call you Claire?"

"You may."

"I didn't invite you here to bring you into this world."

If lying was on a sliding scale, Luca Bernardi had just slipped into a pit of untruths. He brushed her knuckles with his thumb and his longing to comfort her was mildly appeased.

He continued, "I need you as my banker. I know it seems like a risk on your end, and if it sweetens the deal, I can help you recruit some new clients. But you don't belong here." He looked away.

Even with the confidence he'd used to deliver the words, he wasn't sure they'd been convincing. It was one thing to train a new sub. It was entirely something else to introduce an overwhelming lifestyle to a driven, yet fragile, woman. She'd lost her husband within the last year. It was too soon. While a few past relationships he'd had had been healing and freeing for the women on many levels, there was a sadness in Claire's gray eyes that told him to proceed with caution.

He would convince her to help him with the purchase and maybe slowly dangle bits and pieces of the Dom/sub dynamic before her over time. He would stay in touch and see how she was when she was more healed. Let her dip her toe in the warm water, not throw the beauty into the deep end. That would be the right thing to do.

He tapped her knuckles with his index finger three times and stood.

"I'll call your car."

He walked toward the archway and decided to turn back and reassure her with a smile. When he did so, he was met with an icy glare. Her reaction was more proof that she didn't understand. Although, he had to admit that the anger *was* slightly amusing. He hadn't seen it on a woman outside his family in so long that it made him chuckle.

He shook his head and walked to security. With a swipe of his card, he entered the darkly lit room and found his phone in a cubbyhole alongside all the other members' phones and wallets. No cameras or money were allowed on the higher floors.

As he dialed and ordered the car, her lonely silhouette haunted him from the closed-circuit feed in the bay, a stark contrast to the twisted bodies in Elias Zwallen's suite on the neighboring screen.

Luca was doing the right thing. As much as he hated to let go of the prospect of helping her, he reminded himself that it was timing, not fate, standing in his way. *Let the poor woman be.* His ego had really become out of control, thinking he could fix every broken sparrow that had fallen from a branch or that he was some expert at finding new subs.

He met her again at the bar and she took the final drink of her wine.

"You were right," she said.

The tension released from his shoulders.

She stood and straightened her dress. With a toss of her hair and her posture stiff, she was no longer Claire. She'd returned to Ms. Claire Favre, partner of Steinmetz and Favre. The change was almost astounding.

"I did prefer the Barolo. My compliments to your family in Italy."

He grinned and escorted her down the grand hall. At the end, the double doors parted and the fall breeze hit them.

The same dark town car waited for her at the curb. He opened the door and she turned to him.

With a hand outstretched for a formal goodbye that he already hated, she said, "Thank you for an enlightening evening, Mr. Bernardi. My assistant will be in touch next week with my decision."

"I look forward to it." His attempted warm smile fell flat with her cutting eyes.

"Maybe you shouldn't." She slid into the car, and before he could push the door shut, she slammed it herself.

Chapter Four

Claire

"No calls, no texts, not even a carrier pigeon. For all I knew, that Italian hunk had you locked in a dungeon somewhere doing wicked, wicked things to your disgustingly toned body." Julien's eyes lit up. "*Did* he do wicked things to your body?"

Claire narrowed her gaze and stepped to the side, holding her door open. "Won't you please come in, Julien?"

He tossed his jacket on the back of one of her sitting room chairs with practiced flair before throwing himself onto her sofa and crossing his legs. "Okay, sweetheart, tell all. Are his lips as soft as they look? Did he toss you onto the nearest horizontal surface and run his big, strong hands over every inch of your body?" His lips curled into a devious grin and he waggled his eyebrows. "Does the hand size match the package?"

With her fists perched on her hips, she said, "No. Apparently, after practically strong-arming me into joining him in his den of depravity, he had second thoughts."

Julien sat up at attention. "He changed his mind? You're telling me Luca Bernardi, economic ruler of all of Italy and half of Switzerland, changed his mind?"

She began slowly circling her left palm with her right thumb. An image of his darker skin against her pale flesh crossed her mind and stilled her movement just as it had the previous night. "Apparently I'm not good enough to be a guest of Mr. Luca Bernardi beyond the basic bar."

The familiar pricks to her heart struck again. 'Not enough' had been her label since infancy. Not enough to garner her parents' attention. Not enough to compel them to attend her piano recitals. Not enough to warrant visits at boarding school. And now, Mr. Luca Bernardi had deemed her not enough for even a romp in the hay.

The thought made her shake her head slightly. *Where in the world did that come from?* She was still in mourning and not even a devastatingly sexy olive-toned businessman who oozed power and charm could ignite the fire in her again.

And she would never, *could* never, want his lifestyle. She ground her molars together at the memory of his abrupt change in attitude when she'd asked to learn more, see more. It wasn't as if she had propositioned him, for crying out loud.

It had all been for research. She'd merely wanted to better ascertain client interest and business viability. It'd had nothing to do with the gleeful looks of anticipation she'd seen on those girls' faces. And it most assuredly had not been related to the purring timbre of Mr. Luca Bernardi's voice hinting at the various acts taking place elsewhere in the club—or the thrum of curiosity that had confused the hell out of her all night long.

Claire sank into a chair and tucked her feet beneath her. Silence descended upon them as she chewed the inside of her cheek. Memories of his warm fingers brushing against her bare back and her cheek made her skin tingle. Flames licked through her veins, despite her determination to deny the fire that existed in Luca's presence—a heat she hadn't experienced since the first time she'd spied Liam across the lecture hall at university, something she had spent so much time believing she would never find again.

"What's your next move?" Julien's voice summoned her back to reality.

She focused on him, a determined smile in place. She hugged the ivory sweater closer to her body. "There's more than one way to skin a cat."

He groaned and dropped his head against the back of the sofa. "Another quaint colloquialism from your American nanny, I presume? Please enlighten me on why Americans would find wisdom in animal cruelty and torture?"

Claire pointed a perfectly manicured finger at him. "I adore your bitchiness in all its glory, but Helen is off limits."

Julien held his palms out facing her. "No offense meant to Nanny Helen. So, what is the alternate plan to best your Italian stallion?"

"He's not my anything, but if the great Mr. Luca Bernardi feels strongly that Steinmetz and Favre is the bank for him, he will need to prove it." She waved a hand in the air, searching for the right words. "Put his money where his mouth is, so to speak." Claire grinned at her personal-assistant-turned-best-friend, liking her new idea more by the second.

He eyed her warily from across the room. "I know that smile. That is a dangerous smile."

She jutted her chin out at him. "You are going to set up a meeting for me and Mr. Luca Bernardi for first thing Tuesday morning."

Julien tilted his dirty-blond head. "*First* thing Tuesday morning?"

Claire hesitated before answering. Julien knew her so well. She'd never be on time, no matter how hard she tried. She was just about to acquiesce and suggest he make it for closer to noon when a thought popped into her head. She chewed on her lower lip, the corners of her mouth curving slightly. He'd made it quite clear the previous night that her perpetual tardiness annoyed him.

"Yes, Julien. First thing in the morning."

* * * *

Claire had spent longer than normal that morning coaching herself in the bathroom mirror and agonizing over her clothing choices. She could handle Mr. Luca Bernardi. He was just a man—a devastatingly handsome man who wielded a quiet authority that was both exciting and unnerving, but still, just a man. She knew how to play the game with alpha men and wind up the victor, all the while leading them to believe success was theirs.

She bit the insides of her cheek just before she pushed open the door to the suite that housed her office. Offering a Cheshire Cat grin at the irritation she was certain would be etched across his face was highly unprofessional, even if a foreign part of her found it fun.

Despite her frustration at his dismissal of her Saturday evening, she drank in the sight of him as soon as she crossed the threshold. She wasn't surprised in the slightest that he sat as silent and still as a statue. Anyone else would be tapping their feet, pacing or leafing through a magazine between irate huffs. She already knew him well enough not to mistake his patience for approval. The displeasure rolling off him in waves was almost palpable.

When she'd planned her attack on the train in this morning, she had decided she would breeze past his sure-to-be-annoyed self without acknowledging his presence then have Julien summon him to her office. It would be a power play, a silent throwing down of the gauntlet. It would be…

Completely impossible. The dark eyes hinted at things Claire wasn't yet ready to admit she wanted. She was helpless to deny the commanding pull charging the atmosphere around him, urging her to offer him her compliance.

Summoning every ounce of pure stubbornness she possessed, she offered a smile. "Please, Mr. Bernardi, follow me. My apologies for being late." He rose from his seat, buttoning the perfectly tailored navy jacket with one hand while waving her ahead with the other. The cadence of his footfalls behind her encompassed everything Luca Bernardi was — determined, controlled, firm.

"I presume this is a habit of yours." His comment followed the soft click of the door as it latched into place, sealing them in the privacy of her office.

Why was the very notion of being cloistered away with him enough to cause the heart she'd once believed incapable of beating again after she'd lost Liam to now pound in her ears? She set her case on the floor beside her desk and took her seat as he mirrored her actions across the gleaming oak surface. Her gaze dropped to her lap of its own volition.

"I... Yes. Yes, it is." She cleared her throat and forced herself to meet his steady stare. "And I do apologize again. But I would like to make a proposal, Mr. Bernardi. A business proposal." She tacked on the qualifier as an afterthought, lest he believe she wanted anything more from him than the connections and traction fees he offered...like the undoubtedly expert hands resting on the arms of the chair to explore her body or the full lips almost concealed by his dark, well-groomed beard to make a trail over her every curve. Certainly not the gleaming white teeth sinking into the sensitive flesh at the juncture of her neck and shoulder, making her knees buckle...

No, she was not interested in any of that and wanted it to be very clear to the great Mr. Luca Bernardi.

His intense gaze didn't falter and Claire fought the urge to squirm beneath his blatant scrutiny. And the heat creeping up her chest, peeking out of the neckline of the lilac camisole she wore beneath her black blazer...

"Luca," he said.

His name wiped her mind clear of every rehearsed word she was trying to focus on. "E-e-excuse me?"

He inclined his dark head. "You will call me Luca, Claire. Not Mr. Bernardi."

Claire struggled to control her erratic breathing. He hadn't requested she address him by his first name. He had demanded. Ordered. Decided.

"As I was saying, I have been thinking over the brief tour of your perspective club. In order for me to align my company with you and risk the possibility of being exposed at some point, thereby putting my partner and my reputation in jeopardy, I simply must insist on seeing the entirety of the building, all you have to offer, to see exactly what would entice one to spend that much money on a membership."

She folded her hands on her desk and congratulated herself on the confident, unaffected, nonjudgmental tone with which she had spoken. She began making circles in her palm with her thumb — of its own volition. His chocolate gaze slid from hers to her hand and back up. Without a word he arched an eyebrow and her finger stilled on its own. Butterfly wings beat a rhythmic pattern in her stomach at his approving nod.

"Your bank is successful, has an impressive client list and will unquestionably become a renowned and highly sought-after home for an array of businesses." He paused and inclined his dark head in her direction. "However, there are many other banks in Europe that could tout each of those points. Why should I agree to your terms?"

That had been the question to trip Claire up as she'd mulled over her plan the previous night. What did she have to offer him? Nothing, other than his own voracious pride.

Claire lifted one slim shoulder and affected an unconcerned expression. "You are undoubtedly correct. And for all I know, some of the partners of those banks may very well already be clients of your future establishment." The corner of her mouth kicked up and she tilted her head to the side. "But you chose me and my bank. And while I don't fully comprehend your reasoning, I believe I do understand your personality — and failure is not an option."

His jaw worked back and forth. It was a small, barely perceptible motion, but Claire found herself highly attuned to his every movement. She kept her calm mask in place while a war raged beneath the surface. She had either made a grave mistake or opened a thrilling door.

The silence was both terrifying and exhilarating as the air crackled between them. Claire fought against the instinctual urge to lower her gaze, instead holding the dark liquid stare with far more conviction than she felt. A taunting voice at the back of her mind reminded her of the girls she had seen at the club. Their easy and immediate obedience to their...whatever misogynistic title those men wore. A vision of Luca in that role flashed in her mind, commanding those under his authority.

A second image followed, making her manufactured confidence falter as her eyelids fluttered. No, no, Luca might have any number of women willing to kneel before him but she was not one of them, not even if the mental picture renewed the fire that seemed to smolder in his presence.

"I shall make arrangements for a more in-depth tour." He held one long finger up. "However, you will be on time for this appointment."

He rose from his seat and buttoned his coat in one smooth move. Claire stood with him, struck speechless by his authoritarian tone — and very annoyed at her traitorous body's response to it. She held her hand out, relying on the manners she had cut her teeth on to save her from giving away one iota of her true feelings to him. "As you wish, Mis— Luca."

Once again his brow arched then an approving smile settled on his face. He nodded before turning on his heel and taking his leave.

Within seconds, before she could have the recovery time she needed after the power struggle with Luca, Julien raced into the room, closing the door behind him and perching on the edge of the chair Luca had so recently abandoned.

"Please tell me that you love me enough to not allow this to be the last time we see that gorgeous specimen in this office."

Claire sat back in her chair, in a daze and a strange combination of exhausted and excited. "I— I don't exactly know. I am getting the full tour of his club..." She realized that even in his concession, he had taken control. "At some point. Then I'll make a final decision."

Julien clapped with glee. "Another encounter with Luca Bernardi and a second chance to dress you up like my own personal doll? It's like Christmas is coming early!"

Claire folded her arms across her desk and let her forehead fall on top of them. "Oh, fuck me, what have I done?"

Chapter Five

Luca

The black Maserati's engine purred as it crept closer to the toll booth. A five-hour drive south in silence had been the perfect remedy for the constant chatter that had overtaken Luca's mind.

He tapped the steering wheel with his middle and index fingers. It was difficult to believe Claire Favre's interest in the club was strictly business. He pursed his lips before forming a tight grin. It was equally difficult to admit his interest in her was only for a financial transaction. Maybe if he let her stew, the real reasons would bubble to the surface.

Toll paid and now well beyond the Swiss border, he checked his mirrors. His shoulders pressed into the dark leather behind him and he stiffened his arms as he accelerated past the right lane of cars abiding by the speed limit.

She would be lovely on her knees, head bent—surrendering. And had she been late intentionally, to rile him up? Perhaps this was already a game neither one of them was fully aware they had begun playing.

But if she were going to see the club, it would need to be with him. There was no room for misinterpretations. Whether or not Claire was curious about the lifestyle, which her body language had confirmed but her words had not, his future business and current reputation now hung on the line.

He guided the impressive steel machine back into the right lane and called Bruno from the speaker.

"I thought you were in Italy." His old friend coughed twice.

"This is what it has come to? You don't even greet me anymore? I'm wounded." Luca would have smiled at their banter if the sign of Bruno's failing health had not reminded him of the precious little time he had left.

"Hello, Luca, my dear. I've missed you." The sugar in Bruno's voice dripped through the car. "Lucerne is boring and Adrian fusses over me too much. Better?"

"I miss you, too, you old queen. I thought you two were headed to Sopra?"

Bruno let out a long breath from the other end. "I didn't have the energy. I sent him alone. I'm sorry. I should have told you, but I was afraid you wouldn't go to see your *nonna* like a good Italian boy." Playful truth wove between his words.

His friend knew him too well. The thought of Adrian, while sweet and well-seasoned on the scene, running Sopra for the weekend was indeed displeasing. Management required a strong hand—so to speak—as there were certain Doms who had unfavorable tendencies when not properly monitored.

But Luca could not turn around. His tiny little *nonna* would be crushed, and that was not worth the gamble. Plus, seeing her calmed him. Her dust-free house and perfectly arranged small statues of saints were the order from his otherwise chaotic childhood.

Three more taps on the steering wheel as his jaw shifted and Bruno waited on the other end. Luca would have to speed up the completion of the sale. The sooner he paid Bruno, the happier they would all be.

"I need you to authorize a non-member for a tour during peak hours. The banker wants to make sure your clients are getting their money's worth."

Bruno chuckled but it turned into a minor coughing spell. Had the phone been close to Luca's ear, he would have withdrawn.

"Claire Favre? The woman you so randomly chose to broker the deal?" The song in Bruno's voice made Luca frown.

"Don't push," Luca scolded.

"Darling, it is my nature to push. That's why I had more male subs than I care to admit." The laugh came back and, thankfully, this time it was hack free.

"Don't push *me*, then."

"Fair enough. I assume she's already signed the non-disclosure. I'll get Elias to confirm and Adrian will send you a message with the green light."

They ended their call and Luca had just enough time for two more before he would arrive at his family's home.

"This is Max." The husky voice rang out over the car's speaker.

"It's Luca. I need you to watch that prick Noah Paulick this weekend. Get one of the unattached subs to work the bar and keep your eyes glued to the cameras. Got it?"

"Yes, sir. No problem. Anything else?"

"Call me on this number if there's an issue. Adrian is coming without Bruno. If something comes up, you may need to act quick. You have my full confidence."

"You got it."

After pressing the button to hang up, Luca glanced at the clock on the dash. She should still be at the bank. And even if she wasn't, her assistant would be.

He made a mental note to get her private number. Hearing Claire's voice and the possibility of one more 'As you wish' could lighten the tension in his neck that a poorly supervised club was causing.

"Claire Favre's office."

"Luca Bernardi."

"Oh. Hello, sir. How can I help you? I'm afraid Ms. Favre is on a call. She'll regret missing you." Her assistant's perk and attempt at coolness were endearing.

Luca grinned. "Please tell your boss I will pick her up at ten tomorrow evening at her house."

"Uh…"

"And please remind her to be ready."

Luca's thumb brushed the End Call button and pushed it down gently. He gazed ahead at the rolling hills leading into his grandmother's town and estate. *Nonna* would not be happy with him leaving early and would probably fuss about him driving ten hours within twenty-four, but she was worth it. Both women were—the short, fragile force of nature with graying hair and the frail blonde who needed to be tamed and worshiped like she'd probably never known was possible.

The gravel crunched under his tires as he drove into the circular driveway until he was directly behind his father's old and abused Aston Martin. Piero Bernardi stood next to his baby-blue car with his shirt untucked on one side, exposing what his son was sure was a larger belly than the last time he'd seen it. It had been one year prior, for the same celebration.

Piero waddled around to the trunk, reached for a duffel bag that dated from Luca's childhood, slammed the metal down and turned to his son. Behind the cloak of disorder, disorganization and occasional drunkenness, there was love.

A horn honked from behind him and the silver SUV of Luca's cousin approached in the rearview mirror. Luca got out of his car and went to greet his father.

"You have paint in your hair," Luca said as he pulled back from the embrace.

"I always have paint in my hair." His father shrugged and looked to the new arrivals.

Children of various ages poured out of the SUV, waved to Luca and his father and ran around the large gray stone house. Soon after, splashes and screams followed from the back, signaling their delight and need to burn off pent-up energy from a long ride.

Luca walked over to his cousin Gianna, who unbuckled her last child from her car seat. The middle-aged beauty paused from her task long enough to kiss Luca on the cheeks then passed him her daughter. He cooed an Italian song in the little girl's ear, bounced her a few times and told her how beautiful she was.

Another car drove up and another group of children sprang free from its passenger doors and ran directly to the pool where their dark-haired counterparts were already laughing. Luca handed the little darling back to her mother, went to say hello to the new arrivals then turned his attention to finding the birthday girl.

* * * *

The recently washed car idled around the corner from the address plugged into his GPS, and Luca leaned deeper into his seat. Nine-fifty-six p.m. After a noisy and hectic Friday night where his father's lack of manners had reminded him why he kept his distance, the quiet inside the automobile brought him calm.

But the anticipation of Claire Favre's reaction and potential true interest in what she was about to see percolated in his veins. There was something. It couldn't be denied. With one small look, she'd stopped that adorable habit she had with her hands. And he'd had to flee the bank and steady his heart rate with her parting words.

Does she have any idea what that phrase does to me?

He put the car into drive and turned the corner to his destination. To his utter delight, Claire stood in a black silk dress with a long V in the front and a tied sash that accented her small waist.

Madonna mia.

She has on red heels.

With her hair up and blonde tendrils grazing her lovely neck, she was stunning. She was also on time. That made two habits she'd already surrendered to him.

Their eyes locked and she walked down the steps of her large, historic house. Luca left the car running and his door open as he circled to the opposite side. The approaching events now beyond a handshake, he leaned in to kiss her three times on her cheeks. The perfect blend of jasmine and geranium pleased his inhale, and when he pulled back, he smiled.

"Always beautiful, Ms. Favre." Luca opened the car door.

With her chest exposed, he caught the light flush of her skin. "Claire. I thought we'd agreed on Claire."

"Quite right. You look perfect, Claire."

The soft, dark fabric of her dress brushed against him as she said thank you and gracefully made her way into the car. He closed her in and a wry smile teased his lips. With a hand resting on the button of his jacket, he strode to his side and joined her.

They rode in silence and he trained his eyes to stay ahead and not gawk at the pale skin exposed to his right. It was within reach. *She* was within reach.

When he risked a glance, he found her staring out of the window as the modern buildings transformed to those full of centuries of stories. Her lovely chest rose and fell at a clipped pace.

Any other woman would have received his touch. But, unable to know if she would appreciate his hand on her very much visible thigh, he gripped the steering wheel tighter.

"*Allora*, Claire." He glanced at the traffic light along the side of the road. "Are you prepared for what you will see?"

"I'm sorry?" She crossed her legs so that the opposite one was on top.

"Well, it was quite obvious from our initial conversation that you were misinformed about what goes on in my soon-to-be club. I was wondering if you had done any research since then?" And if so, he'd like to hear all about it.

"No. I haven't. My eyes have remained virgin to sex clubs."

He shook his dark head and turned down the long, traffic-ridden street next to the river.

"Have you ever watched pornographic videos?"

The lights of the city twinkled off the water and the car came to a halt.

"Excuse me?" She'd practically choked on the words.

"Claire," he said, turning to her. Thankfully the endearing term he'd wanted to say had stayed on his tongue. "You are about to witness live sex. It's one thing to see it on a screen. It's quite another to be in the room with it. The energy will seep into your skin. Your reaction to those three women last week was one thing. What you are about to experience is entirely another."

"What do you mean my reaction? I didn't have a reaction."

Luca grinned and fought back a laugh. *She didn't have a reaction?* Her body temperature had risen, and she'd practically panted. Hell, he'd thought she might go over and join the trio.

"I don't know what you're talking about." Claire sat up a little straighter.

"Okay." He let her have her small victory.

The cars in front of them sped up and he put the signal on to turn down the street to his building.

She pouted — *just divine* — next to him until they were in the underground parking and he'd killed the engine.

"Claire," he said and shifted toward her, "I know you're a strong woman. And I admit I read that article about you in the magazine a month ago, so I know you've been through a lot. At any moment, if you are uncomfortable, you just need to tell me. We'll find a quiet place and talk about it. Do you understand?"

Safety, increasingly Claire's alone, was at the top of his concerns.

The gravity of his words must have hit something inside her, because the adorable frown was replaced by her biting the inside of her cheek—something to add to his future unattainable wish list of things the beautiful woman should stop. But for now, it was just a sign of her true unease.

Luca reached out to brush her cheek and their eyes met.

Softer, he asked, "Do you understand, Claire?"

Regretfully, he drew back his touch from her simply made-up skin.

"Yes. I understand."

Quiet. So deliciously quiet.

The air between them thickened and Luca licked his lips then let his teeth rake across the bottom one.

"And you're sure you want to go up there? Sure you're ready?"

"Yes." There was no flush in her skin, no stagger in her breath. Just her eyes. Her piercing, damning, perfect blue-gray eyes.

He turned back and reached for the door handle. "Okay."

Chapter Six

Claire

Two glasses of wine, the same deep red color as the Barolo — his family's vintage, as he'd informed her last time with more than a hint of pride — sat near the corner of the bar where the firm hand on her back was guiding her. Claire's gaze went from the glass to him and back again as she perched on the tall chair.

Luca inclined his head and unbuttoned his jacket, taking the seat next to her. "Yes, my Barolo again."

The dark liquid slid smoothly down her throat with the first sip. She attempted to quell some of the nerves she'd been fighting since Julien had pranced into her office to deliver Luca's message. His order, really, complete with the command to not be late.

"Thank you, Mr. —"

His brown eyes tightened and his mouth thinned.

"I mean, Luca. Thank you for sharing your wine with me again. It's exceptional."

A part of her—a part growing smaller by the second—wanted to beg Luca to take her home and forget this entire preposterous deal. But the fire of curiosity that had been lit at her first visit was so much stronger than her fear. She lifted the glass to her lips again, hoping the alcohol content was high enough to help her see this through to the end. She almost choked on the mouthful of wine when she caught his gaze tracking her every movement.

He mirrored her action, draining his glass. Rising from the chair, he held an arm out. "Shall we?"

Yes? No? The war of uncertainty raged beneath the surface, but she was determined to present an unconcerned face to him. One more swallow and she placed her empty glass beside his on the bar to be whisked away by the ever-present yet mostly invisible Max. She affected an even tone. "Yes, please."

Luca tucked her hand into the crook of his elbow and led her to a wide mahogany staircase. He paused just before they began their ascent, turning his head to pin her with an intense stare. "Do you trust me, Claire?"

"Yes." The answer stunned her nearly as much as her immediate, instinctual response. It had only been a couple of weeks since the man had entered her world as anything more than a hypothetical businessman she'd read about in the latest financial publication. "Yes, I do."

His gaze left hers, surveying the crowd over her right shoulder for a moment before focusing on her again. "Stay by my side tonight." He held up a single digit just as she opened her mouth. "You said you trust me, and while our members are welcoming and adhere to the strict code of conduct of Sopra, there are occasionally guests I do not know, that I am not certain I can trust." He snapped his jaw closed, cutting off his own statement. He tugged her arm, encouraging her to begin the climb.

Claire jutted her lower lip out slightly and furrowed her brows. *Is this unsafe? Am I at risk of being hurt? What was Luca about to say before he so abruptly ended his speech?* Lost in her own thoughts, she jumped when a finger gently pushed on her protruding lip.

"No pouting, Claire."

Was... Was that a smile? Did Luca Bernardi just flash a genuine, damn near playful smile?

They crested the top of the staircase and her mouth went dry. If she had found the first-floor bar boring, this one more than made up for it...and there were two additional stories to explore.

Luca waved to the left where there was another bar, smaller than the one below. "Would you like another drink, Claire?"

She shook her head wordlessly, unable to find her voice. While the gleaming wood surface surrounded on three sides by tall stools was nothing out of the ordinary, the table in the middle of the room certainly was. Nearly the entire length was covered by a flawless blond man surrounded on all sides by various cut fruits, his body covered in chocolate and caramel sauces, whipped cream and even a bowl of maraschino cherries was centered on his navel.

Men and women in various states of dress and undress circled the table, nibbling on the offerings — both the food and the human platter — and making small talk as if this were a normal occurrence. The young man at the center of it all remained completely still, not moving, not speaking, not reacting to any touch.

"His Mistress has instructed him to behave that way." Luca's deep voice purred on her left. "And the single greatest joy for a submissive isn't sexual gratification. It's pleasing their Dominant."

Immediately his words triggered memories for Claire—the approving nod when she'd stilled her silly little habit of focusing her attention by making circles on her palm with her thumb, the gleam in his eyes when he'd seen that she had not only been on time but had been waiting for him tonight. Pleasing him in those small moments had caused an unusual warmth in her belly—and a raging fire roaring through her veins.

He gently pulled her arm to steer her to the right. She scanned the open floor plan laid out before them but quickly pulled her focus to the next area, overwhelmed by the activity. Luca paused, grabbing two glasses of champagne off a passing tray and dropping her arm in the process. He handed her one and Claire gripped the stem, afraid she would drop it as she stared at the scene before her.

A curvy brunette had her wrists and ankles bound to two horizontal pieces of wood in the shape of an X. The only clothing Claire could see on her body was the back of a bustier and spiky black heels. A tall, muscular man dressed in pants matching the black leather the woman wore spoke directly to her in a low tone before turning to address the small group surrounding them.

Luca moved slightly behind her and leaned close, his breath warming her ear with each word. "That is Stefano and his submissive. She has been disrespectful by sitting on the couch beside him rather than on the floor at his feet. Since she insulted him publicly, he feels her punishment should be public as well."

Claire swallowed once. Twice. Her breathing became shallow and she had to concentrate on pulling air into her lungs. With the first crack of the riding crop, she jumped and her hand fluttered to her chest in a futile effort to still her racing heart.

Luca's palm came to rest against the small of her back and he rounded her, his very presence at her side pulling her attention from the continued discipline. "Would you like to leave?"

She shook her head. The excitement — the unexplainable, all-consuming excitement — racing through her veins confused the hell out of her, but the last thing she wanted was to leave. If anything...

"N-no. I-I was just wondering... You've mentioned the rigorous background checks, health forms and membership fees, but how does one begin this process?"

Her cheeks were on fire by the time she'd finished speaking. She downed the contents of the glass she'd almost forgotten about, hoping the action and the lowered lighting would conceal her blush. His eyes darkened, turning into intense black pools. Claire tightened her fingers on the crystal once again as she fought the urge to lower her gaze.

If she'd thought he had perfect posture before, it had been nothing compared to the ramrod straightening of his back that her words had caused. His jaw flexed and he remained silent for so long that an involuntary tremor ran through her.

Luca moved his hand to her arm, running the tips of his fingers down the length before lacing through hers. "Come."

A single word shouldn't carry that much power. The unfamiliar desire that had been building in her the entire night ramped up to an unbearable level and she bit her bottom lip as she struggled to keep up with his clipped, purposeful cadence.

Claire cursed her impatience in blurting out the question. He was going to pack her back into his sexy-as-hell car and drop her at home like some disappointed father who'd caught his underage daughter at a seedy pub, three sheets to the wind. Why in the world did the thought of his rejection lance through her like a dull knife?

He marched them both up another series of steps to a floor lined with closed doors. Echoes of moans, pleasured screams and smacking flesh greeted them as they made their way down the hall. Claire was certain she'd never been this turned on in her life. A small spear of guilt hit her gut. She'd loved Liam, adored every inch of his lanky, six-foot-two frame and had been more than satisfied by their sex life. But every part of tonight spoke to her on an entirely different level.

Luca made a sharp left, sequestering them behind a thick oak door that silenced every sound from the hall. A massive bed stood against the far wall, a deep red velvet couch on the left and a case housing an array of toys Claire couldn't fathom being used on her, yet... Her nipples puckered as an avalanche of possibilities flooded her mind. She tugged her hand free from Luca and crossed her arms.

He stood in the middle of the room, once again fixing her with his silent, intense gaze. After a few moments, he pointed at the sofa. "Sit."

Her body had already taken residence on the soft surface before it clicked in her brain that she'd followed his order. Again.

Luca slid off his suit jacket, folding it carefully and placing it on the chair that matched the couch before sitting beside her. With an amount of precision Claire had never seen accompanying the simple act, he slowly rolled up each sleeve of his crisp white shirt, every inch of exposed olive skin exciting her more than the one before. "This is not an easy question that you ask, Claire."

He smoothed his hand across the material now gathered around his elbow and she willed her mind to focus on his words rather than his movements, a nearly impossible task. He tapped her exposed thigh twice with his index finger. "Look at me, Claire."

Immediately her gaze met his.

"Why is this so difficult? I am in perfect health and am a partner in what is projected to be one of the most successful private banks in Switzerland. I am obviously capable of meeting the fees associated with membership."

The corners of his mouth twitched. "It isn't your physical or financial condition that concerns me. This lifestyle is all about transcending into a mental state based on trust in your Dom, your Master, your owner."

Claire's heart skipped a beat. *Owner.* She was the product of the boarding schools, top universities and social breeding that rivaled royalty, but the very concept of being owned caused a level of exhilaration to course through her that she'd never known before. It was both foreign and welcomed — and incredibly right.

He gripped her hands. "You need to understand what you are asking, Claire."

She curled her fingers around his. "Can you teach me, Luca? Explain it?"

His eyes widened a fraction, his mouth dropping open slightly before he schooled his features once more. "You would need to be trained, need a trainer." Luca lifted his gaze to the ceiling for a moment before pinning her with his stare once again. "You need someone who will teach you everything you need to know, how you need to behave and so much more than we can cover in one conversation."

She tilted her head to the side and bit her lower lip again. If they had been in the boardroom, she could negotiate a deal easily, with confidence, assured of the fact that she would get her way. She always did. But here she was helpless. And Luca seemed determined to talk her out of it at every turn.

Before she could think of anything to say, he tugged her lip free from her teeth with his thumb. "It would be a shame to cause damage to such a beautiful mouth, *cara*." He cleared his throat. "Claire, if you are intent on embarking on this journey, exploring the lifestyle—*my* lifestyle—you need to find someone you trust implicitly to train you, someone who will act with only your best interests at heart, someone who will protect you for as long as you belong to him, someone who will respect your every desire and fear."

His jaw tightened, working back and forth. "There are some who claim to be experienced, knowledgeable Dominants...trainers." He snorted and shook his head. "They are not to be trusted. I've seen many removed from this club in my time here and have all intentions of banning a few more. Because of this, you need to be exceptionally careful who you entrust with your body and, more importantly, your mind."

Claire blinked, absorbing everything he said. It was as informative as it was confusing. Who were these people? Clearly, they didn't walk around with signs around their necks declaring them dangerous. And even if they did...there really was only one option in her mind for a trainer, only one person she trusted to a degree that was perplexing, considering their brief time together.

She licked her lips and took a deep breath. "Luca, would you be my trainer?"

Chapter Seven

Luca

Yes. No. With pleasure. Not now. Right now.

Luca brushed his thumbs over Claire's soft knuckles. She may not have fathomed the enormity of her question but its weight was not lost on him. Her light eyes glistened with insecurity. She knew not what she'd done.

"You are in a state. You've seen things that have perhaps awoken something inside you, that charged a dormant energy you didn't even know you had."

Claire's hard swallow confirmed his suspicion.

"Tonight is not a time to make a decision like this," he said in a soft voice and caressed the sweet skin again.

She dropped her head and pulled away. "You're saying no."

Luca reached inside the collar of his unbuttoned shirt and rubbed through the modest chest hair then up to his shoulder, where he squeezed the tight muscle. He angled his head to find her eyes. He waited.

Yes, he wanted to train her. And yes, it would bring him unreal pride and pleasure to be the one to introduce the power of a true Dom/sub relationship—selfishly, because she was exquisite and he knew he could take an uncut jewel and craft a stunning result, but for her sake as well. He'd seen too many other subs who'd had terrible beginnings. All had had male Doms, to be fair—men who reveled in punishment, who didn't understand the chrysalis of a sub or the cocoon their Master must provide to ensure success.

And his ego would not allow anyone else the honor.

"I don't believe I said that word." His voice brought her eyes, her sad, fragile yet powerful eyes. "I'm saying I want you, that I need you"—he slowed his breath—"to be sure."

As if understanding an argument would be futile, she nodded once.

He continued, "I'll send you some reading material. This lifestyle is not to be chosen on a whim."

"I—"

As soon as her mouth opened he raised his eyebrows and, reading his intent perfectly, she stopped herself. It came as no surprise that the intelligent, beautiful woman in front of him was a quick learner.

Luca stood and unrolled his sleeves with brisk turns of his wrists. He smoothed out the fabric along his forearms—once, twice, three times on each side.

As he crossed to reclaim his jacket, he said, "You've seen enough for tonight. I'll drive you home."

She rose and threaded her fingers through his outstretched hand as they'd done before. Her energy shifted, and he allowed himself to credit his touch.

The echo of their shoes married with the satisfied groans down the hallway to the stairs. For a brief moment, in the darkness of the stairwell, he considered stopping.

To push her up against the wall and kiss her madly, to claim her right then and there, to mark her as his own. He marveled at the oddity. Of all the subs to kneel at his feet, kissing had never been the first thing on his mind.

Upon arriving at the second floor, Luca took quick stock of activities. The sub buffet had been cleared away and a small crowd had formed in front of the glass of the public shower. The slithery Noah Paulick, with his arms crossed and a far-too-smug face, observed the scene of two subs giggling as they washed each other.

Luca gripped Claire's hand a little tighter and hurried her down the next flight. In front of the bar, he told her to wait as he collected his phone and wallet from security. He joined the lovely blonde again and ushered her to his car in the garage.

Once they'd left the lights of the city behind and were on the empty, dark road toward her home, she said, "I've decided to help you with the sale. I'll open your account on Monday."

Luca shifted his jaw. "I hope that's not an attempt to get in my good graces."

"No. I promise it's not. You have money and you want to make more. I can do that. In fact, I'm quite good at it."

His quick glance was enough to catch her smile.

"So I've heard. And that reminds me to tell you something else." He lifted his finger to the blinker and clicked it up. "Honesty is a fundamental requirement in a Dom/sub relationship. Sometimes telling your truths is more painful than any punishment. But if there are lies, or omissions, the foundation crumbles."

The sleek car slowed and crept to a stop in front of her house. He killed the engine and got out to open the door for her. With a hand on the alluring curve of her lower back, he guided her to her front door. She paused and turned around to face him.

Reaching out for her was beyond his control, and he framed her cool face with warm hands. He titled her chin up.

"When it happens, *if* it happens" — he smoothed her pale skin with his thumb — "make no mistake. I choose you. I want you." He stepped back and smiled with pride. He ran a hand over her blonde hair, enjoying the softness and contrast to his own coloring. "If you choose me, Claire — if that's where this goes — you can be sure my dedication will be only to you."

The gentle kiss on her forehead was a sad replacement for his desires but a nonetheless chilling sign of the connection they had already formed. He held it longer than he should have and cursed both the withdrawal and need for more. Wanting her was the easiest thing he'd ever done.

That tender fierceness, her fragile strength... It was all a mystery he needed to unravel.

"Thank you," she said, and turned around to unlock her massive front door. Claire's eyes met his once more from over her shoulder and she went inside.

Once he'd heard the sound of the lock, Luca walked down the steps and went back to his car.

On the drive back to the club...well, home, since his residence was on the top floor, he contemplated playing with one of the free subs to release a bit of his energy but he knew he wouldn't. Putting a scene together while wishing he was with someone else would be a disservice to any sub. Plus, while he was sober enough to drive a car, he had drunk earlier. No, he would have to take care of himself the old-fashioned way. He snickered in the otherwise silent and pristine car.

Haven't done that in a while.

* * * *

Claire's assistant—Julien was his name—was turning out to be a trusted ally. He'd not only confirmed the receipt of Luca's money in his brand-new bank account, but he'd also sent Luca Claire's private email and telephone number and cleared her schedule to accompany Luca to the purchase of the club.

She didn't need to be there. In fact, really only Bruno, Luca and the notary were physically required, but Luca hungered to see the woman in action.

On the cobblestone sidewalk outside the notary's office, she stood in a dark gray suit that subtly hugged her curves. The light blue silk blouse underneath matched her eyes and Luca thanked whatever historical genius had required the Swiss to kiss three times for hello. When her light perfume, still the jasmine with a hint of geranium, stroked his senses, he put aside the thought that he'd missed it.

Desire to kiss, self-gratification and now longing for her smell? The sooner he got an upper hand on this situation the better. And she wasn't late. In fact, she was early.

Luca stepped back. "Shall we?"

He held the door open and Claire passed through with a warm smile. When the small elevator doors closed in front of them, she cleared her throat.

"I got your email," she said.

He'd sent her a long list of reputable blogs he'd discovered over the years. They were not just a good start for a curious mind but also a helpful reminder to Doms/Dommes everywhere — provided that one took the time to read them, which he was sure some did not. Haste was the enemy of care.

The doors opened, and Luca once again grazed the spot on Claire's lower back. In the waiting room of the notary, they found Bruno, dressed in an admirable bright blue suit with a pink tie, and the younger and thinner Adrian in a V-neck tight sweater and even tighter dark jeans. Introductions were made, and Luca left them to inform the receptionist that the party was complete.

In a small conference room, Adrian and Bruno took seats opposite Luca and Claire, with the middle-aged notary and his thick glasses at the helm.

Claire crossed her legs at the ankle. She lined up her own paperwork directly in front of herself and interlaced her fingers in her lap. They all sat through the formal reading of the document of sale and Luca, transfixed by the utter stillness of his banker, was thankful he'd already had his lawyers scour the document. If she hadn't blinked, he would have thought her a statue.

After forty-five minutes and with the document signed, it was her turn for action. She accepted her copy and reached to retrieve her phone from her bag.

"This is Claire Favre for Evan in Transactions, please." She smiled over to Bruno, who was not just ready to be done with the club but to tie up all ends of his fortune. He would stay later at the notary to ensure that his final testament included the proviso that the newly acquired funds go to Adrian in the event of his death. And his death approaching was a real possibility if his illness did not slow its progression. The rush for the sale and the need for Luca to take over the club were more out of duty than desire.

"This is Ms. Favre. Please transfer the ten million francs from account number E47A89 to the recipient in the notes."

She'd memorized his account number. *Why am I surprised? And why am I touched?*

Claire thanked the employee on the other end of her phone and placed the device face down in front of her. "Congratulations, gentlemen. The transaction is complete." She rose, and the men in the room did the same. She shook hands with them all as Luca gathered his paperwork. He tapped the file straight three times and tucked it into the soft leather case he used for his affairs.

After saying his own farewells and wondering if he would ever see Bruno in Zurich again, he trailed Claire out of the office and back to the small elevator.

Luca twisted his wrist and noted the time. "It's a bit early for a drink. Do you have time for a coffee?"

"I do," she said, without checking her own watch or phone.

They exited the building and walked across the square to a café, where they found a table in the back.

With two small espressos in front of them and half a packet of sugar in each, Claire tapped the tiny spoon on her cup and cleaned it off in her mouth before storing it on the saucer.

"As I was saying, I got your email."

"I heard you the first time." He smiled. How could she doubt that he missed anything about her? She was exceptional in every way.

She twisted the small platinum watch around her wrist, and Luca sipped his coffee.

"And I want to thank you. You were right."

Undoubtedly, but he looked forward to her explanation about what.

"It was rash to jump to the conclusion that I could be a"—she leaned down even though there was no one around them—"sub."

No. No thank you very much. He did not want to be right about that. Lord, he might even admit to being wrong. But if he'd saved her from making a commitment to something she wasn't ready for, then he had acted with principle. And she was what mattered, not his longing.

"You've changed your mind?"

"I don't recall using those words." Her flirtatious tone erased the fact that she was using his own retort against him.

He smiled. *Touché.*

"As I said, you were right to stop me. And, for that, I am grateful."

He finished his coffee and slid the cup and saucer to the edge of the table. "It's a big step. One that merits proper consideration."

"I understand that now. And I even dug a little deeper, to try to figure out what was pulling me toward it."

That…? That was pleasing. It was also information he was desperate to acquire. Oh, to be the flame to her nighttime butterfly.

"Turns out," she said with a little shake of her head that freed a lock of her blonde hair. "Turns out, I'm in it for the sex."

"Excuse me?" Luca looked around. *Is this heaven?*

With a giddy smile and a blush in her cheeks, she continued, "There was a test — well, a survey — in one of the links you sent. My results all pointed to sexual submissive. And I have to tell you, I was relieved. I'm not sure I've ever cleaned my house and I have no idea how to cook. So a domestic servant was scaring the shit out of me."

Information overload. But while those tests were a generally helpful way to steer one in the direction of their potential identity, they were not the be-all and end-all.

"Anyway, again, I just want to say that I appreciate what you did that night. And if it's okay with you, I would like to take some more time to think about this."

"I think that's an excellent idea." Or a terrible one, depending on which body part of Luca's was doing the talking. But, deep down, he was proud of her. She had taken his advice and was applying it, just as he'd suggested. Whether or not this went anywhere between them, she had listened. He daresay, obeyed his wishes.

But the gnawing at the inside of her lip told him she wasn't done.

"Ask," he said.

"I'd like to come back to the club, but only if you're there — in case I have questions."

Did the beautiful woman understand that she'd already pleased a Dom? "Another excellent idea."

Chapter Eight

Claire

"A submissive must trust their Dom completely, implicitly, with as many aspects of their life as they negotiate. This can and may include everything from what they wear and what they eat to whether they take a bath versus a shower. A submissive is not merely submitting to the Dominant's sexual and physical demands but also offering their free will, confident in the knowledge that they will be cared for and respected."

Claire took a long draw from her ivory cup of black coffee, not even noticing when she caught her lip in the small divot along the rim. The more she read—even though the very last thing she should be doing in the middle of a Thursday afternoon was reading about kinky sex acts—the more she wanted to experience things she'd never dreamed were for her.

And, without a doubt, she wanted to experience them with Luca, further confusing her already-flustered mind. How had he come to be so important in her life in such a short time?

"Your trust is a gift. Be certain to choose who you give this to wisely." An evocative chuckle erupted from Julien's lips. "Oh, what has that dastardly Italian done to my sweet, little Claire?"

She jumped as soon as Julien began reading the words over her shoulder, the cup clattering loudly against the saucer in her hand. "Julien! Has the word 'privacy' ever entered your vocabulary?"

He set a stack of papers in front of her before rounding the desk and taking residence in the leather chair. With a flick of his wrist, he dismissed her complaint. "Honey, we crossed the privacy barrier off the list when I helped your skinny braless ass shimmy into that sequined dress for the grand opening of whatever-the-hell that restaurant was last year."

"My ass is not skinny." She rolled her eyes. "And by 'whatever the hell' I assume you mean Verkosten? The most exclusive restaurant in Zurich? The deal that landed Steinmetz and Favre multiple other accounts and corporate profiling by several influential trade magazines?"

Julien huffed and crossed his legs, folding his hands around a kneecap. "Yes, yes, we are all thoroughly impressed with your business acumen, Ms. Favre. Now, let's discuss important stuff, shall we? Are you a top or a bottom? A Master or a slave?" He wrinkled his nose in disgust. "You would probably look amazing in black leather, you gorgeous bitch."

She bit down on her bottom lip then quickly released it as the image of Luca gently tugging it free and softly correcting her behavior flashed in her mind — as well as his approving smile. His words rang in her ear, the soft rumble of his deep voice explaining that submissives find joy in pleasing their Dominants. Yeah, she could relate to that.

Claire met the steady, steely gaze head-on, ignoring the heat creeping up her neck. "I am Claire Favre. I am a privileged daughter from one of the finest old-money families in Zurich. I've studied at the top boarding schools and universities in all of Europe—hell, probably the world. I've had etiquette classes, for fuck's sake." She covered her face with her hands. "And right now I want nothing more in the world than to let Luca Bernardi tie me up and beat my ass red with…whatever he wants, because I want to give him every bit of control."

She loved Julien deeply. He had become so much more than her assistant in a very short period of time. He was the only person she'd ever dared to confide in…but she also knew him better than she knew herself. She expected laughter. She expected sassy comments. She expected almost anything other than the silence she was greeted with. Her hands fell and she drew her eyebrows together. "Tell me what you're thinking."

Julien's face remained uncharacteristically stoic. He leaned forward slightly in his chair, his gray eyes glittering with unshed tears. "I think you need this. I think you deserve this. I think Luca may be the best thing that has happened to you in a very long time."

He startled slightly and tapped the black earpiece he always wore to answer calls when he was away from his desk. "Steinmetz and Favre Banking, Claire Favre's office." His impassive expression quickly morphed into a devious grin. "Good afternoon, Mr. Bernardi. Let me check to see if Ms. Favre is available."

She swore simply thinking of him had summoned his presence. "Transfer him. Right away. He doesn't like to wait." She laid her hand on the phone receiver, ready to snatch it up as soon as Julien hit the button.

His smile widened. "Sub. You are definitely a sub."

She glared at him, pulling the phone to her ear, mouthing 'Go' and shooing him away. She closed her eyes, swallowed and forced her voice into an even tone. "This is Claire Favre." She mentally patted herself on the back for pretending she didn't know exactly who was on the other end.

"Good afternoon, Claire."

She pressed a hand to her chest. The man had spoken three words and wasn't even in the same room as her and her body had immediately responded to his voice. "Hello, Luca. I-I didn't expect to hear from you." She jutted out her lower lip. "There isn't a problem with the sale, is there?"

A small chuckle echoed across the line. "No, no, you are too thorough for that. You truly left no room for errors. But I believe we have some unresolved business of a more personal nature."

Her heart stopped beating then began racing. "Yes, yes we do. I was actually reading through one of the articles you sent. It was quite informative."

"Having a late lunch, are we?"

Claire's stomach chose that exact moment to growl in protest at yet another missed meal. "Oh, lunch, no I… I skipped lunch today. Well, missed it. Worked through it would be a more accurate description, I suppose." She placed her fingers over her lips at the admission. Why did she feel the need to divulge so much information to him? Her eyes landed on the screen in front of her as she read the second bullet point in the submissive guideline. Right beneath '*Trust is honesty*'.

Silence. Her response was met with a heavy, telling silence. The disapproval practically oozed through the phone line. A lack of reply from Luca was nearly as intense as his voice.

After several beats, he sighed. His voice became muffled but the words 'salmon' and 'asparagus' stood out. "I am sending a meal. I expect you to eat the entire thing. We will discuss your eating habits at a later date."

Rebellion fired up within her and she opened her mouth to do battle with the great and powerful Luca Bernardi. She wasn't a child and could certainly manage to take care of herself and...

"As you wish."

The words fell from her lips and warmth spread through her as she envisioned his approving nod — and the fire in his eyes each time she said that phrase. What was it about those three little words?

He cleared his throat. "You mentioned wanting to return to the club, with me. I will pick you up tomorrow evening at nine."

What was it with Luca and that day? "I can't Friday, but please, Saturday? I-I also have questions for you."

Another pause. Shorter. "Saturday it is, Claire. Continue your research. There are some aspects we will certainly need to discuss. Enjoy your lunch, *cara*." Without waiting for a response from her, he ended the call.

Before she'd had time to process the whirlwind that was the end of her call with Luca, Julien swung the door open, leaning against the frame with that incorrigible smirk on his face and a to-go bag dangling from his index finger. "A Mr. Luca Bernardi requested a meal delivery for Ms. Claire Favre...or so said the delicious little delivery boy who dropped this off" — he winked, sauntering in the room to drop the food on her desk — "and gave me his number."

Claire tore the lid from the container, suddenly ravenous, and attacked the food with gusto. Swallowing the mouthful of glazed salmon and risotto, she waved her fork at Julien. "Then go call him and stop tormenting the payer of your salary."

* * * *

Claire shoved her hands deeper into the light jacket she wore, shivering a little in the brisk fall air as she stood on her porch waiting for the sleek black Maserati to round the corner. He'd be pleased she was on time, early even. A hum of joy surged through her veins.

The already familiar roar of the engine as Luca pulled up to her house sent a chill down her spine that was completely unrelated to the dropping temperature. When he rose from the vehicle, he pinned her with an intense stare, hanging one arm over the open driver's door. The corners of his mouth twitched. Claire couldn't help but smile as she stepped down to the sidewalk. *'Joy in pleasing your Dom'*...indeed.

Even in her impressive heels, Luca still had to bend slightly to kiss her three times on her cheeks. Be it wishful thinking or a figment of her overly active imagination, he seemed to linger ever so slightly on the common greeting tonight. "You look stunning, *cara*."

She ducked her head. "Thank you, but I'm wearing a coat. For all you know, I could be wearing an orange leopard print pleather mini dress."

He laughed. Luca Bernardi, who rarely even cracked a smile, laughed. "I cannot imagine you in such an atrocity." He held her door open and ran his fingertips down her sleeve, causing her to meet his steady gaze. His voice dropped to a rumbling whisper. "And I have a very good imagination."

Claire's mouth went dry and she slid into her seat before Luca could spot the pink creeping up her neck. The short ride to the club passed in silence, the air thick with all the unspoken thoughts.

With her hand once again tucked into the crook of his arm, Luca paused at the door. "As before, one word and we leave."

Claire lifted a shoulder and offered a small smile. "I know, but I'm looking forward to watching. Again. With you."

He held her gaze for barely another breath, but it was enough to reflect the fire in the chocolate depths. He turned to swipe his card and gain access. They paused on the main floor long enough to check her jacket with the attendant. He swept his gaze over her body, clad in a short white dress with a neckline that dipped dangerously close to her navel. He gave a nod before leading her to the stairs.

With each step her desire grew. Knowing what she'd see—or at least having a basic understanding—only seemed to ramp up her excitement, to increase the need she'd never known she had but was helpless to deny.

Tonight's tour led them in the opposite direction and Claire found herself standing before a wall of glass shower doors. Some of the stalls stood empty, but the others... Claire couldn't fight the heat burning her cheeks. Women, men, couples and threesomes filled the various cubes. A few merely bathed with little attention paid to the onlookers. Others pleasured themselves or their partners as spectators stood, commenting, admiring, lusting.

"You like this, *cara*?"

She turned her head and only noticed then that while she'd been drinking in the public showers, Luca had been studying her. "H-how…" She summoned her courage and recalled every article she had read. If she truly wanted this—and him—she had to be open and honest. "How long… How much training would I need before I could do that?"

His eyes widened, but before he could answer, Max appeared from nowhere with a harried expression. "Mr. Bernardi, I'm sorry to interrupt you, but we have a situation downstairs. It's rather urgent."

Luca held her gaze for several moments. "Let me take Ms. Favre to my room first then I'll be down."

The V between Max's eyes deepened, but he nodded in acquiescence. He scurried away and Luca turned them toward the mahogany steps leading to the third floor.

Claire dug her heels into the plush red carpeting. "Luca, please. I can wait for you here. It sounds important and I don't want to be the cause of any issues for you."

He shook his head then muttered something in Italian. Although she was fluent in several languages, she couldn't hear him well enough to translate, but she was fairly certain there was more than one expletive.

He straightened his shoulders, dropped her hand and moved in front of her. "If I am gone longer than twenty minutes, you are to go to my room upstairs and wait for me. Do you remember which one it is?" At the movement of her head in the affirmative, he gave a quick approving nod. "Until you go upstairs, you will stay on this side of the floor." He hooked an index finger beneath her chin and dropped his head, his mouth millimeters from hers. "We shall consider this a test of your obedience, *cara*."

Without another word he released her, turned on his heel and walked away with confident, purposeful strides. A level of need she'd never experienced before pooled between her legs.

With a shaky inhale, she walked to the bar, needing to soothe her parched throat. She took a stool recently abandoned by a shirtless man wearing black jeans, who was holding a leash attached to a collar attached to a petite blonde who had been sitting at his feet. Not brave enough to request Luca's wine, she ordered a margarita. She smiled to herself as the drink was set before her. Seeing a person being led around like an animal would have shocked her sensibilities before Luca Bernardi had come into her life.

She nearly choked on her first sip. *What would Liam think of me?*

Ice ran through her veins and she struggled with the unsettling thought. Lost in her own mind, she never registered the person who took the seat beside her until his hand landed on her thigh and she jumped. A small amount of the frozen drink sloshed over the side of the glass.

"I didn't mean to scare you." His full lips split into a self-deprecating smile and his blue eyes crinkled at the corners. He was gorgeous. "Aren't you here with Luca?"

Something about the concept of belonging to Luca chased away the ghosts haunting her. "Yes. He will be back any moment." She scooted on her seat to angle away from him slightly, her instincts throwing out warning signals.

He winked and, despite the fact it was charming, her stomach refused to settle. "Lucky for me I picked this moment." He stuck a hand out. "Noah. First names only, as you know. And you are?"

Chapter Nine

Luca

If Max had insisted, there had to have been a reason. Luca jogged down the circular staircase and as soon as he caught a glimpse of the bar, he knew his employee had been right to interrupt him.

A male submissive who Luca barely knew was curled into a corner of the bar with his arms crossed over his face for protection. Above him stood another male submissive — recently replaced by the ball on the floor — who Luca knew too well. And between them, with her hands perched on her wonderfully curved hips, stood Luca's close friend and fellow Domme, Caroline Cartier.

"Everybody out except you," Luca growled to Max.

As Luca stepped closer, his skin tightened around his normally steady frame.

Blood.

They were all bleeding.

The sub on the floor had a crack over his eyelid and red dripped down his wincing cheek. A drop of blood from Caroline's nose crawled closer to her already deep red lips. But the worst culprit of the dripping red was the wrist of the familiar sub, Damien. He held a broken tumbler glass in one hand and stared at his former Mistress with glazed eyes.

Caroline shot Luca a look of warning. She clearly wanted to handle this herself, but from the crimson blots on the rug below, she was failing.

The bar officially cleared out and Max started to head to Luca's side. Luca raised his arm slowly, giving him the signal to wait. With his military background and dedication to safety, Max was proving to be an incredible asset.

Caroline narrowed her eyes and found her voice. "On your fucking knees. *Now*, sub!"

Damien's face dropped, the poor man obviously craving the order more than even he could have realized.

This is why I don't want any sub of mine to fall in love with me.

The broken glass tumbled from his hand and landed with a quiet thud on the rug. Damien crumbled to his knees, gaze falling with him, and wept.

Tension defused, but blood still dripping, Caroline knelt down to her new sub. He softened at her touch on his forehead. She whispered into his ear and kissed the back of his hand.

Max trotted over to the bar, grabbed a stack of towels and returned. He dropped them on the low table in front of him and waited with Luca for Caroline's sign to move in.

Instead, the Domme looked to Max and said, "Please take him upstairs. Call a doctor if he needs stitches."

Luca did admire Caroline's way. There was no hint about future plans with her and the new sub, even though there most certainly would be. She had chosen her words perfectly in front of a suffering and out-of-control Damien.

Damien, who was whimpering at her feet and needed medical attention... But the calm of her voice was better than any Band-Aid that could be offered. It wasn't the first time a sub had come back to his Mistress and caused a scene. Caroline Cartier had a way with men, and while Luca couldn't relate to being addicted to it, he could appreciate it.

"Damien, Luca is going to wrap your wrist. I need you to be still for me."

Luca is going to do what?

With no time for grumbling, Luca reached for a towel and found himself in the very unlikely position of kneeling in front of a Domme. Had the cut not been so deep, they would have laughed at the absurdity.

Blood wept onto Luca's suit and into his white sleeve until he was able to apply enough pressure to control the wound.

Glad he didn't have to be the one to deal with the next decision, he asked Caroline, "What's your move here?"

"I'm going to call my doctor and get him patched up. Wait here while I go get my phone."

Luca arched an eyebrow. He was on the wrong side of taking orders.

"Please," she added in a low voice.

As Luca continued to press into the towel, he thought about the impact this might have on his club.

While blood didn't bother the average member, drama did. 'Not his sub and not his problem' had quickly flipped into 'his club and now his problem'.

Max returned with a drained look on his face. He scratched his neck and let out a forceful exhale through his mouth. He shook his head slowly from the doorway all the way to the corner where Luca and Damien were on the floor. "I'll take it from here, boss. Knowing you, you'll want to attend to the bar upstairs."

Max leaned down and replaced the bloodstained towel with a new one while Luca pushed on his knees to stand.

Christ.

His hands were covered in blood—not his and not his sub's.

On any other day, that would have been enough for Luca Bernardi. He'd already thought about how many times he would need to wash his hands with antibacterial soap while he'd held Damien's arm. But the real concern, the true problem in that moment, was the tone in which Max had spoken. He needed to get back upstairs. It could only mean one thing. What in the ever-living-hell of this disastrous night was Claire doing?

And the fact that Max still hadn't made eye contact did nothing for his heart rate. Luca wiped his hands on his ruined suit and marched out of the bar.

"Luca," Caroline called from down the hall.

He steadied his breath.

Caroline tossed her long red hair over her shoulder and clipped toward him. "I'm sorry. I didn't know he'd taken it like that. I checked in with him several times last week because I sensed something was off, but he lied. And I will talk to him."

"He can't come back."

"I know," Caroline said. "A car's on its way. I'll be back later. Obviously, I'll replace the rug." She grimaced.

"Obviously." Luca turned on his heel and climbed the stairs. When he reached the second floor, he glanced toward the empty spot where he'd left Claire twenty minutes prior.

Heat slithered up his spine as his gaze shot left to the bar. There she sat, cradling a margarita, next to the grinning novice.

Weasel. Noah Paulick was a wanna-be-real Dom and a fucking weasel. And Luca had left Claire alone for easily twenty minutes and in a state the lovely lady could barely cope with.

Luca reached to pull on his cuffs and stopped himself. Instead, he walked slowly behind the bar and over to the sink, conveniently located directly opposite Noah. With the back of his hand, Luca pushed on the water and slid the faucet to warm. He pumped the soap, again mindful of the residual blood on his skin, and he lathered up. The foam, hidden by the bar, turned pink and he repeated the process again—and again.

With the towel in hand, he looked up once at Claire and read her briefly. Whatever her conversation with Noah may or may not have been before his arrival, it had ceased. At least there was that. After a long blink, his gaze wandered over to the young blond who thought he knew something about the lifestyle.

Luca folded the used towel and set the perfect cloth square next to the sink. "Were you aware, Noah, that you were speaking to my guest?" he asked in a low, too-calm voice.

"I was, although she said you'd be right back. That was a while ago. I was beginning to think you'd abandoned her. Maybe she was, too." Noah licked his lips, the little bastard obviously ready for a challenge.

"What she thinks does not concern you." Luca leveled his gaze and shot it back to Claire. "Follow me."

He walked out from behind the bar and down the hall. Her heels clicked at a steady pace behind him. *Good.* She had listened to him.

Out of his jacket, he found his key card, which opened a nondescript door. He motioned for her to enter, and when she saw the buttons, she said with wide eyes, "Oh my God. Are you taking me home?"

"Yes. Mine." Luca jabbed the button to the penthouse and they rode in silence.

The doors opened to his massive loft. Soft lighting illuminated their walk to the kitchen, where he motioned to a stool around the dark granite island.

"Sit," he said as he turned around the counter and opened up the trash drawer below the stainless-steel sink.

He slipped off his jacket, gathered it in half at the neck line, then brought the sleeves in along its length. One, two, three times he folded it and shoved it into the plastic-lined receptacle.

Behind him, he reached into the dark wood cabinet for a water glass. After releasing his cuff links, he dropped them inside. Sterilized. They would need to be sterilized.

As if the clink of the platinum had broken the silence, Claire chose that moment to speak, and when she did, her tone was cautious. "Are you mad at me?"

Luca unclipped his thick watch and slid it into the glass with the cuff links. He unbuttoned his shirt, folded it exactly as he had the jacket and it met the same destiny.

His exhale stuck in his tight throat.

She did not cause the blood.

Calmer, with less evidence of the fiasco on his body, he was ready to look at her.

She bit her lip, and when his eyes dropped to the infraction, she released it immediately.

"I…" Claire brought a thumb to the opposite palm, appeared to rethink herself and sat on both hands.

Through squinted eyes, he asked, "Did you think speaking to another man in my club would make me happy, Claire?"

In truth, it could have been anywhere. It was unlike him to be annoyed, and jealousy wasn't an emotion he was familiar with. But the blood… It had made him panic—panic like the day he'd seen his mother's unstoppable nose bleed, panic like the day he'd realized he had no mother.

"I didn't want to be rude. And I honestly didn't think you would be gone that long." She swallowed but held her gaze until her focus fell to his bare chest.

He allowed her to gawk. Hell, he enjoyed it. And when her bottom lip curled in and she trapped it with her teeth, he didn't care.

Slowly, Luca reached for his belt. She continued her voyeuristic ways as he pulled it tight against his hips then released it. It slid through the loops and he wrapped it around his knuckles. *No contact.* The belt had been under the jacket, so there was no chance of blood.

With the leather strip still around his hand, he placed it on the counter and leaned a little closer.

"Eyes up, Claire."

After a flutter of her lashes, he had her attention.

Luca worked his jaw. "Are you implying that I was the reason you were speaking to Noah?"

Her lovely face fell and her posture sank. "I'm sorry." She shook her head slowly. "I didn't know."

"No. No, you didn't know. And no, you don't. And while I may be disappointed that your instincts were off, I'm not mad. Not at all." Luca studied her and, satisfied he read relief, spun around to the large refrigerator. He found two bottles of water and set one in front of her.

Leaning in, too close — he knew it was too close — he said, "I need a shower. Take off your heels and go get comfortable on the couch. We'll talk."

He pushed away, the cool counter poking into his back. Claire nodded her understanding and slid off the barstool. Her tiny hips swayed all the way to the other end of the loft, where she stopped and stared out of the window at the shimmering city lights.

Luca walked around the counter, kicked off his shoes and dropped his pants. After he'd folded them, he piled them on top of the other clothes he could never wear again. With a gentle push, the bin was back under the sink and the cabinet closed, all evidence to be locked away and forgotten. In his socks and black boxer briefs, he carried his belt back to his bedroom.

Under the hot stream of the shower, it hit him. He'd let a potential sub into his private apartment. The shocking events from the bar and the need to deal with blood had thrown him off his game. That was not good, not good at all. If — and that was a big if — she really did want to be trained, there was no more room for error. He could not let her down.

He dried himself off and changed into a pair of track pants that hung off his waist but tapered at the heels. It occurred to him that negotiations would be far more interesting if he was bare chested. The little minx had obviously liked what she'd seen, but his Dom voice cried foul.

Barefoot and thick hair still wet, he padded back to Claire. She hadn't sat as he'd asked—well, told—but her high-heels were next to the cream sofa. The urge to set them straight instead of one up and one on its side, as they were, would have to wait.

It wasn't just that she'd lost height without the shoes. With her focus still out of the window, the beautiful blonde was somewhere else. He stepped closer.

Claire closed her eyes and her posture relaxed.

"Are you okay?" he asked.

"I think so." She stared forward again.

Luca hesitated but stepped back. He tidied her heels and sat down on the L-shaped sofa. "Come on. Sit."

"You say that a lot." She turned around and smirked.

"Would you rather I say something else?" He'd thought she'd liked the direction. Perhaps he'd been wrong.

Claire sat at the far end of the couch and tucked a foot under her rear. "You're the one with the imagination—or so you claim."

Is that some kind of challenge? Accepted. And he would get back to it. In spades.

Luca hid his smile. "I know you said you have questions and I'm ready to answer them all. But first I have one very important one to ask you."

Claire shifted in her seat. "Okay…"

"When was the last time you ate?"

Chapter Ten

Claire

She parted her lips, preparing to suck the lower one between her teeth when she caught herself. *No.* She had spent more time than she cared to admit researching everything Luca had sent her. Each article varied slightly, but they all centered on the same precepts — honesty, trust, confidence. She would answer his question honestly. "I told you I'm not much of a cook…" She sighed and rolled her eyes. "Okay, I don't cook at all. I could burn water. So, yes, I ate around seven. *My* type of dinner."

Luca's deep chocolate gaze darkened. "Explain 'your' version."

After his reaction to her lunch the other day, she was certain her response would be met with disapproval and that bothered her far more than she wanted to acknowledge. "Popcorn — and wine." She straightened in her seat, flustered by the censure written all over his face. "I don't drink a lot, just a glass or two in the evenings sometimes."

His nostrils flared. "That is not anyone's 'type' of a meal. If you want to be under my tutelage, you need to behave in a way that displays my ability to guide you into the fulfillment of yourself. You need to show the world the very best version of yourself that I am helping you achieve. Popcorn and wine do *not* achieve that end, Ms. Favre."

Ms. Favre? Had she undone everything simply by being truthful? A bubble of anger roiled through her stomach. She jutted out her lower lip and furrowed her forehead. "In all the research I have done, both through your guidance — which I appreciate very much, if I have not mentioned that — and on my own, the importance of open communication between a Dominant and a submissive was stressed repeatedly. I understand that this" — she gestured between the two of them — "if you agree to it, is a temporary proposition. Only training. But the same rules would apply, no?"

His jaw flexed beneath the well-groomed beard. "I do not believe I said anything contradictory."

She paused for a moment. She had already disappointed him twice this evening — once with whatever-his-name-was downstairs and again with her eating habits. Did she really want to incite him again by arguing? "Then why did you call me Ms. Favre? Was it not you who demanded the familiarity of first names?"

Did… Did his mouth just twitch again? Is he trying to avoid smiling? Claire blinked. She was so certain he'd be seething.

His gaze washed over her, pausing for just a moment on her mouth. He stood abruptly. "Follow me."

Claire had no doubt in her role. She was a submissive. With each bit of information she gleaned, she was learning to embrace the title, and it made so many pieces of her click into place like a long-abandoned puzzle. But if Luca did agree to train her and they did have a conversation, she would need to address these mood swings of his before she got whiplash. Although seeing the hint of a smile, knowing what it meant, she pushed aside the feelings that stirred.

She trailed after him into the kitchen, assuming this was yet another one of his obedience tests. He laid eggplant, red and yellow peppers, zucchini and an onion on the counter. He reached into an overhead cabinet and pulled down a dish before grabbing a length of Italian sausage from the refrigerator, setting it on the plate and placing it soundlessly on the granite surface as well. When he bent down to reach beneath inside the island, she pressed her lips together to prevent the gasp from escaping. There wasn't an inch of this man's body that wasn't perfect.

He set a thick, wooden cutting board beside the vegetables and turned to face her. Claire's cheeks flamed as soon as his eyes met hers and he sauntered over to stand in front of her. The left corner of his mouth kicked up and he leaned close to her. She assumed he would kiss her—prayed he would—but the soft whisper of the drawer opening on her right told her that every hope was in vain.

"Here is your knife, *cara*." He held the short blade between his thumb and forefinger, pointing the silver stainless-steel handle toward her.

Claire blinked, darting her eyes back and forth between Luca and the utensil. "M-my knife? I told you I can't cook."

"I was listening." The three words rumbled through her body, exciting her in ways they shouldn't and reaching parts of her she wasn't ready to acknowledge. He nodded toward the counter. "But you are going to cut those for me."

A test. This must be one of Luca's tests. She took the knife with a steady hand that belied her true emotions. "As you wish."

The entire length of his body stiffened at the words. Yes, she would need to investigate that reaction a little more.

She focused on her task, driven by the overwhelming urge to show Luca she could be obedient, *would be* obedient. For him. Hearing him address her formally had left her unsettled and uncertain about where they would go from here. Perhaps this was a second chance to prove herself?

Cutting vegetables was something she could easily manage. Nanny Helen had allowed her to assist with small things in the kitchen when her parents hadn't been showing her off at some social obligation she'd had no desire to participate in. Slicing and dicing various items had often been her job — something that could be quickly abandoned in the event of either parent approaching.

And that experience afforded her the ability to watch nearly every move Luca made out of the corner of her eye. He pulled a stockpot and large pan from somewhere behind her, filling the pot with water and coating the pan with olive oil before placing both on the stove at various heat levels. Every movement was efficient, smooth and focused.

Finished with the peppers, she grabbed the zucchini. "Does this mean you've decided?" Her voice was barely above a whisper, but she knew he could hear her, just as well as she knew he would know exactly what she meant.

"We shall discuss it over the meal."

The answer must be no. He had some weird fixation on her eating habits and didn't want to give her the answer now to ensure she would eat. A lead weight dropped in her stomach. She slid the zucchini to the side and began to chop the eggplant into bite-sized pieces with more ferocity than it required.

Luca deposited the cut vegetables from the board into the warm oil with a sizzle. Resigned to the fact that he wouldn't be her trainer and there was no need to display her willing obedience any longer, Claire plucked a strip of pepper from his hand as he collected the remaining pieces and popped it into her mouth before she returned to her duty. He looked at her with a mixture of disapproval and humor.

"If you were that hungry, perhaps you should consider having a normal person's version of a meal rather than your own."

The scent of the herbs he sprinkled into the pan with casual precision made her mouth water. She grinned playfully. "It's actually all your fault. I was quite content with what I'd eaten earlier until you started making this delicious meal."

He emptied the remaining bit of penne into the boiling water, folding the empty plastic bag before placing it into the trash with more care than Claire had ever seen someone handle garbage. "Concern for your wellbeing is considered a fault, is it?"

Several clever retorts were on the tip of her tongue, but instead of offering them, she simply moved to cut the sausage into angled discs. When she'd finished and he'd added the meat to the sautéing vegetables, she carried the knife and cutting board to the sink, but Luca intercepted her. He carefully loaded the board into the dishwasher, washed the knife in the sink and wiped the countertop she'd abandoned — three times.

Claire tilted her head. Perhaps it was a good thing he didn't seem interested in training her. There were some things about Luca Bernardi that would take getting used to and wouldn't meld with her life.

Even with her growing certainty that he didn't find her good enough to train, just watching him cook with that focused intensity — not to mention the bare chest her fingers itched to touch — was a gift. Hell, watching him breathe was better than a square of her favorite chocolate. She couldn't tear her eyes away as he combined the pasta with the vegetables and meat and filled two plates.

"Set these on the table." He inclined his head toward the dishes as he washed the pot and pan.

With the first bite, Claire moaned and closed her eyes. Garlic, rosemary and an array of spices she couldn't place exploded on her tongue. A chuckle startled her from her reverie and made her lids pop open.

"That is quite the compliment." He speared a piece of eggplant with his fork and lifted it to his lips. Claire was helpless to look anywhere else. Luca's mouth, his hands, his everything, had her hypnotized. "Eat, Claire. We will talk after."

She shook her head slightly to try to break the spell he had over her. She focused on the rainbow of food on her plate and tried to formulate the most logical response to his forthcoming dismissal that she could. Thankfully, her years of smiling and assuring her parents she didn't mind that they missed yet another major event in her life had prepared her well for this moment.

They finished their meal in relative silence and, when done, Luca immediately collected their dishes. He added them to the cutting board in the dishwasher and set the cycle to sanitize before wiping the nearly spotless glass-top table — three times.

He folded the disposable wipe into a square and put it in the trash before he held an arm toward the couch again. "Let's get more comfortable, *cara*."

She rose from the table and followed him without thinking. She sat closer to him. If this was the last time she'd see Luca Bernardi outside of her office, she wanted to enjoy it.

"What have you learned in your research?"

Claire blinked several times and pulled her feet up beneath her. This wasn't the way she had anticipated the conversation going. "As I said, open and honest communication is critical — and trust." She swallowed as Luca turned toward her slightly, stretching an arm across the back of the couch. "Because I would be giving control of...everything to m-my D-Dom."

He nodded slowly. "And how do you feel about that prospect?"

Claire lifted one shoulder slightly. "A little nervous but mostly excited."

"If I train you, I will expect you to answer phone calls or text messages within a fixed period of time.

Your eating will change and your habits will change. Depending on where your limits lie, your clothing may even change. I will punish disobedience, but only within guidelines we establish. I will show you how to find pleasure through pain and stretch your boundaries, but I will never break them." His chocolate eyes softened. "I will always have your best interests at heart. Your protection and personal growth will be my number one priority and color every decision I make while you are mine."

Goosebumps appeared on her arms, at war with the fire of need raging through her, both reactions caused by his words. *His. I would be his.* "If? So, you still haven't decided?"

His lips twitched again and Claire fought her own smile. "It is you, Claire, who makes the decision. While the outside world sees a submissive as weak, the truth is that they hold all the power. They are the ones who call 'red' to stop everything when they feel it has gone too far. They set hard and soft guidelines for what they are and aren't willing to try. And they choose their Dom."

There wasn't an article or blog or video that had prepared Claire for Luca's speech. He'd said everything in less than five minutes that she'd never known she needed to hear. She scooted toward him on the couch, her knee nearly touching his. "I want you to train me, to be my Dom for as long as that lasts."

His arm fell from the back of the couch and he grasped her hand in his. "There was one thing, one very important rule I didn't hear when you explained all that you'd learned."

She frowned. Did he want her to recite every detail from every page she'd read? She opened her mouth to respond but quickly closed it at the arch of his eyebrow. He wasn't finished.

"The very first rule is meant to guard and protect *you* more than me. And as I said, the mental, emotional and physical wellbeing of a sub — *my* sub — is a top priority to any good Dom. Since this is training, you can't fall in love." He breathed the final word on a heavy sigh, as if the very concept of love was a burden.

"I've had love…and lost love. That's…" Claire shook her head. "You have no concerns there." A bright smile lit her face. She loved winning, no matter the setting, and Luca had all but said the words. "When do we begin?"

"Tomorrow." He inclined his head downward, his free hand gripping the side of her neck. "But from here on out, you are mine. In the club especially." His eyes hardened and his jaw flexed. "You speak to no one other than me unless I give you explicit permission."

She nodded rapidly. "Yes, Luca. As you wish."

This time her silly little saying was met with a more passionate response than ever before. His lips met hers, firm and possessive — moving across every inch, claiming them as his. The soft hair of his beard brushed against her top lip and chin, ramping up her desire to an almost desperate level.

She lifted her hands, needing to touch him. But as soon as her fingers met the skin of his shoulders, he placed them back in her lap. He continued to kiss her with nearly the intensity his eyes held when he was reading her. Dissecting her.

He swiped his tongue across her lower lip before snaking inside her mouth and taunting hers with a dastardly game of tag, retreating every time she hesitantly reached to him. She reached his chest, itching to thread her fingers through the short hair smattering across it. But, just as before, he removed them from his body after only a few seconds of contact. She growled in the back of her throat.

He pulled back, breaking the kiss. He returned one hand to grip her neck, running the thumb of the other across her lower lip. "A small preview to our lessons, Cara. A sub doesn't touch their Dom without express permission." He rested his forehead against hers. "And we shall learn more tomorrow, but for now, I must find something more appropriate to wear to drive you home."

Claire stared at his retreating back as he sauntered back into his room. She pressed her fingers to her lips. She belonged to Luca Bernardi...at least for the time being.

Chapter Eleven

Luca

Four.
Five.
Si-

The joints on the wooden door of Luca's suite squeaked open and Claire slipped in. She pressed her lips tightly together. In her Burberry overcoat, black heels and with her hair in a well-groomed ponytail, she was impeccable.

"There was traffic."

At least she'd acknowledged her tardiness. And in the six minutes she'd kept him waiting, he'd concocted the most perfect first lesson around her self-inflicted theme.

Luca tapped his fingers on the armrest of the leather sofa and grinned. "Last chance to back out, Ms. Favre."

Her eyes widened at the name. "No, Mr. Bernardi. I'm ready to learn."

Was that her attempt at sass? *Tsk. Tsk.*

"Sir," he corrected with sternness. "In this room and wherever else I take you during your training, you will call me Sir."

"Yes, Sir." Her hands twisted just below the cinched belt of the taupe overcoat.

The desire to address her fidgeting was overpowered by the fact that she'd called him 'Sir' for the first time. His chest swelled. Had he known he'd been addicted to the sound of that word from her mouth, he would have sought her out sooner. But just as she'd helped him with the purchase of the club, this arrangement was serious. She wanted to train, was willing to devote herself to him. He had a responsibility to do it right.

Luca continued, "Good girl. And from here on out, when I want your eyes, I will ask for them. Do you understand, *sotto*?" *Sotto?* Surely, he'd meant 'sub'. Had she endeared him so much that it warranted an Italian nickname?

Her gaze dropped to the floor and she said, "Yes, Sir."

He needed to return to the basics. Formalities would bring him peace. "*Brava.* Claire, what do you say to me when I approach a limit and you think you need me to stop?"

"Yellow, Sir."

"Yes." *Good.* This was all good. "And what do you say to me when I've gone too far, and you absolutely need me to stop?"

"Red, Sir."

Even better.

"Correct. I'm putting all my trust in you to use these words whenever you need to. All my trust. *You* hold the power. Can I trust you, *sotto*?"

She swallowed and licked her lips. Her surrender was enchanting. "Yes, Sir."

"Take off your coat and dress and hang them in the closet. Put your shoes in there as well." He stood and rolled his white sleeves. "When I walk into this room, you will already be here. You will kneel next to the bed and your eyes will remain on the ground. Show me how I will find you, *sotto*." The Italian word for 'bottom' slipped off his tongue yet again before his mind could stop it. Apparently, the nickname was hers now.

In her assigned—and beyond pleasing—white lace bra and matching panties, Claire obeyed. Luca brought a hand to his cheek and rubbed his soft beard in circles. He smiled.

There she was, the beautiful, smart and successful Claire Favre, below him. He'd been right all those weeks ago when he'd seen her picture in the magazine. She was even more stunning on her knees.

"I read your email. Every word." *More than once.* He might just do the same every night before bed for the rest of…her training. The rest of her *training.*

"Your limits are impressive and, I must admit, inspiring. I had a delectable first lesson planned for you."

Her face pinched. *Good.* She'd caught the past tense.

He continued, "But it seems you had other plans. You thought I should wait."

Luca stepped around his sub, trailing a finger on her bare shoulder as he went. Goosebumps peaked to life along her upper back.

"It is a pity, this foul habit of not being on time, making people wait." He drew his hand back, but Claire stayed still. "I do wonder why you would think your time is more important than mine. And now, my plans have been changed. Quite inconvenient." He clicked his tongue.

Luca leaned down and took in her lovely light scent. In her ear, he whispered, "And I am quite disappointed. I'd been imagining for weeks the look on your face when I make you come the first time."

She flinched, and Luca stood back up.

"Oh yes, *sotto*. Many weeks." He sighed dramatically and crossed his arms. "But you decided to make me wait. You see all the power you hold?"

She stared at the ground and her chest stuttered on her inhale.

"I asked you a question. But today seems to be a day of firsts—the first lesson for you and the first time a sub has dared to be late for a first meeting with me. So, I shall commit another virgin act and repeat myself. Don't get used to it." He slowed his speech. "Do you see how your actions—your decisions—hold power?" He walked back in front of her.

"Yes," she said in a meek voice.

"Eyes!"

Her blue beauties snapped up.

He corrected, "Yes, *Sir*."

"Yes, Sir," she said with more strength.

Better. "You may return your gaze to the floor." Luca checked his watch. He had only intended on spending an hour in the scene then however long she needed in aftercare. It was her first day. He reminded himself to be gentle. No ropes.

"I am a strong believer that the punishment should fit the crime. So yours should, too. You shall wait."

Luca's dress shoes scuffed over to the end of the large four-poster bed.

"Stand."

Claire did as she was told, keeping her eyes down. She was doing well. Very well.

"Lie down on your stomach in the middle of the bed and spread your legs. Put your arms overhead and cross your wrists."

Again, his new sub followed his orders. He checked his watch and stood silent for three minutes.

When the needle ticked the final second, he sat down on the side of the bed.

"Close your eyes, *sotto*." A rasp had taken over his stronger commanding voice and he reached to the curve at the base of her spine. He trailed his fingers along an aimless path on her soft, creamy skin.

His discovery continued, sometimes brushing over the hem of her underwear, but mostly central to the little dip in her back.

"Did you learn, in all your reading, that your orgasms now belong to me?"

"Yes, Sir." Her faint voice matched the quiet energy of the room.

"*Brava*. You understand that there will be none without my express permission for the duration of our time together."

"Yes, Sir."

He ventured his fingers south and ran them up and down the outline of her white lace. The hint of heat between her legs called to his depths.

"This color is perfect for you, Cara. Always wear white unless I tell you otherwise."

Claire wet her lips and said a breathy, "Yes, Sir."

He touched her inner thigh and she whimpered. "Do you like my touch?"

"Yes, Sir."

"Good." Luca slipped his middle finger inside the seam to find his sub dripping in anticipation. He spread her need in a slow circle, careful not to contact the one spot she would most definitely want him to tease.

"You were six minutes late, Claire. And for that, you will not have an orgasm for six days." His sleepy torment continued, still eluding her clit. "But every night you will come here at seven p.m. and we will repeat this act—except Friday. That has been established as a limit for you. But you will not climax until Saturday. Do you understand?"

"Yes…"

He stopped his fingers and sat up straighter.

"Yes, Sir," she corrected herself.

He retraced the path one more time. "There is only one catch. You have to tell me when to stop." His circle narrowed, approaching what he knew would be an aching nub.

"When you are about to explode, you must say 'stop'." He kept his lingering pace but added pressure.

Claire squirmed under him. Being still would require an entirely different lesson.

He found her clit and tapped it once.

"Stop! Oh my God! Stop, stop, stop."

Luca ceased all movement and regretfully removed his hand. The spell was broken, and he already longed for more. His sub-in-training wormed away and shuddered.

"You did well, Claire. A little too much wiggling, but you did great." He smiled as he stood up. "Get under the covers. I'll be right back."

Luca walked to the en suite bathroom, washed his hands, refolded the towel just right and went back to find Claire. In the minutes he'd left her alone, her energy had changed. On her side, she faced away from him and had already assumed the fetal position. The mighty high of a scene, her first, had vanished, the unfortunately reliable sub-drop too present.

He cornered around the bed and bent down so they were face-to-face.

"Look at me, Claire."

She stared at the door.

"Claire, I need your eyes. We're not done."

She drew her eyebrows together but met his gaze.

"Thank you. Please tell me you read about aftercare. It's incredibly important."

She nodded.

"Good." He stroked her hair and tilted his head. "You can look me in the eyes as long as you want now. You can even touch me." He winked. "But, most importantly, you need to talk to me. What's troubling you?"

She worked her jaw and blinked away the tears puddling in her eyes. If this had been a mistake, he would regret it. But deep down, something in her called out to him. Was it lust? Certainly. But more so, it was truth—their true natures reaching out to connect. She was new to all of this, and when one begins to uncover stones, one might find crushed flowers.

"Trust, Claire. You *have* to trust me." He kissed her brow and pulled back.

She let out a long breath. "I don't want to spend the night with you." Her head shook back and forth. "I don't want to sleep in the same bed with you."

A lonely tear fell down her temple and landed on the white cotton pillowcase supporting her head. He touched her splotchy cheek with the back of his hand.

In a soft, understanding voice he said, "I don't remember asking you to do that, *cara*. But I assure you it's not a problem. What I'd really like to do is hold you, because you've been so brave today. I want to show you how proud of you I am."

The words settled between them and her jaw continued its small movements.

"You didn't get me naked. Is that, like, a thing for you? Or do you not want to see me that way?"

There she was, the spunky Claire. He smiled down, and she sniffled.

"Well, one… You are absolutely stunning like that. Better than I imagined. And, as I've already told you, I have an excellent imagination."

She nuzzled into the pillow.

"And yes, I have a thing for you in white. I'm not even sure why. Probably that dress from the other night. But not getting you naked was also for you. You're new to all of this. I'm trying to go slow."

She reached out from under the covers and interlaced her fingers into his. Her light skin threaded into his olive counterpart and he reveled at the sight.

When he searched for her eyes again, he found her staring at him.

Just above a whisper, she said, "I liked it, Luca. I felt more right than I have in a long time."

He squeezed his fingers around hers. "You're a natural."

"So, aftercare. This is where I get whatever I want to feel better? It's like me being the Dom?"

"Ha. Not quite, *sotto*. But certain rules are suspended, like the looking, until I'm satisfied that you are in a good place physically and emotionally. I won't let you back out into the world without having made sure you're okay." Luca moved from kneeling and sat on the side of the bed.

"So, if I ask if you'll hold me, I can touch you back?"

He narrowed his eyes. She negotiated huge financial deals for a living, so maybe his guard needed to go up.

"Within reason," he answered. "But you can ask. I can always say no. I have limits, too."

A twisted grin pulled at her lips. "I do want you to hold me. Desperately, truth be told."

Thank every heaven. One small brick of her wall had tumbled. The only problem was that Claire's bricks usually came with stipulations, like the whole Friday night thing. *What is that?*

"But..." Luca arched an eyebrow, anticipating her next statement.

"But I want you to do it with your shirt off." Claire bit her bottom lip.

Luca reached out and tugged it free with his thumb. "Is that all?"

"For now."

There was a reassurance with her request. It was physical—safe, out in the open—not like the sliver of emotion in his heart that he was doing everything in his power to ignore. Because his pride for Claire went deeper than seeing someone obey and surrender.

No, that tiny thread would need to be nipped in the bud. The enormity of what she'd asked him to do—

train her and introduce her to what one should expect from Doms—was not a task he took lightly.

Luca stood up from the bed and untucked his dress shirt. He unbuttoned it and straightened the sleeves. After he'd stowed it away on a hanger next to Claire's coat, he walked back to the bed.

"Am I allowed to take my shoes off as well?" he joked.

"As you wish."

His three favorite words. There was no way she could understand their power. Luca kicked off his shoes and met Claire in the middle of the bed. He leaned against the headboard and she moved into him as if they'd done it a million times before.

He let her squeeze into him nice and tight and he played with her ponytail while her cheek rested on his bare chest.

"It's pretty normal to come down hard after the adrenaline of a scene, Claire. And today was small. It's obligatory that you let me care for you after."

"Okay."

Luca pressed a kiss into the crown of her head.

"Are you feeling better?" he asked.

"Mmmm. I am."

"Good. Let's talk about what you had for lunch."

Chapter Twelve

Claire

Julien's jaw dropped as Claire stormed through the front door at eight o'clock on the button — for the fourth day in a row. "My, my, my…"

She held a hand up. "Don't start." She bit the words out as she sailed past him and locked herself in the relative sanctuary of her office, pressing her back against the cold door. She could text Luca, call Luca or send a fucking carrier pigeon to his doorstep, begging him to see her tonight and end the torture.

Every day her desire was ramping up higher under Luca's talented and taunting hands, literally. Showering this morning had been an exercise in futility. All she could envision were olive-colored fingers touching her, caressing her, bringing her just shy of the pinnacle she craved more than oxygen.

Shirtless. Every night this week since her admission in their first aftercare session that she liked having him shirtless, that fucking bastard had made her watch as he took his time unbuttoning his shirt, had folded it three times and laid it on the chair before beginning his exploration. The short, soft hairs on his chest would dance across her back, her stomach, her thighs as he leaned in, his body brushing lightly against hers while she lay helpless in whatever position he'd ordered her into.

She crossed the room, dropped her case and her purse on the floor beside her desk and slumped into the seat. Today could be her one of freedom and pleasure. She'd technically be allowed a release under Luca's six-day punishment. The throbbing at her core intensified, remembering the purring orders that she was not allowed an orgasm due to her tardiness. In that moment, she was certain all Luca would need to do was to dip his chin, pin her with the look that always set her body ablaze and give permission. She would be screaming from a climax without even having his hands on her body.

Her breath stuttered on an exhale. She propped her elbows on her desk and dropped her face into her hands. But today was Friday. She couldn't do that to Liam, no matter how much her traitorous body cried for relief.

Three taps brought her head up. Julien stood in the doorway with a handful of papers and one eyebrow — more perfectly shaped than Claire's — arched in question. "Has Medusa tamed her snakes or should I come back another time?"

Claire narrowed her gaze. "What do you want, Julien?"

He closed the door behind him and took a seat in the cubed chair across the desk from her. "You have three contracts to review, two conference calls and correspondence to answer." He set the papers in front of her. "But first you need to tell me why your face is more pinched than the old lady who lives beneath me and why the bitchy side of Claire that is normally reserved for brokering the big deals has come out to play."

Claire leaned back in her chair. Her bottom lip found its way between her teeth for a moment before she popped it free. Even when Luca wasn't here, she couldn't allow herself to fall into the habits she was working to break. He would be disappointed if he caught her.

She tilted her head and regarded her assistant, her friend — the closest thing to real family she had left in this world. But as much as she loved and trusted him, could she possibly disclose… this? "It's been a long week."

Julien snorted and crossed his legs. "Tell me about it. In the past five days I have gone from dealing with a confused Claire to an angry Claire to a bitchier-than-I-ever-thought-possible Claire." He held a hand out in front of him, inspecting his nails. "If I didn't know better, I'd think someone needed to get laid." He grinned around his fingers. "But I believe a certain Italian stud has that all handled."

No. No, he most certainly did not. Claire squirmed in her seat and thinned her lips. Each day seemed worse than before and today was the most tortuous of all. Knowing that a simple acquiescence, less than a one-minute phone call, would put an end to the ache… A thrill shot through her as she envisioned Luca's body on top of hers, undoubtedly creating a new and very welcome ache as he thrust into her…

Fingers snapped in front of her face, making her jump. "Is the sex so good you've gone braindead?"

She swallowed and forced the heat to leave her face as she composed her expression into something much more appropriate. For better or worse, Julien was all she had and had proven himself reliable and trustworthy time and again. If she needed anything in this moment, other than Luca Bernardi naked, it was his advice.

"We haven't had sex."

Julien resumed his seat, jaw slackened. He stared at her in silence for several moments. "Claire, sweetie, I know losing Liam..." He shook his head. "I remember...every minute. From the very first second he was diagnosed you were a pillar of strength. You never failed to stay on top of the latest and greatest treatment and pushed so hard to get him entered into clinical trials. You never made a single decision without weighing all the options and researching the hell out of it. You were his champion."

Moisture collected in the corners of her eyes remembering those hellacious days. Seeing the love of her life fade away and his light-filled eyes, the cornflower blue orbs that had carried her through each day, grow dim and weary had changed her. She'd had to find an inner reserve of strength to be the wife and partner Liam needed. And when all medical intervention had proved fruitless and she'd had to say goodbye, only Julien had seen her fall apart.

His soft voice pulled her back to the present. "But, sweetie, this is for you, for your happiness. And you and I both know damn well that Liam wanted nothing more in this world than to see you happy." He scooted to the edge of the chair, stretched his arm across her desk and laid one hand on top of hers. "If he can't be here to give that to you, there is nothing wrong with finding it with Luca." He tapped his fingers against her knuckles three times before he pulled away and settled back in his seat again. "And let that man rock your world."

Her lips turned down. "It's not that, Julien." She rolled her eyes and ran her hands down her face. "Well, it will always be that. I will always miss Liam and he will always be the only man I'll ever love." She shook her head. "But this… This isn't me. It's him. Luca. I-I was late. Six fucking minutes late. So, this is my punishment. Teasing, playing, touching but no…finishing." She folded her arms across her desk and dropped her forehead onto them. "For six days — one for each minute I was late."

She barely registered Julien's sharp indrawn breath, lost in a mixture of perpetual sexual frustration and embarrassment. She did not, however, miss the quiet giggles that soon erupted into cackling laughter. She looked up and glared across her desk. "What exactly is so funny, you pretentious little queen?"

After several minutes, he swiped a tear from his eye and offered a few lingering chuckles. "Oh, Claire, sweetie, trust me. It's worth it. So very, very worth it."

She groaned, letting her head fall to her arms again. His reassurances meant nothing when the very idea of Luca Bernardi running his fingers across her hot flesh raced through her mind and amplified the need coursing through her body.

This is going to be a very long night.

* * * *

The brisk fall air was decidedly more cold tonight and Claire burst through the door of her house, grateful to feel the warmth against her icy skin. She cursed herself the entire walk home for not wearing something heavier than the white cardigan sweater she was gripping tightly. Her gaze landed on the fireplace as she passed by the living room, heading toward the kitchen, desperate for a hot cup of tea.

Liam would have built her a fire and taunted her perpetually cold state. He'd kiss her nose and rub her hands between his before wrapping her in a blanket and cradling her in front of the roaring blaze. She set the kettle on the burner with more force than necessary. Why hadn't she ever paid attention and learned how to build one herself?

Because Liam was never supposed to die. The tugging in her heart brought the pain of her loss back into acute focus. They were supposed to live happily ever after and grow old together.

The kettle chirped, pulling her back from the darkness that hovered at the edge of her existence. She swiped at the errant tear running down her cheek and poured the scalding water over the round, silver infuser. She wrapped her hands around the delicate blue cup gingerly, avoiding the edges where the handle used to reside and which were still sharp, despite her attempts at filing them.

Claire carried her drink into the living room, curled her feet beneath herself on the couch and tugged the blanket down from the back. She flipped through the channels, prepared to lose herself in the most ridiculous reality show she could find, when her cell phone rang out from the stand next to the sofa. Excitement warred with irritation when Luca's name flashed across the screen.

"So much for respecting my boundaries." She rolled her eyes and swiped her finger across the glass. "Yes?"

Silence. Luca's silence was shrouded in disapproval and she hated the effect it had on her. She immediately wanted to correct her tone. Hell, she wanted to invite him over right this very minute to put an end to her torment.

"I take it your evening is not going well, Claire."

She bit her lip then quickly released it as if he could see her disobedient behavior through the phone. "It's going fine." She twisted her mouth to the side. "I didn't expect to hear from you tonight. I thought this was a boundary. What did you call it? A 'hard no'."

"Yes, *cara*." The deep rumble echoed through her veins. "It is a boundary. It is a hard no. It is a line I will never ask you to cross." If it were at all possible, his voice dropped another octave and had a power over her she wasn't comfortable admitting to yet. "However, you are my submissive, my *sotto*. As we have discussed, your well-being is a top priority to me. Since we are not meeting, I need to check on you to make sure you have...behaved today."

She arched an eyebrow. *Behaved? As if I am a child?* Her anger quickly faded as his words sank in. He was checking on her. When was the last time anyone other than Julien had checked on her? The answer came just as quickly as the question. *Liam.* Well, Liam when he was well.

"H-how do you mean 'behaved'?"

There was a brief rustling before he responded. "Have you eaten? And I think we've already determined when I ask this I am most certainly not referring to *your* type of dinner."

A grin tugged at the corners of her mouth. "Yes, I have eaten — beef lo mein and an egg roll."

"Very good, *sotto*." The affirmation washed over her, and her skin tingled with the praise. "And to drink?"

He'd told her during a previous lesson that he had no problem with wine — he was Italian after all — but he required his submissives not to drink to excess. To remain poised, in control of their faculties and ready to serve willingly without making decisions they would later regret. "A glass of Pinot and now I'm drinking tea."

"And was your Pinot as good as my Barolo, *cara*?"

Claire held the phone away from her ear and stared at the screen, needing visual confirmation she was still speaking with Luca Bernardi. Was it possible he was teasing her? "Um, n-no. No, it was not."

He sighed heavily. "Confidence, Claire. When you address me within the walls of the club, over the phone or anywhere else we may be together, I want you to speak with confidence. I will never harm you. When you search for words, when you stammer, when your voice quakes, it implies distrust, and trust is the very foundation of this relationship, *sotto*."

The nerves that had been frazzled and frayed all day had calmed as soon as she'd heard his voice, but now they simply disappeared. They were just as helpless to resist the power of Luca Bernardi as she was. Claire was fairly certain the man could lull a prowling tiger to sleep simply by speaking in his authoritative, yet soothing, tone.

"I trust you."

"Very good, *cara*." His obvious pleasure washed over her and made her smile. "It is nearly time for bed, *sotto*. You need to be very well rested for what's to come tomorrow."

Tomorrow. The seventh day since her punishment was enacted, the sixth day of her training and the day she would finally be allowed to find some peace with her body. Desire pulsed through her, collecting at her core and making her throb with need.

"Same time?" She was proud of the nonchalance in her tone when she wanted nothing more than to beg for an earlier meeting, a sooner release.

"Ah, no, *cara*. I will pick you up at five and we will have an early dinner first."

Dinner? Was she truly supposed to sit across from a man who oozed sex from every pore on his body for an undetermined length of time after he'd spent the past week working her to the brink of orgasm with no relief? *No.* That was not acceptable or funny or even the slightest bit fair.

"As you wish."

Chapter Thirteen

Luca

"You're spoiling her."

Luca grinned up into dark brown eyes that matched his own and set his phone on the woven gray couch.

"I can't help it," he said, just above a whisper and with a true smile.

"You can't help it." His cousin Gianna swooped her arms in a massive gesture. "You're not here every night. The second I take her off her precious Cuca's chest, she will cry and cry. And who sneaks out the door while I listen to the pleas for Cuca, eh?"

Luca tucked his chin and shifted his gaze down to the brown-haired angel who mangled his name so beautifully and was indeed snoozing on his stomach. *Madonna mia.* He'd even welcomed the warm puddle of drool seeping through his shirt.

Gianna studied her daughter again before saying, "She does love her godfather."

"What's not to love?" Luca, with a wink in his eye and loving the taunt of his younger cousin, kissed the little head for the umpteenth time that day.

But instead of serving back a zinger, Gianna reclined in her chair and crossed her arms. "One does wonder."

He rolled his eyes. Never a girl brought home... Never a date beyond a pointless charitable event — not because they weren't worthy, not that they were boring, but none of the previous had been... He hated to admit it, even to himself, so he would not. He willed that blonde and her perfect mind and body — an apparently lethal combination — out of his thoughts.

Luca stretched to his left for the cream throw blanket and covered little Ilaria. With a natural gesture he'd only discovered since he had held her above the holy water in the church at her baptism, his forearm met his goddaughter's spine and he stood. "I'll put her down."

Gianna rose as well and collected the espresso cups and remaining pink frosting-stained plates from her daughter's birthday.

In the privacy of his goddaughter's room, Luca ran his bearded cheek along the sweaty brow of the toddler. What was that smell? In her three tiny years, it had remained unidentifiable yet intoxicating.

He pulled back the white duvet with its dusted rose design of her 'big-girl bed' and snuggled her in. When she stirred, he stroked her soft Italian locks and sang her their song, the same song his mother had sung to him. Once convinced she was in a deep sleep, he stood and tiptoed out of her room.

Gianna wiped down the counter in the kitchen and tossed the crumbs into her massive gray marble sink.

"This is my favorite time of the day," she said with warm eyes and a contented smile. "Everyone is asleep, healthy and — "

"Fed," they said in a quiet unison. Being fed was a staple in their family. *Nonna* had always assured it.

"One more coffee?" Luca gestured to her espresso machine.

"For you?" Gianna reached up and squeezed his cheeks. "Anytime." After a little shake, she tapped his jaw and busied herself with the grounds and the machine.

Luca walked over to the breakfast nook in the corner of her kitchen and waited as the coffee hummed its arrival, the aroma of the strong blend reaching him first.

His goddaughter's party could not have been on a better day, the distraction a blessing. And while he'd not crossed the line of seeing Claire on her 'red day', as he was now referring to it, she had answered her phone — a fact that he not only appreciated but one that had also brought him relief. And even though she seemed so perfect, especially without the risk of love, Claire Favre was clearly haunted. There were hints of it in her eyes and it seeped through her bones.

Calling her, while risky and a technical loophole he'd sniffed out the second he'd read it, had been mandatory. He needed her to know she was still very much on his mind, even though she was out of sight. His. She was his. *For now.*

Gianna slid the small coffee onto the table then sat opposite him. "We have the hospital fundraiser at the end of the month. Antonio changed his plans and can go." She fiddled with a bracelet to hide the clasp on the inside of her wrist. "But that doesn't mean you don't have to come." Her dark eyes narrowed and she fought a smile. "I don't know, Cuca, maybe you could even bring a date." Her manicured fingers spread, feigning surprise.

Luca stirred half a sugar cube into his cup, tapped the spoon thrice, took a cautious sip and replaced it in its saucer.

"You'd love that, wouldn't you?"

Gianna was torturously predictable.

"I would love it, Luca." Her eyes bugged out and her shoulders wiggled. "Shoot me. I want my favorite cousin to be happy."

"That's assuming I'm not. A day with my goddaughter and your cooking? I'm beyond content." He sipped again, knowing Gianna had more words for him.

"Do you want *me* to be happy, Luca?"

"Always." The rest of his coffee went down in one quick turn of his wrist.

"Then bring a date to the fundraiser at the end of the month, someone I can talk to while old women beg my husband and you for more money." Gianna smacked the table and stood, swiping the small modern cup and saucer out from under him.

"No need to get cranky."

* * * *

Cranky. He laughed to himself. Poor *sotto* had indeed been cranky when he'd spoken to her earlier as well. Luca bounded off his heels and stuck his hands into the pants pocket of his suit. A hungry moan brought him back to the hall and the scene in front of him.

He couldn't imagine what Caroline Cartier's sub had done. In truth, he didn't care, but as she trailed the black leather flogger down his chest in the public punishment room, it was clear the Domme had also surpassed her own level of cranky.

Spread out and nearly naked, the sub hung his head. The rest of his body formed a perfect X, bound to the impressive dark wood behind him.

The tasseled ends of Caroline's whip fanned around his caged cock. In a loud voice, the Domme said, "I bet you'd like some relief, sub. Is that why you thought it wise to look at pornography when I had strictly forbidden you from doing so?"

"Yes, Mistress." His voice, while quiet, was still confident.

A Dom next to Luca tugged on the silver-studded leash of his sub, who was on all-fours at his feet. "You may watch now."

"Thank you, Sir." She lifted her blonde head and licked her lips.

Sir. Three letters that when strung together brought order to his world—and an emptiness to his duties. Where was his own sub? Luca hoped she was snug in her bed sleeping. Resting. Not seeing her for one day had already forced him to move up their scheduled time. He craved the moment he could reward her.

A crack of the whip snapped his attention to Caroline.

"Who decides when you come, my pet?"

The sub swallowed and rolled his shoulders back slightly, the punishment soothing a call from his soul. "You do, Mistress."

"Correct." Caroline's high red heels clicked against the dark tiled floor as she paced in front of the sub.

"And while you may be disobedient, you are honest." With her free hand, she trailed her black nails down his torso and around to his ass.

"Tell me, sub. What type of pornography were you watching?"

"Male, Mistress. Gay men."

"I see. Is your Mistress not enough for you? Am I lacking without a cock for you to suck?"

"No. My mistress is all I need."

Whack! The whip smacked his torso and small red traces of contact appeared at its withdrawal.

"I don't believe you."

Luca stepped back from the small crowd and walked as silently as he could to the stairs. There was no doubt in his mind what was next and watching that sub suck cock was not on his 'to do' list.

He knocked on the door to the security office, where he found Max and the two muscle heads who normally flanked the entrance.

Max nodded his greeting and Luca squinted at the many screens in front of him. A twinge of relief hit when the one designated for Noah Paulick was black.

"Everything okay?"

"All good. Calm night. The subs said a lot of their Dom/Dommes are out of town." Max shrugged and went back to watching the public scene. "If that dude isn't sucking a dick in ten minutes, Caroline's lost her touch."

"I'm going for a nightcap then upstairs. Call me if anything changes." Luca smoothed the front of his suit and let himself out of the secure room with his key card.

At the bar, Gwendelyn, with her long dark hair around her shoulders, twisted a stemmed wine glass in a white bar towel.

"Hey, boss," she said with a smile. "Grappa?"

Luca pulled back a bar stool and sat. "Am I *that* obvious?"

"I'd like to think that I'm *that* observant." She placed the glass next to its matching counterparts in a perfect line. She might not have known as many drink mixes as Max, but Gwendelyn's attention to detail was a welcome ending to his day.

She pulled the grappa and its glass out of the freezer, served up just the right amount and set it under a napkin in front of Luca. He tipped it in her direction and let the cool sting hit his palate.

With the bar empty and her duties complete, Gwendelyn stayed across from Luca.

"So…" Her red lips twitched. "New sub?"

Luca narrowed his eyes. *Nosy.* Gwendelyn had always been too nosy.

She raised her hands in a surrender then shrugged. "Worth a try." The amusement from trying to tease Luca fell from her face. "Actually, I wanted to talk to you about something."

"Elias treating you okay?" Luca set his drink back into the sweat ring on its napkin.

"The best. You know that." She smiled but it was brief. "You know that girl you trained not too long ago?"

"The one you got to play with?"

Again, a smile flashed then faded on the sub's pale face.

"Yeah. Well, I don't want to get anybody in trouble…" She glanced around as if someone might overhear her.

Elias may have been her Dom but beating around the bush was not acceptable.

"Speak, sub."

Gwendelyn set her shoulders and looked Luca in the eyes. "She told me she played with Noah Paulick and he took off the condom for anal."

A stuttered exhale fogged his glass when he brought it up for another drink. *That novice. That fucking irresponsible neophyte.* And the information was secondhand. *Christ.* Now he had to police safe sex? Wasn't that the entire point of his club? A safe place for sex?

"I'll keep an eye out. Thanks for the heads-up."

Relief. He needed some fucking relief. Not only had Claire not come all week, but neither had he — some sort of weird mirroring desire where he wanted his release to be as powerful as hers. And yeah, now he was cranky.

He set the drink down and flipped his wrist to check the time. Technically no longer Friday night. Another loophole. Worst case, she could say 'red'.

Luca pushed the unfinished drink toward the other side of the bar. Situation resolving, he said goodnight to Gwendelyn and walked to the elevator that led to his top floor residence. On the way up, he closed his eyes. His. She was his. For now.

A reminder and a release. She wouldn't deny needing it as much has he did. Hell, she'd whimpered into a puddle Thursday night. And if the lesson hadn't been so important, he would have considered an early reward.

He found his phone charging on the counter and scrolled to C.

Cara.

He swiped a finger, his decision solidified.

Three rings. A good sign. Everything good came in threes.

"Hello?" Claire's groggy voice brought a smile to his face. She'd been sleeping. "Luca? Is everything okay?"

"No, *sotto*." His grin deepened. "It is not. And it's no longer Friday night. I want you on your knees, in only white lace panties and next to the bed in my suite in one hour. You can nap tomorrow to make up for your rest."

"Did I do something wrong?" Her confusion was understandable. He had changed their plans and woken her up.

"I certainly hope not. A car will fetch you." Luca's hand rubbed past his beard and into his shoulders that were already unknotting from the sound of her.

"Does this mean…?"

"In my suite. In one hour."

She paused and her exhale crackled into his ear. "As you wish."

He hung up the phone and placed it carefully on the counter, face down. With a quick roll of his shoulders, his jacket fell off halfway. He finished the job and hung it on one of his bar stools.

In a large ceramic bowl in the middle of his dark counter, he found a ripe banana and peeled it. Energy. He was going to need it.

After a shower and a scrub of his teeth, putting a suit back on in the middle of the night when he was most definitely going to take it off — all off — again within thirty minutes seemed futile. Instead, he slipped into the same track pants he'd worn when Claire had been at his apartment and added a tight workout shirt.

Luca rode the elevator to the main floor. Down the hall, the bar was dark, but security was twenty-four hours. He let himself into the little room.

Max raised one of his dark eyebrows. "I thought you went to bed."

"Change of plans," Luca said without a grin.

"I noticed." Max turned back to the screens and gestured to the feed dedicated to Luca's suite.

Sure enough, his precious *sotto* awaited. And she was early. "How long has she been there?"

"Five minutes."

"Kill the feed to my suite."

"No problem, boss." Max typed in a few commands to the computer and the image of Claire blinked to black.

Luca stretched his arms overhead. What the hell was he going to do for the next seven minutes until it was time to go tie up his blonde banker? Because she would be his *exactly* how he'd been dreaming—on her back, arms secured and him inside her.

"You're not going up?" Max side-eyed him.

"In a minute." Luca grinned.

Chapter Fourteen

Claire

Her brain was still clearing the last remnants of the fog that sleep had left her in when the mechanism in the knob activated and the tips of black leather moccasins entered her peripheral vision. The upturned hands resting on her thighs shook, and keeping her eyes fixed on the floor was nearly impossible. She snuck a quick glance up when she saw him turn to the closet, toeing his shoes off and placing them beside hers. She swallowed a groan at the tight shirt outlining each perfect muscle and the loose sweatpants hanging on his impossibly lean hips. Claire dropped her eyes back to the floor before he caught her, the need to obey almost as strong as her need for him.

"Well done, *sotto*. You were early."

She swallowed. "Yes, Sir."

He began slowly circling her, trailing his fingers along the tops of her shoulders as he walked behind her. "Do you know why I called you here, *sotto*?"

Because you want to fuck me senseless? "No, Sir."

He hummed and stopped in front of her. The rustling of fabric begged her to look up but Claire was certain a violation would only lengthen her torture. When his pants hit the floor in front of her, she nearly choked. If she thought sitting in the back seat of the car Luca had sent for her, cataloging all the ways he could touch her, was torture, knowing Luca Bernardi was standing a foot away from her without his pants on when her eyes couldn't feast was damn near intolerable.

"Stand."

She rose to her feet in one movement that was growing smoother with practice. Her gaze was still focused on the lush carpet but she caught the edge of his boxers and a shudder ran through her body. Black had never looked so vibrant.

He traced the swell of her breasts, trailing his fingers down the front of each before landing on her nipples. He rolled the hardened buds between his index fingers and thumbs and her breath left her body on a short, stuttered exhale in response. When he pinched both sides at the same time with more pressure than he had before and held them longer than previous times, Claire couldn't control the small 'eep' that escaped.

Luca chuckled lightly before replacing his hands with his mouth. He licked and sucked the right side before switching and repeating the exact same actions on the left. He traced the outline of her panties across her hip bones and between her thighs. His wandering and incredibly talented digits dipped beneath the lace material and between her folds. "My *sotto* is ready for me so soon?"

Claire licked her lips. If she abided by the total honesty rule she would confess to having been ready all day, every day, since Sunday. "Yes, Sir."

"Eyes."

Even though every instinct in her body screamed at her to gawk at the naked, perfectly defined chest a breath away, she met his stare head-on. Her gray gaze collided with his chocolate one and the desire she read there made her heart forget to beat. He held the look as he continued his fingers' teasing path, skillfully avoiding the area where she needed him most. "Yes, Sir?"

The left side of his mouth twitched. "You have done well your first week, *sotto*. Exceptionally well. It would be unfair for me to force such a willing and obedient sub to wait until this evening." He withdrew his hands from her body and the hot flesh screamed at their absence. More. She needed more of him, not less. He snapped his fingers. "Eyes down, and as attractive as it is, underwear off. I want you on the bed on your back, arms above you, holding the headboard."

Her entire body shook, but she did exactly as he'd said. Within minutes, he had both ankles restrained on opposite sides of the mattress and her wrists bound together firmly, with little wiggle room. It was the first time he had ever tied her down. The excitement of the unknown quickly overrode the brief surge of nervousness that had prickled her skin when he'd clicked the straps into place.

"What is your safeword, *sotto*?"

"Red, Sir."

"And what do you say if I am pushing a little too far?"

"Yellow, Sir."

He hummed his approval. "Eyes."

She pulled her gaze from its position on her own body, indescribably turned on by the sight of it locked into complete submission for him, to where he stood beside the bed. The need that had set fire to the brown orbs lingered but was tempered by softness.

"There is a safety mechanism in place on all the straps. One word from you and you will be released in less than a minute. You will not disappoint me if you call red. You will *not* be a failure. We are both learning your limits and your desires. Do you understand, *sotto*?"

The burning in her chest was...unexpected. She was grateful to learn and train for this part of her life with someone as conscientious as Luca, but his words hit a place on her body much more neglected than the throbbing need between her spread thighs — and much more unwelcome. "Yes, Sir."

He moved to stand at the foot of the bed, a smile tugging at the corners of his mouth. "You are beautiful, *sotto*. Stunning." Before she had a chance to respond, he knelt on the bed. "You have been so very patient and that is a trait I greatly admire, in business and in pleasure. Now I would like to reward you."

He moved his hands up and down her legs, turning the appendages she rarely paid attention to after her daily once-over with the razor into highly erogenous zones. She whimpered under his expert touch. He traced the outside of her slickened core, dipping inside once, twice, three times.

"This time, *sotto*, when I tease you, when I touch you, you may come." He paused, holding her eyes captive with his. "But you must look at me. Understand and acknowledge who is bringing you this pleasure."

He dipped his dark head between her thighs, drawing intricate patterns on her needy flesh with his tongue. He closed his lips around the swollen nub that had been screaming for attention for several days, but his gaze never once faltered from hers as he licked and sucked her to a screaming pinnacle. She thrashed her head against his pillow and struggled to keep her eyes open and trained on him. When two fingers slid inside her, she quickly hit a second peak. "Fuck!" The curse was ripped from her lungs with the force of her orgasm.

He slowed his ministrations but kept his hands and lips in contact with her trembling flesh. Stars danced before her eyes and relief mixed with an undeniable urge for more.

Luca moved up her body, tasting every inch as he went. "Ah, *sotto*, I was so very wrong. I thought you were beautiful before, but now I know you are truly breathtaking when your cheeks are flushed and you are screaming your release from the effect of your Master's touch on your body. *Assolutamente mozzafiato*." The words were whispered against her skin, which had no business catching fire once again.

"T-thank you, Sir."

A hand collided with her left ass cheek. He leaned close to her ear, pressing his hard length against her reignited core. "Confidence, Claire." He rubbed against her, eliciting a needy moan as her body cowed to his silent instruction. "You are my sub, my *sotto*. Prove that I have your trust and speak to me with confidence."

He moved his lips from her ear to her breasts, making a trail of light kisses along the way. He lavished attention on her nipple — licking, sucking, nibbling. He tormented the opposite nub with his hand, pinching it. She arched into his touch, her body still humming from two mind-blowing orgasms, yet also begging for more.

"Sir, please." The whimpered plea surprised her. She was quickly growing just as desperate as she had been when she'd arrived. *What the hell kind of dark magic does this man deal in?*

Luca ground against her, the cotton material of his boxers a thin barrier that provided an exciting texture, overwhelming her senses. "Yes, *sotto*, yes. You may come."

His permission allowed the hovering wave of release to crash over her again. She screamed. She swore. She bucked her hips against him as much as she could within the confines of the straps. As she hovered in the fog of pleasure, his touches turned feather light, his kisses no more than a whisper, and all too soon he abandoned her body.

She snapped her eyes open and, permitted or not, sought him out. *More.* She still fucking wanted more. She had no idea how it could be possible, but the truth couldn't be ignored. Claire opened her mouth to ask, to beg, to have him inside her. She needed that more than she needed oxygen at this moment. But the arch of his eyebrow quickly drew her lips back together and warmth spread through her at his approving nod.

Luca released each of her ankles then stood beside the bed, grazing his fingertips over her cheek. "We are not done, *sotto*. Remember…trust. You do not question because you trust that your Dom, your Master, will make the right decisions, the very best decisions, for you."

"Yes, Sir." She nodded, drinking in every inch of him while she could and desperately wishing his boxers would disappear.

As if reading her mind, he hooked his thumbs beneath the waistband and slid them down, walking to the other side of the bed naked, with more confidence than most men affected in a three-piece suit. Claire's gaze drifted down his body, stopping just below his finely tuned abdomen.

Oh.

Luca pulled a foil packet from the drawer and donned the condom without preamble or embarrassment. He climbed onto the bed, stretching his body across hers and extracting a needy groan. "Next time, *sotto*, you will sheath me."

Next time. Her body and mind sang out in unison at the words. Her ecstasy was only allowed a moment to linger as he slid his thick cock inside her. The shudder from his body rippled through hers and she smiled slightly, proud to have even a modicum of the effect on him that he had on her.

"You have been exceptional." He repeated the affirmations he had been speaking to her all night. "You have outshone the brightest star in your obedience and willingness to please your Master."

Claire focused on controlling her words. "Thank you, Sir."

He rolled his hips against hers as he moved in and out, his shaft brushing against her rapidly swelling clit. "Lock your legs around me, *sotto*. You need to feel your Dom on every inch of you."

In a short period of time, her body had come to recognize and respect Luca's authority and control. For that she was grateful, because her brain had no input in the actions of her body as her thighs tightened around his waist. She moaned as he went deeper with the next thrust.

"*Troppo bella per le parole.*"

His voice vibrated against her chest, causing her greedy nipples to beg for more attention. Claire tried to translate what he'd said in her head but quickly abandoned the notion. There was no hope for intelligent thought when Luca was hitting every sensitive spot on her and discovering a few more she'd never known about.

His breathing was shallow and labored. "You will come with your Master and you will say my name. Remember, *sotto*, who owns your orgasms, who knows your body." As always, Luca demanded. He did not request.

"As you wish, Sir."

Her words were met with a final hard thrust and a loud roar that pushed her, once again, over the edge that he'd had her teetering on. She screamed his name so loud that she was certain she'd lose her voice. And she couldn't imagine a better reason for becoming temporarily mute.

He rested his damp forehead against her shoulder. For the first time since he'd locked her into place, she cursed the restraints around her wrists, keeping her from touching him. After several minutes he pulled himself from her, disposed of the condom and disappeared into the bathroom. He emerged moments later with fresh pair of sweatpants slung low on his hips, carrying a basin of water and a cloth. Luca wiped warm water across her shaky flesh before drying her with a towel.

The drop she was learning to anticipate and identify began to claw at her mind and she was very close to calling him to release her from the straps, suddenly battling an unfamiliar panic. Before she could utter a word, he placed one knee on the bed beside her and freed her from the black cuffs. He tugged down the covers, pulled her close to his side and wrapped the soft material around them both.

Claire laid her head on his chest, threading her fingers through the short smattering of hair and finding comfort in the steady, rhythmic beat of his heart. While she was certain she'd never get used to the crash of falling from the adrenaline high, this was her favorite part.

His hands massaged her biceps. "Your arms may be sore tomorrow, *cara*. You are not yet used to being restrained for so long, and you were bucking against them for a while. I will book a massage appointment for you at one. That will give you time to nap when you get home."

She nodded against him, having already learned that once they hit aftercare, he allowed her whatever she needed, be it silence or chatter.

Luca gripped her chin and tilted her head up. It was criminal for a man to be that attractive, successful and talented. *Truly.*

"*Cara*, I am extremely proud of you. I had high expectations for you when we embarked a week ago, but you have exceeded each one. You continue to astound me in the very best ways possible and I continue to feel grateful you chose me to walk this journey with you." He pressed his lips to the crown of her head before pushing it back down to his chest. "I shall drive you home whenever you are ready, *cara*. But there is no rush."

She sighed slightly and nodded against his chest again. "As you wish."

Chapter Fifteen

Luca

With her blonde head on his chest, Claire was obviously content—for the moment, he knew. But the descent and inevitable low became more apparent with every exhale from her spent body. And while, yes, her arms and legs might be a little sore in the hours to come, it was her mind that concerned him.

Whether Claire acknowledged the shift of the sacred energy between them was hard to tell, but Luca's experience and gut told him to look for a sign before pushing her any farther. He stroked her head, studied her breath—and waited.

It was possible his motivation to savor the quiet was selfish. Having the beautiful and successful woman to himself, not just sexually, was proving to be addictive.

While aftercare was always a priority—he and his friend Bruno had discussed it many, many times over the years—and he'd enjoyed the satisfaction of making sure his previous subs departed while in a stable place, holding Claire's warm, fragile body stirred something else.

A small movement at his waist drew his eyes. Claire's left thumb rubbed the base of one of her fingers. Instinct told him to correct the fidget, but experience stopped him. *Her ring finger.* She was fondling the absence of her wedding band.

Luca had wondered if or when Claire's widow status might come up. He slowed his breathing, calming himself even more, and hoped it would penetrate her being. As her jaw worked against his stomach and the twiddling continued, he decided to tackle the issue.

"When?" he asked in a breathy voice.

"When what?" The whispered question did not cease the movement of her hand.

"When did you stop wearing your ring?" Luca's hand skimmed over the back of her head and stopped between her shoulder blades. With the pads of his fingers, he circled the center of her back at a lazy pace.

"The day of the photo shoot for the article. The PR asshole said a grieving widow wouldn't incite confidence in potential clients." Her hand stilled but her head remained down. "I thought that if I left it on, I wasn't alone."

"I'm sorry for your loss," Luca said as he continued the reminder of his presence on her skin.

"No. I'm sorry." Her light lashes tickled his chest as she blinked. "You just gave me four amazing orgasms and my pillow talk is of a dead man."

He let her words settle into the air then responded as earnestly as he could. "I don't need you to be sorry, *cara*. I need you to be okay."

She looked up and tears puddled in her gray eyes. Her bottom lip quivered and her face flushed. "I'm not okay." Her words were choked out and she sat upright. With her head shaking, she said, "I feel like I just cheated on my husband."

Claire pivoted away from Luca and grabbed a pillow from the other side of the bed. She pulled it to her stomach and sobbed in the fetal position.

He reached for her shoulder, but as soon as he touched her, she smacked him away twice.

"No! I don't want you to touch me."

That stung, but Luca rolled away from her. And while it pained him to withhold his comfort, it was nothing compared to the agony of seeing her sadness. He lifted the duvet and covered her naked back, a feeble gesture.

Her wails continued, each one breaking his heart and rendering him even more helpless. He wanted to tell her to let it out, hold her, share her pain, but it was foreign. What could he possibly have to say that could relate to her emotions?

But sitting idly by was not an option. He stood up, and the action brought a pause to her cries.

"I'm not leaving," he reassured his dear little *sotto*. Luca walked around the bed and knelt by the opposite side. Careful not to move too quick, he leaned in to face her. In a soft voice, he said, "Eyes."

She blinked several times but lifted her gaze.

Still quiet, he said, "Don't shut me out, Claire."

She sniffled and new tears filled the corners of her eyes.

"Tell me what you're thinking."

A lone drop made its way to the pillow beneath her cheek and the urge to wipe it away tore through him.

But she'd said she didn't want to be touched and that needed to be respected.

"You can trust me. Remember, I serve you." He gave the smallest of smiles.

She closed her eyes, and the space the lids created between them was unbearable.

"I'm not leaving you." There was no need for an 'until' or an 'if you don't'. His words were his bond and they came free of ultimatum. He repeated them, just above a whisper.

"It's taking everything I have not to turn away from you right now," she said slowly.

"I know." Reaching out and touching her rang selfish. What she needed was his steady voice. "And I'm so proud of you for facing me, for facing this. I can't imagine what you've been through. But *I'm* here now. And *I'm* not leaving you, Claire."

She gripped the pillow tighter and opened her eyes before closing them again.

"I don't want to go home. I'm not ready to face the memories."

He smiled. There was absolutely zero chance of him driving her home in her current state. At least that battle wouldn't need to be fought.

"And you don't want to sleep with me."

She shook her head no. Why did that pester him? It was her desire. Respecting it was mandatory.

Her eyes opened and their anguish broke his throbbing heart.

With the first sign of clarity on her face, she said, "I need to get out of this room."

She also needed to sleep, most likely eat and stay close to him.

Luca trailed his arms to the edge of the bed as he leaned back. Relieved to have her regard, he said, "I'm not leaving you."

He stood and fetched the robe from next to the shower in the bathroom. Back by her side, he laid it on the bed.

"Do you want some help with that?" He nodded to the robe.

Claire stared at the white terry fabric, signaled no and gingerly put it on. Still no touching.

"No sudden movements, *cara*. Your head must be spinning."

Her hands shook as she tied the belt at her waist.

"Follow me." It came as no surprise to Luca that the one thing she responded to was commands.

She shuffled behind him, out of the room and up the elevator to his condo. The first light of the day hinted from the wall of windows.

"Couch," he said with a tilt of his head.

Her zombie-like walk continued to her destination. As she curled up in the corner of the plush L, he reached for the fur throw blanket. Without contact, he covered her and sat at one of the ends.

She blinked with heavy eyelids.

"Sleep, *cara*. I'm not leaving you."

Order given, his precious *sotto* obeyed. Her head dropped on the back of the sofa and this time he welcomed the closing of her eyes. Luca swiveled his legs onto the leather and crossed them at the ankles.

Over the years, he'd seen subs with all kinds of issues and subs with just a healthy curiosity about sex, but a widow was a first. He'd assumed that grief, in all its forms, was universal. Losing his mother had created a hollow space in his heart that even his *nonna* couldn't fill, but he'd never really thought about how his mother's death had impacted his father.

Sure, Piero had been sad. But had he been as devastated as Claire? Would his father have cried after sleeping with one of the many women who had served Luca breakfast on the mornings after their loud romp in the bedroom across the hall?

Luca liked to think he'd been conceived out of love, but if loss was a measure of greatness, what Claire'd had with her husband must have been more profound than his parents' relationship.

Claire, whose breathing had calmed, who might wake up and no longer wish to be his.

He retraced the previous week and analyzed his every move. He must have done something wrong. Their first sexual encounter had ended with her no longer wanting to be touched by him.

His head bobbed a few times until he surrendered to his own sleep. He would not leave Claire.

* * * *

A warm hand met his cool chest and woke him with a start. The light from the windows stung his eyes and Claire snuggled into him, complete with the blanket under her chin. Destabilized from his inability to touch her, he willed his hands to stay down.

Her shoulder pushed into his stomach and she laid her head on his chest. It was rare for Luca Bernardi to not know his next move. So—as was the case with his *cara*—he waited.

In a whisper, she said, "I'm so sorry, Luca. I never anticipated something like that happening."

Lord, how he wanted to gently kiss the top of her head. Even without the faint scent of her perfume, she was intoxicating.

He cleared his dry throat. "I told you. You don't need to be sorry. How are you feeling?"

"Better. C-confused, maybe."

The indecisiveness was noted but the correction would have to be put on hold — or perhaps never mentioned. It wasn't clear if he would ever see his *sotto* on her knees in all her beauty again. While the healing aspects of the Dom/sub relationship were many, readiness and timing were essential elements of its foundation.

And while he'd thought Claire was ready, the pain of her loss had been greater than he'd anticipated — an unfortunate error on his part and one he was sure would rob him of future moments he had been looking forward to and planning and randomly smiling about just walking down the streets of Zurich.

"What has you confused, *cara*?"

She brushed her cheek a little harder into his skin.

"This tugging of past and present. My heart and my body. It's left my mind…blurry."

"Well, if it helps your mind, you should know that there's nothing blurry here. I very clearly see an intelligent, successful woman seeking guidance for something that suits her perfectly. And it's an honor that she's allowed me the week behind us." Again, Luca craved initiating contact to reinforce his words, but he remained true to her desires.

He continued, "And look at the progress you've made in one week. You're respecting time for others and yourself. And you're taking better care of your body. Not all subs succeed to these levels. There are many who find it to be a game and lack the commitment you've shown. I know I'm proud of you, Claire. But you should be proud of yourself as well."

She shifted her head and focused on the bright sky from the window.

After a few minutes she said, "I thought it would be just sex. And I thought I was ready for that. But when you lay it out like that, I see how wrong I was. It's not just sex. And I wasn't ready for it to be so profound."

Luca closed his eyes. She'd said it. She wasn't ready. And even though she was lying on his stomach, she was slipping away.

"I'm sorry, Claire. I made a mistake. But I was afraid if I didn't agree, you would find someone else who would. I understand if you'd like to stop."

Her silence brought more torment. But he would not leave her or ask her to move — no matter which path she chose.

Finally, she asked, "Is that why you aren't touching me? Kissing me? Because we're done?"

"*Cara*," he said and was pleased that one word had brought back her lovely smile, "you told me not to touch you. I'm respecting your wishes. You hold the power, little one. Not me."

She popped up and stared him in the eyes. Her face bore the first signs of normalcy in hours. "I never said that! You touching me is what gets me to work on time." She smiled.

The stress fell from Luca's shoulders and he rounded his stiff neck.

"You did. And you hit me twice last night. Three times I would have forgiven, but twice…" He thought about teasing punishment but wasn't sure if it would be an option.

"Ah, your love of the number three." Claire playfully tapped his bare shoulder. "Better?"

"So much." He grinned. The glimmer in her eyes had returned. Whether or not she was going to continue remained unknown, but at least she was stable and had survived her mighty drop. That was everything.

She squinted and tilted her head. "How long does aftercare last?"

"As long as it takes."

"In that case, I need more. I need your arms around me." Claire returned to her previous position, her cheek just above his heart.

He wrapped his arms around her and squeezed just a little. After a kiss on the top of her head, he rubbed his beard on her temple.

"Then I'm going to need breakfast."

His scoff shifted to an airy chuckle.

"My, my, we are a demanding little sub in the morning. Lucky for you, feeding you gives me great pleasure."

"Lucky for you it's not the other way around or you'd be eating burnt toast and raw eggs."

Chapter Sixteen

Claire

Luca's words played in her head for the hundredth time since he'd dropped her off at home two days before. What had been the thing Nanny Helen had compared her to when she'd repeated the same pleas for an extra cookie after dinner? Oh yes, a broken record. Luca was a broken record in her brain. A deep, deliciously seductive one.

His eyes had burned with sincerity and he'd held her hands firmly between his. "I cannot guarantee this won't happen again, *cara*. In fact, I am confident it will. Although next time we will both be far better prepared." He reached up to cup her cheek. "But with this new information in mind, you need to once again decide."

She opened her mouth to object. Claire Favre wasn't some indecisive little debutante. She knew what she wanted, what she needed, for this stage in her life. But his fingers slid to cover her lips before she could utter a word of protest.

"Consider each step carefully, *cara*. If we continue, our physical interactions will only increase." The corners of his mouth twitched, and the familiar butterfly symphony played in her stomach, the cadence of their wings causing a small shiver to race through her body. "With the amount of times I've caught those stunning eyes rolling, I'm certain a little physical punishment will be on our training schedule soon. Our next steps will be even more intense than those we've taken. I want—I need—you to be certain this is what you want. I need you to choose me again, *cara*."

He pressed his lips against her forehead then he walked away. A smile curved her mouth. She didn't miss the fact that he'd waited in his idling Maserati until she'd entered her house and closed the door behind her.

She sighed, tucked the knitted purple blanket under her chin and snuggled deeper into the couch. Every part of her was still locked in a battle two days later. Loyalty versus discovery.

The slamming of her front door made her jump and dragged her back into the present. Julien stood in the doorway between the living room and the front entry with his hands on his hips, breathing heavier than if he'd just competed in the Ironman. "Since you seem to still be alive, would you care to explain exactly why you didn't come into the office today or answer your fucking phone? Dammit, Claire, I've been worried sick about you."

Julien's admonitions restarted the flood of tears she'd barely been able to contain. Before the first drop landed on her blanket, Julien's mask of anger melted and he knelt on the floor in front of her. He gripped her hands tightly. "Oh, sweetie, I'm sorry. I didn't mean to yell. I was just so scared when you didn't show up at the office and didn't answer your phone and —"

Claire shook her head vigorously, a blonde lock escaping the messy bun she had piled on top of her head. "It's not that. It's not you. It's… It's…" A sob choked off her words. She pulled her hands free from his and threw her arms around his neck. She needed to talk. She needed advice… and if not Julien, then who? "I had sex with him, Julien." She whispered the words into his neck like a dark confession.

He squeezed her waist before moving his hands to push her away slightly and squinted. "Was it that bad? Did he hurt you?" His jaw tightened. "Did he force you?"

Claire's eyes widened and her mouth fell open. "No!" The need to defend Luca both shocked and confused her. "No, he would never. He was…"

Luca's unwavering respect and persistent concern flashed through her mind again.

"He was perfect."

A deep V formed between Julien's eyebrows. "But?"

She disentangled herself and settled against the back of the couch as Julien took a seat on the coffee table right in front of her. She rolled her eyes to the ceiling. "I lost it, Julien. One minute he was this sexy Italian god who'd brought me pleasure I'd never dreamed possible and the next…" She lifted her hands helplessly. "I lost it. I sobbed. I screamed. I… I pushed him away in every possible way."

Julien held up his index finger. "First, we will be revisiting that whole pleasure thing." Claire twisted her lips to side in an irritated half smile. "Second, talk to me, sweetie." He reclaimed both of the hands she'd been wringing in her lap.

A stray tear rolled down her cheek unchecked. "It was Liam. I was lying there and Luca was being...Luca, holding me and telling me everything I didn't know I needed to hear. The next thing I knew, I couldn't think of anything but Liam." Claire stuck out her lower lip and furrowed her brow. "I started wondering if he'd be disappointed in me, if he'd be hurt that I'd had sex with someone else. But the worst part of all was that until that moment, I hadn't thought about him in hours. I was so completely consumed by Luca that I forgot about my fucking husband."

Julien moved to sit on the couch, pulling her back against his side and sliding an arm around her waist. "Liam was the best thing that could've happened to you when you were at University. He gave you everything your parents had withheld — unconditional love, open affection and the kind of appreciation you deserve."

Claire's cheeks flamed at the compliments and the mantle of guilt on her shoulders grew even heavier. He was right. Liam was the most wonderful thing to have happened to her. How could she betray him in this way?

Julien stroked her forearm, moving his thumb in soothing circles, oblivious to her building inner turmoil. "But there is nothing more in this world Liam wanted than to see you happy. And, sweetie, Luca makes you happy. He brings a light to your eyes that has been missing since Liam was first diagnosed." He pressed his lips against the crown of her head. "Enjoy this, enjoy *him*, for as long as he's in your life. Don't block him out and don't limit...whatever this is."

Claire swallowed and digested everything Julien had said. The near-constant anxiety and shame she'd battled for two days slowly began to disappear. She squeezed the arm that still held her. "Could you just pretend to not know me better than I know myself?"

He chuckled. "I'll fake almost anything for you, darling." He straightened behind her. "And speaking of faking it—which I'm sure you didn't have to do—I think I've earned all the tasty details... Wait!"

Julien scrambled off the couch, causing Claire's head to collide with the arm. "What the hell, Julien?"

"We need wine for this," he called from the kitchen right before a loud cork pop echoed into the living room.

* * * *

The nondescript simplicity of the main floor of Luca's club never ceased to amuse Claire, now that she knew what the subsequent floors contained. Her heart sped up as she approached the glossy bar, gratitude washing over her at seeing a familiar face on the opposite side. "*Guten abend*, Max."

His warm brown eyes crinkled. "*Guten abend*, Ms. Favre. Can I get you something to drink?"

Claire shook her head, tapping her fingers against the smooth wooden surface and shifting her balance from one spindly gold heel to the other. "I'm looking for Luca, er...Mr. Bernardi."

Amusement danced across the man's face and he nodded toward the staircase. "He just went upstairs to make his rounds. I'll call him down to—"

"That's not necessary. I can find him." She smiled and the familiar excitement bubbled as her mind raced with the possibilities of what she'd see upstairs tonight.

Max's mouth turned down. "At least allow one of the security team walk you up and help you find him. It's...pretty busy tonight."

Claire waved him off with one hand, smoothing the other down the front of her cherry red dress. "I know my way around. Thanks." Before the overzealous bartender could offer any additional arguments, she slowly ascended the stairs.

As soon as her foot reached the top step, a curvy brunette—clad in a black leather bustier and fishnet stockings—crossed in front of her, pulling an ebony leash studded with silver rivets, attached to a young blond man wearing nothing more than a burgundy thong. Claire swallowed, the sudden desire for more than what she'd experienced overwhelming her. Maybe she would have to beg Luca for that kind of training.

Claire scanned the crowd before turning to the left and beginning her search in earnest, much less confident than she had been. Perhaps she should have let Max call Luca for her. But she wanted to surprise him and...

"Well, well, lovely to see you again."

The voice from behind her right shoulder was familiar. When she spun on her heel, she frowned. The man from the bar the other day, the one Luca clearly didn't like, was standing with a hand in one of his pants pockets and a charming grin on his face. *Nathan? Nick?* As soon as Luca had returned she'd forgotten his name.

Years of breeding and business helped her affect a mostly genuine smile. "Yes, hello. I'm just looking for Luca."

A look of horror passed across his face. "Looking for him? He didn't accompany you? That isn't very good Dom behavior." He shook his head and casually walked toward her.

Claire took an involuntary step back and cursed the wall her ass collided with. He continued moving closer, boxing her in. "He is an excellent Dom. And he didn't know I was coming tonight."

"But it is a most welcome surprise, my *sotto*."

The deep purr that radiated from behind Noah caused a tidal wave of relief to wash over Claire. The low-level unease she'd experienced all week in his absence fled. When he reached around the startled blond, she didn't hesitate to slide her hand into his and be pulled firmly against his side.

Noah's shock melted into a smirk that made Claire inch even closer to Luca, gratified to feel his arm tighten around her. "Losing your touch, Luca? It seems your new little sub hasn't learned about venturing through the club, alone and unclaimed."

He grasped her hip harder and she barely silenced a moan. "*My* sub is not alone or unclaimed." He sneered and Claire fought the urge to strip her dress off right that second. Everything the man did was sexy as hell. He dipped his chin, pinning Noah with a stare. "Have a lovely evening, Noah. Please don't forget to avail yourself of the room service options. We have a wide variety of condoms you should enjoy."

The sharp intake of breath from the other man barely registered for Claire as Luca dropped his hand from her waist. He laced his fingers through hers and all but dragged her after him. At the base of the staircase leading to the third floor, he spun her, pressing her back against the wall. He placed one hand on either side of her head. Unlike when Noah had crowded her personal space, very similar actions from Luca caused a spear of fire to lance through her body.

"Why are you here?" He pressed his forehead against hers. "Why were you looking for me?"

She swallowed, one shaky hand reaching up to stroke down his face. "I choose you, Luca. Again."

He crashed his lips into hers as soon as the last word had left her mouth. His facial hair tickled her skin, heightened her excitement. She pressed her body against his, snaking her arms behind his back, stroking the soft white shirt.

He pulled away slightly, hovering his lips a breath above hers. "My little *sotto*, we need to review a few items, but the first thing we need to discuss is your collar."

"M-my collar?" Simply speaking the words made molten hot desire pool between her legs. She couldn't imagine actually wearing one.

One corner of Luca's mouth kicked up and he clicked his tongue. He pulled her closer to him, creating enough space between Claire and the wall to plant a firm smack on her ass and steal the breath from her body. "Have we so quickly forgotten our confidence, *sotto*? It's only been a week."

"I trust you. I have confidence."

His eyes lit like flares in the desert. "You are not to enter the club again until you have a collar. Everyone needs to understand that you are taken, that you are under my protection. And even then, I need to be with you. Do you understand?"

The shift between them was nearly palpable in that moment. She thrilled at the concept of wearing an outward symbol to show their bond. When he spoke of his protection, his claim on her, an ache she'd never known was present was immediately soothed.

She smiled up at him and nodded before dropping her eyes to the floor. "As you wish."

Chapter Seventeen

Luca

Luca squeezed Claire's hand tighter. A deep moan seeped out of one of the suites as they strode down the hall to his own. From his pocket, he slipped out his keycard.

He held the door open for her, regretting the lack of contact as he released her hand, but nonetheless calmed to have his *sotto* back where she belonged...with him. She crossed the threshold and the knot he'd had in his upper back for six torturous days smoothed out.

"Dress and shoes off. On your knees."

Claire moved over to the closet, and when she toed out of her heels and lined them up perfectly next to each other, he grinned. Her attention to detail was exceptional.

Luca, with the desire to savor each moment the night would bring, crossed the room and sat on the couch.

At the first sight of the dark dress, he'd clocked her understated but overwhelming beauty — then, a burning curiosity about what she was wearing underneath. She'd always come to him in white, as he'd requested, and the night needed to be about reward for returning. He hated the thought of clouding it by her not following his rules.

Her arm bent at an angle as she worked the zip down her divine back. The little vixen was taking her time. Luca's lips twitched with a small smirk. She was such a good sub.

The deep red material caressed her light arms on its way down, revealing a bare back. No bra. His *sotto* had been speaking to the novice without half of her underwear. His exhale warmed his inner throat. That would need to be addressed. *Later.*

Claire stepped out of the dress and his heart sang. *White.*

Madonna mia, she is perfect.

Even her hair had been tied back.

With the dress stored away and her eyes ever down, she walked to the side of the bed, knelt in one graceful movement — *has she been practicing?* — placed her palms up on her knees and waited.

She truly was a sight to behold. Fair, unmarked skin, perky breasts with hardened pink nipples that led to a flat stomach and narrow hips, she was his blank canvas. A future masterpiece, to be sure.

With a slow tilt of his wrist, he checked his watch. Six minutes for six days. A more than reasonable wait, he bartered — and a far more acceptable amount of time than the original six-day wait of her first lesson. He unhooked the platinum clasp, slipped the timepiece down his hand and propped it up on the armrest to study.

Six days of worry, stress and more self-control than he'd ever had to conjure. Not calling her, giving her space, had been the right move. The proof was kneeling in front of him. But it had been treacherous—not knowing if she'd dropped again, thinking she was struggling without him... He'd never hated six days more. And Luca had lived through dark times with his absent father and ghost of a mother.

At the halfway point, her breathing stabilized. Clever *sotto* understood. And while the anticipation would be her only punishment, she would need to hear his words and be reminded of the weight of their meaning.

When the needle ticked its final second, he stood.

"My *sotto*," he said with his hands on his hips and a purr in his voice, "I can't tell you how relieved I am you've found your way back to me."

Luca strode until he was behind her then bent down. He brushed a finger from the waistband of her white lace, up the arc of her lower spine and caressed the short free hairs on her neck. She shivered.

"I missed touching you, *sotto*." The whisper brought another small shudder.

Luca rose and, with a side-eye on his sub, crossed to hang up his jacket. He thought about asking her if she'd missed him, but it seemed obvious that she had.

With the jacket smoothed and hung, he unbuttoned his white shirt.

"You should know, *sotto*, that you can call me whenever you need me. I hated thinking you were suffering. Your solitude was, and now is, unnecessary."

She stayed silent, so smart. When he reached to open his pants, his hardened cock begged its relief. *Soon enough – or not.* The return of *sotto* needed to be celebrated. She deserved a reminder of what he could do for her.

Pants hung, shoes aligned and naked, he said, "Tell me, *sotto*. Did you have an orgasm without me?"

"No, Sir."

Bless her, she sounded practically offended.

"That's a very good girl." He smiled and approached her. He brushed his hand over her collar bone and cupped her left breast. After he fondled the stiff nipple, he pinched. Her bottom lip quivered but she otherwise remained still.

Luca slinked around her and his erection pushed into the cool skin of her back. He cupped both breasts and ran his bearded chin along her bare neck.

"Would you like me to make you come tonight, *sotto*?" He nipped her soft lobe.

"Yes, Sir." She pushed her head back into his and intensified the haze between them.

Using his thumbs and index fingers, he twisted again, and a small moan was her plea for more.

"How? How, my precious sotto? How would you like to come?" It was a test, one he was sure she would pass.

"As you wish, Sir."

Another double pinch of her nipples served as the reward for the perfect response. His need ached inside him and he rubbed his cock into her spine. *Not nearly enough contact.*

"That's right, my little *sotto*." He twirled his tongue around her flawless jawline and kissed down to her shoulder.

"Because who is your Master?"

"You are, Sir." Her faint voice signaled she'd drifted farther into her glorious sub state.

"And who decides when you come?"

"You do, Sir."

With every 'Sir' she whispered, his need grew. But the heavy air in the room and his desire to own, please and dominate her could not fog the formalities of his role.

He released her breasts and smoothed his hands down her stomach. As he threaded his fingers in and out of the seam of her underwear, he asked, "What does my *sotto* say when her Master is approaching a place where she's not comfortable?"

"Yellow, Sir."

"*Bene.* And what does she say when she needs him to stop and he's crossed a limit?"

"Red, Sir."

He dipped his right hand into her soaking panties and traced a slow circle around her clit with his middle finger. "Oh, *sotto*. Six days is a very long time for you to be away from your Master. But I'm so pleased you have returned." He spread her wet lips and, with a slow wiggle, slipped the digit inside her core.

"Are you pleased to be back with your Master?"

"So pleased, Sir," she said with a muted purr.

"Mmm... Would you like to show your Master how pleased you are?" Luca reached his free hand back up to one of her breasts and matched the slow tease from between her legs.

"Yes, Sir. Please, Sir." Claire's back pushed into his chest and he pressed his lips into her temple for a long kiss. He inhaled and exhaled then repeated two more times.

"And how would you like to please me, *sotto*?" Another wicked test, he knew, but one she was certain not to fail. It had been apparent from their first meeting.

"As you wish, Sir."

His smile beamed pride. "You are exceptional. So smart. So beautiful." Once again, he rewarded her with linked pleasure from his touch, sure her desire was climbing as steadily as his own.

"You Master wishes for your lovely mouth around his cock, *sotto*. Would that please you?"

"Yes…" Her airy affirmation was almost enough for him to forget his own place.

"Yes, what?" A nipple pinch married his question.

"Yes, Sir. Pleasing you is all I want." Her powerful declaration spoke to his soul, the very essence of his being. It promised understanding, acceptance and more—more of this undeniable connection, more of *them*.

"An angel, *sotto*. You are an angel. I knew it the moment I saw you." He leaned back and brushed his hands along her ribcage. "It's why you wear white. You are a piece of heaven on earth."

He stood and realized his sub had been on her knees for quite a long time. And while breaking her into finding comfort there was important, he wasn't going to leave her too sore to play again the next day. He had his *sotto* back and he fully intended to make up for lost time.

He dipped onto the bed and stretched in the middle.

"Come, my sweet. Come and show me how you missed me. You may use your mouth and your hands."

With too much grace for a beginner, she rose, eyes still fixed down. Claire crawled onto the bed and settled between his spread legs. A wry smile lifted her cheeks as she looked down at his erection, but she traveled her fingers up his knees and skimmed the dark hair on his legs. She ran them back down and let out a deep sigh.

Luca quirked his brow. "Are you teasing your Master, *sotto*?"

"No, Sir. I... I like touching you."

"While that does make me happy and the feeling is quite mutual, this moment is about your Master's pleasure. Your mouth, my cock."

"Yes, Sir," she said before leaning down and rolling the tip of his aching erection with her warm tongue. She reached for the base and her tight grip tugged him closer. Without warning, she opened her mouth fully and the head of his cock touched the back of her throat. As he'd imagined, her lips around his shaft brought equal physical and emotional bliss.

Up and down she pumped as she hollowed out her cheeks and teased with her tongue. It was almost too much. *Almost.*

"Eyes," he said in a quiet command.

When their gazes locked, happiness danced behind her baby blues. She truly was a sub, taking pleasure by giving it. What a magical gift the gods had bestowed on him.

"Slow down, *sotto*. I'm going to feel your orgasm when I'm inside you."

Her pace turned lazy and the urge to explode into her mouth simmered.

"Fetch a condom from the drawer and put it on me."

Claire licked the length of his shaft one last time, as if regretfully saying goodbye, but she obeyed.

"Take off those lovely panties, sit on my cock and ride me."

Was it unusual for him to have a sub on top so early into their relationship? He couldn't remember and didn't care. Giving Claire the reins and proving to her that she could grab hold of her desires was essential for the moment. And the slow decent of her hips over his entire length was impressive.

She let out a long breath that hit his chest and cooled his skin.

"Are you okay, *sotto*?" The question was two-fold and he hoped it would be received as such.

"Yes, Sir," she said and swallowed. "You're a lot to take in." Perhaps her own words had a double meaning.

"Take your time. Remember your safewords."

Her eyes closed and she hovered for a moment before she spread her hands below his navel and gripped his hips.

Gently, she rocked forward and whimpered as she pulled back. He put his pleasure aside and stared at her face. Another exhale forced from her mouth and she glided again.

"You're doing so well, sweet *sotto*. So well. Your Master is so proud of you." Luca reached for her knees, but instead of pushing, he held them in place. "There is no rush."

The base of her palms pushed into his stomach and her wonderful sway strengthened. Forward and back she went, and the tightness of her walls urged Luca's building climax. As she quickened, her whimpers morphed to moans.

"Touch yourself, *sotto*. It's time for your reward for returning to your Master." Luca squeezed her knees and amplified the pace even more.

Claire reached for her breast with one hand while the other found her clit. She cried out, "Please! Please! I need to come."

Luca dug his fingers into her flesh. The beautiful agony on her face was too much to deny. He counted to three in his head then said, "Come, my *sotto*. Come on my cock."

Her mewling scream and clenched pussy ignited his own release and his balls ached as he came. He groaned through his climax and Claire collapsed on top of him.

When their panting settled, he said, "Kiss me, *sotto*."

Claire trailed her soft lips from his shoulder and pecked up his neck. She was doing as told, but it wasn't how he'd imagined. *My fault for not being specific.*

With a quick movement that pulled him out of her, he flipped her onto her back. He found her lips and closed his eyes. He claimed her mouth and trailed his fingers through her loose hair. He pulled back, but the need to keep kissing her overcame him. *Three more kisses*, he scolded himself. Then he would turn all his attention to her and everything she needed.

"You are divine, *cara*." He looped a lock of her blonde hair and marveled at its softness. "Heaven on earth. And you did so well. Your Master is so proud of you. Even with our time apart, you excel at everything you do."

"Thank you, Sir." After a long blink she opened her eyes. "I owe it all to you."

"Flattering, but untrue. All the change is coming from you. I'm just giving you a safe place to do it." He kissed her brow and spun around.

Before he could stand, she said, "Is this aftercare?"

"Yes, *cara*." He smiled and wondered what she'd ask for. Maybe food. Dear lord, had she even eaten in the last six days?

"So, I can ask for whatever I want?"

Luca spun around to find her bottom lip between her teeth. As soon as he'd clocked it, she let it go. "Yes, *cara*."

"Will you kiss me again?"

He would. He absolutely would. Again, again, and again. Then he would hold her and ask her when the last time was that she'd eaten.

Chapter Eighteen

Claire

"Fuck!" Claire tried to control the volume of the expletive as pain seared through her finger. She pulled the digit to her mouth, ridiculously incensed by the offending sheet of paper in front of her. The clicking of a tongue from the doorway that led into her office made Claire jump to her feet, her hand falling at her side. "Luca?"

Impeccably dressed as always in a navy suit, white shirt and perfectly coordinated tie, Luca strolled into her office, softly latching the door behind him. "Such language, *cara*."

"W-what are you doing here?" She fought the urge to tap her fingers against the desk — or bite her lip or any of the other dozen little insecure tics she knew Luca would pick up on and chastise her for. *Oh, hell.* She'd stuttered.

One dark, thick eyebrow arched. "Forgetting to watch our language, as well as forgetting our confidence? *Cara*, it has only been a few hours since we were last together. Should I be concerned about your memory?"

The plastic bag Luca deposited on the desk in front of her stole the response forming in her brain. "And this is?"

The dark smile that hinted of every seductive thought running through his head — and simultaneously sent shivers down Claire's spine — curled his lips.

"Your lunch, *cara*. When I called thirty minutes ago, it was brought to my attention that you have not yet had lunch — and it is nearly three." He tilted his head. "We have discussed this, *sotto*."

Sotto. She dropped her eyes, took her seat again and obediently began pulling the meal from the bag. "Yes, Sir."

"Good girl," he crooned from the opposite side of the desk.

In her peripheral vision, she caught him taking the seat across from her and she bit back a groan. He was going to ensure she ate the entire meal. The warmth that spread through her at the realization had little to do with the man oozing testosterone and sex appeal and much more to do with his care and concern.

Claire popped the lid off the bowl-shaped container and stared at the contents. Chunks of chicken, something green and...meatballs? All were swirled into a soup that both looked questionable and smelled divine. She hesitated briefly, her spoon poised over the meal. She wasn't certain if she was his *sotto* or just

Claire in this moment, but she dared to lift her eyes to his. "What is this?"

He chuckled and propped his ankle on the opposite knee. "It is Italian wedding soup, *cara*. My *nonna's* secret recipe. Trust me. You will like it. Eat."

Cara. Sotto. It didn't matter. She was helpless to do anything but obey. She took a spoonful of the amber liquid, lifting it to her lips cautiously and painfully aware of his eyes tracking her every move. An explosion of flavor burst on her tongue and her eyelids dropped closed. A moan rumbled the back of her throat. "This is amazing."

"See, *cara*? Aren't you glad you trusted me?" He stood from his seat, buttoned his jacket and leaned across the desk. He traced her jaw with his fingertips. His voice dropped to little more than a whisper. "As much as I would love nothing more than to sit here with you for the rest of the afternoon, relishing every little sound you make and knowing I am the cause, I have an appointment." He moved his head closer, hovering his mouth just above hers. "Make me proud, *sotto*. Eat every morsel."

With that, he dropped his hand away and turned on his heel. He paused at her door, holding it open slightly. "We will revisit your little rebellions tonight, *sotto*. Seven o'clock."

Claire struggled to keep her grip on the utensil in her hand. Hell, she struggled to draw oxygen into her lungs. Anticipation. Desire. Need. All mingled to cause her temperature to skyrocket and her blood to sing as it raced through her veins. She had no idea what was going through Luca's mind and she didn't even care. She knew that whatever his plan, her pleasure was at the center.

Her trust in him was implicit.

She broke a corner off the length of Italian bread he had included with the soup, popped it in her mouth...and nearly choked when she was hit with a sudden realization. His *nonna's* secret recipe? That meant... No, no, it wasn't possible. Certainly he hadn't made this simply for her. She shook her head and dug back into the soup with renewed gusto.

Until cackling laughter hit her ears and forced her gaze to the doorway once more. "And what is so funny, Julien, you nosy little rat?"

His eyes glittered with amusement. "Oh nothing...*cara*. I just adore being right."

* * * *

She was never as grateful for her habit of forgetting to put on a watch as she was when she was kneeling beside Luca's bed. Not knowing how much or little time was passing added a level of excitement and, oddly, comfort to the ritual.

A bolt of lightning shot down her spine as the mechanism in the doorknob activated. "Good evening, *sotto*."

This was...an unusual start to their sessions. "Good evening, Sir."

"You have done so well, *sotto*, so very well." He stood in front of her, heaving a sigh that sounded awfully dramatic. She fought to control her smile. "But we must address some issues."

She swallowed. Her body shook from excitement and just a hint of nervousness. She remained silent but began screaming inside to experience something, anything, *everything* that she'd seen in the public punishment rooms on the floor below them.

"Stand."

The command brought her to her feet before her mind had registered the word. She wondered if she would react this way to any Dom ordering her or if it was unique to Luca. And her stomach recoiled at the thought of any other, which thoroughly confused her.

"Front against the wall, arms over your head, palms flat."

Facing the wall allowed Claire the freedom to look around. She didn't see any restraints hanging from the smooth surface. Her mind raced, wondering what Luca had planned. But the rumble of his voice behind her, so close to her ear, quieted every thought. She trusted him, whatever his plan.

"This is our first time at this, *sotto*, so you will not be restrained. I expect you to keep your hands as they are, flush against the wall. I am trusting in your obedience and desire to please your Dom." He trailed his fingers down her spine and traced the outline of the white thong she wore, running along the seam of her ass and stealing her breath. "You are such a good little submissive. Anticipating your Dom's needs and wants down to the underwear you selected. *Brava*, sotto, but this does not mean you will not need to face some consequences for your previous actions."

"Yes, Sir."

He gripped her hip firmly. "What are your safewords, *sotto*?"

"'Yellow' when it is getting to be a little too much and 'Red' when I need to stop, Sir." Every time they added a new dynamic to their playtime, he required her to recite her safewords. The ritual brought comfort and...something else she was only beginning to acknowledge.

He wound his hand around her long blonde ponytail and tugged slightly. "Eyes."

She turned her head and met his gaze. She'd expected the intensity, the desire, but the concern tinging the edges of the chocolate-colored orbs was...surprising. "Yes, Sir?"

"Your safewords are not just to be used when you are reaching your physical limits. If at any point you are struggling with mental and emotional reactions that are overwhelming, I am trusting you will use them."

The tears stinging the back of her eyes were more confusing than his proclamation. He had never before reiterated the necessity of her safewords. Fear of another crash as epic as the one she'd experienced nearly two weeks ago made the hair on the back of her neck stand at attention. But...

"I trust you, Sir."

He melded his mouth against hers and she found herself so lost in the bliss it created that the crack of his hand against her ass startled her, but she didn't dare move away. His lips were a drug that kept her coming back for more. After a final swipe of his tongue against hers, he drew back. His gaze washed over her face, scrutinizing every inch so thoroughly that Claire fought the urge to look away.

Whatever he saw on her flaming hot countenance clearly pleased him as he offered an approving nod and moved behind her. "Do you believe I want to help you become the very best version of yourself possible, *sotto*?"

Without a moment's hesitation, she replied. "Yes, Sir."

"Brace, *sotto*."

She planted her feet more firmly and pressed her palms against the creamy-colored wall, battling the uncertainty bubbling inside and clinging to the fact that she knew Luca would never hurt her.

Something smooth collided with her ass and she was grateful for his warning that kept her from stumbling. A soft string of Italian hit her ears, but the mounting adrenaline-induced euphoria made translating impossible. The initial pain couldn't be denied, but the speed at which it melted into blissful pleasure shocked Claire.

"*Rosso. Assolutamente mozzafiato.*"

That was one she didn't need to decipher, and hearing him call her stunning once again warmed her chest.

He cleared his throat. "Your language, *sotto*. I expect better." Another smack hit squarely across both cheeks. "And we have discussed your eating habits. In order to perform at your best in all areas of your life, you must nourish your body in the proper way."

This time there were two stinging swats in rapid succession and Claire bit her tongue to contain the moan threatening to escape, fearful he would interpret it as anything other than the hedonistic joy that was her reality. Never before had she dreamed physical punishment could elicit such a response. Now she couldn't envision living her life denying this side of herself.

"Lower your arms."

He snaked his olive hand in front of her and affixed silver clamps to each of her nipples. The breath escaped her lips on a low hiss and the chuckle from behind her caused a ripple to run through her body. He turned her to face him, his eyes shining with delight. "*Madonna mia*, I've been dying to put these on you, *sotto*."

Claire fought irritation at the fact that he was still clothed. Seeing Luca naked was a gift she treasured each and every time. She nodded, uncertain what to say. Her breasts had always been sensitive to the touch, but the pressure on the hardened nubs was delicious. *Exquisite. Unexpected, but wholly welcome.*

"You never cease to amaze me, *sotto*."

The back of his hand trailed down the side of her face. She was grateful to keep her gaze fixed on the floor, anxious he would see every emotion written across it and all the things she couldn't admit to feeling. He would know she wanted no Dom but him. "It is because of you, Sir."

He skimmed his hands over her clamped nipples, eliciting a low moan she was helpless to prevent. He rested them on her hips first, making small circles on her hip bones with his thumbs, yet another area on her body she had always taken for granted brought to life by Luca's expert touch. Soon he was on the move again, creating a path of fire along the edge of her thong. He ran an index finger down the front, delving beneath the thin material, the evidence of her need thoroughly soaking the lace.

"Is this because of me as well?" He slid one digit between her folds, teasing the aching nub. "And this, *sotto*? Is this also my fault?"

Her breathing had shallowed with his slow, tortuous ministrations. Her breasts had grown heavy with the clamps. Every inch of her was crying out for him. "Yes, Sir."

His normally deep voice dropped another octave. "On the bed, *sotto*. On your hands and knees."

The rustling of material behind her caused her brain to scream out a litany of curses in three different languages. *Aftercare*, she reminded herself. She would see him and touch him in their aftercare. The drawer to her right closed, followed by the familiar tearing of the foil packet. Her arms shook with anticipation.

The bed dipped behind her and his warm finger slid the thin material covering her to the side.

"*Mozzafiato*."

It was whispered with more reverence than she'd ever heard and was followed by a hard thrust as he entered her. He kneaded her aching backside, amplifying the pleasure as he moved in and out.

"Please." The single word was spoken on a sob. "Please, I need…"

He reached in front of her, teasing her swollen clit. Her clamped nipples rubbed against the satin material of his duvet each time his cock pumped inside her, making her whimper from the foreign sensation.

"Please what, *sotto*?" His own breathing was labored, his voice hoarse. "What do you need?"

She choked, overwhelmed at every angle. "I need to come, Sir. Please!"

"*Si*. Yes. Yes, *sotto*." He pinched the aching nub with the clamp and her release followed immediately. Three more hard thrusts inside of her and his own guttural moan mingled with hers as she peaked a second time.

As always, Luca quickly disposed of his condom and wiped her gently with warm water. She gasped as he released her nipples from the clamps, sucking them lightly as the blood flow returned. He pulled her close to his side beneath the blankets and pressed his lips against her temple before he pushed her head down onto his chest.

Claire hung in the space between ecstasy and slumber, barely registering the words he spoke beneath his breath in his native tongue.

"Mio Dio che cosa ha fatto questo sottomesso a me."

She promised herself to ask what it meant. Soon.

Three hours later he deposited her back at her house, insisting he drive her rather than rely on the car service that had brought her to him. He held her against him with one arm around her waist, staring at her with the intensity she had come to welcome, as the one person she knew understood every part of her.

"You will remember that from this point on, whether we are together or apart, whether you are negotiating a ten-million-franc transaction or we are exploring your boundaries within the walls of the club, you are a representative of me. Your actions, your words, your every movement is a testimony to the training you have received. You will show the world a version of Claire Favre that you never knew existed." He cupped her cheek, the corners of his mouth curling slightly. "And you will take their breath away."

Chapter Nineteen

Luca

Luca pressed his lips together as his mouth twitched to smile. The picture on his phone, of his sublime Cara's lunch on her desk at a reasonable hour set his mind on fire with ways to reward her. He wrote back.

Your Master is very pleased, sotto. *I'll see you tomorrow night in my suite, as discussed. Wear a short dress, keep it on and wait for me on the couch. You shall be rewarded.*

With his phone stored securely in the inner pocket of his suit, Luca scanned the entry to the quiet but upscale restaurant overlooking the lake of Lucerne. Bruno—more relaxed than he'd seen him in years—entered with a wide grin. They made eye contact and Luca rose as his old friend strode in his impeccable attire to meet him. Long past the days of a formal handshake, the two exchanged a happy tap on the shoulders with a narrowed distance between their chests.

Bruno ran a hand over his combed-back thinning brown hair and Luca gestured for him to sit.

"I already ordered the tasting menu for both of us and told them you'd be drinking my wine," Luca said with a smirk.

Bruno frowned, but the lightness stayed in his dark eyes. "You would. Always trying to top." He shook out his white linen napkin and placed it on his lap. They toasted each other with the sparkling water and Luca grinned.

"Retirement agrees with you."

Bruno waved his hand as if brushing the comment off the table. "Adrian is taking massage lessons and has me going to yoga." The last part of the sentence was barely above a whisper and he sat back deeper into the leather chair. "So, while my life may be relaxing, it's incredibly boring. Tell me about the club. Any new male subs I would like?"

Luca shook his head and raised an eyebrow. "Old habits dying hard? I thought you were committed?"

"Don't cock that bushy eyebrow at me. I can still look. Hell, he's free to come down and have a go and I would too if my damn health allowed it."

Yes. His illness. Luca's face dropped. "What are your doctors saying?"

"The same damn thing they always have. Did you know that in the United States they actually give you a deadline? Ha!" Bruno's head shot back. "That's ironic, a *dead* line. But no, here they won't say how long. Probably better, for Adrian's sake."

The waiter arrived with their first course and the two men stiffened their posture to accommodate the service, including Bruno's wine that Luca was no longer sure he should be drinking.

"For all our sakes," Luca said with a wink.

The fork in Bruno's hand stopped midway to the plate below it.

"A wink? For me? From Luca Bernardi? My God, I must already be dead. Although I never expected to go to heaven."

Luca swallowed his bite with a playful sneer, but before he could find an acceptable rebuttal, Bruno continued, "Are you flirting with me, Luca?"

After a drink from his water, Luca smiled. "I think we both know better than that."

"New collar?" Bruno eyed the bag next to the table bearing the mark of the most exclusive leathermaker in the country.

"Yes," Luca said with warning.

"For the little blonde banker?" Bruno's tongue rolled around his cheek and over his top teeth. He didn't wait for a reply and asked, "What color? Mmm... Let me guess." The old man perked up and stabbed the last bite of his starter then sat the fork next to the plate. He stared at Luca as if he possessed the psychic power to read minds.

Not going to work.

"Definitely not black. You've always been partial to blue." He tapped his empty wine glass and the movement brought a refill from the waiter.

His guessing would be futile. Luca had never given a white collar before and he suspected he never would again. Purple, various shades of blue, pink and many browns. Certainly not red. But white? There had never been a sub he'd trained who'd received white. The meaning, while Luca understood it on a cellular level, remained deep inside him. It was in a safe spot he refused to acknowledge that he held the key to unlock.

"Pink," Luca lied, "like her rosy skin."

"Oh, my dear friend, you truly have a gift."

Luca tilted his head in acceptance. "A compliment from the Dom of Doms. Master of Masters." Luca grinned. "Thank you."

Bruno raised his hand and pressed two fingers under his chin. The small drama, the ruse, was typical. Comical. And welcome. "Not dead," he said with a quick shrug. "You calling me 'Master'? I was sure of it."

They made way for the next dish and instead of the lingering issue of Noah Paulick's membership, which Luca had hoped to discuss with Bruno, they spoke of politics and the weather. After an espresso and the bill Luca insisted on paying, the two walked out into the bright fall sun. Luca waited until Bruno was secure in his car service and watched the dark sedan pull away. With the thick paper bag dangling from his wrist, he strolled down the bustling sidewalk to the parking garage where he'd left his car.

Once inside the clean security of the Maserati, he opened the bag and unwrapped the collar from its tissue paper. His fingers brushed the engraved letters with care.

Sotto.

His *sotto.* His, for now. He blinked and re-wrapped the leather band. It was necessary. Protection and safety. There was no way he could risk any other Dom touching his *cara.* Speaking to his *cara.* And the only way to gauge where she wanted to go next, was to take her into the club. But she had to be protected. It was essential.

Before cranking the car, he reached inside his jacket for his phone one more time. Three simple yet perfect words were his reply from Claire.

As you wish.

* * * *

Taking Claire into the club that Saturday night had a twofold purpose. Most importantly, it was for her. But as the manager on a busy night, Luca would be able to survey the scene and let his presence be known, not that he could imagine his eyes on any person but *sotto*. But Gwendelyn had arranged for a group of German female subs to play for the night, their bill having been negotiated and paid for by one of the male Masters who had met them in Berlin.

Luca smoothed the front of his black suit and rode the elevator, the bag he'd stared at too much over the prior day in his hand. The corridor on the third floor remained quiet, but the energy from his staff's preparations bubbled up the stairway at the opposite end of the hall.

His trust would rely heavily on Max for the evening, as well as the eyes of his security team. With a swipe of his keycard, the heavy, massive door to his suite clicked open and he found his *sotto* exactly where he expected her to be.

In a white short-sleeve dress, inappropriate for the season but delectably perfect for the evening ahead, with nude high heels on her feet, Claire sat on the edge of the couch, her eyes fixed on the floor.

"Good evening, *cara*."

"Good evening, Sir."

"You may give me your eyes until told otherwise."

Claire's posture straightened with her gaze and she smiled.

The urge to return the warmth suppressed itself, and Luca rubbed his lips together. "You're stunning, as always. You never cease to impress me."

"Thank you, Sir. As are you."

He dipped his chin and again hid his content. While the compliment was noted, appreciated and charmed his ego, it was her confidence to give it that pleased him most. He crossed the room, placed the bag on the floor and, with a quick unbutton of his jacket, sat next to his *sotto*.

"You must be confused as to why you are dressed — and so perfectly in white."

Her fine neck begged to be kissed. Her toned legs were pure beauty. When had his own restraint battled him so much?

"A little, Sir."

He reached over and ran his thumb over her impeccable cheekbone.

"Tonight, I want to take you into the club, let you witness more, discover…"

Her slate blue eyes danced over his face, confirming that he'd read her longing correctly.

"But it is my opinion that you are not ready to do that as *sotto*. My calculation is that you would be more comfortable as Claire."

She blinked a few times.

"For now" — he held her hands in her lap — "we must make small steps together. And they will result in a large stride for you."

"Thank you, Sir."

"Now, there are three very important things we must do before crossing that threshold."

He waited for her long exhale and the little roll of her shoulders.

"One, you must understand the rules."

"Yes, Sir." The affirmation came with a quick nod.

"*Cara*, you are not to leave my side. You are not to speak to any other Master. If you become uncomfortable with what you're witnessing at any time, you are to communicate that to me immediately. Do you understand?"

"Yes, Sir."

"*Brava*. Now, to ensure that you are safe, as I mentioned before, you will need a collar." He reached down into the bag and pulled out the bundled tissue. Before opening it, he met her eyes again. "You need to be clear about what this is, *sotto*. One day, when you find a permanent Dom, he may offer you a collar to seal your connection. This is not that. This is a training collar to keep you safe within the walls of this club. It stays here, in my suite, and if deemed suitable for you to return to the public area, will be worn at that time. Or in here, if I decide to use it as part of your training."

Claire's regard fell to the paper on his lap.

"Eyes."

They fluttered up to his own.

An unfamiliar pain stabbed his gut. Something was off.

"Do you not wish to see the club tonight, *sotto*?" he asked.

"I do, Sir. I do. Thank you for understanding."

"Would you like to see your collar? It's custom for your training."

The trace of worry he'd thought he'd seen disappeared with a smile of her pink lips.

"Yes, please."

Luca presented Claire with the package and she delicately unwrapped the layers. With care, she lifted the white leather collar from her lap and examined it.

"It says '*sotto*'."

"So it does. Would you like to try it on?"

She nodded.

"Words, *sotto*. You must use your words."

"Yes, please, Sir."

Luca took the neckpiece from her hands and she lifted her tied-back hair. The breath she let out allowed him to tug it tight and he fastened it in place. A tension left his shoulders and hers at the same time and pride swirled in his chest.

"Would you like to see yourself?"

"Yes, please, Sir."

He stood from the couch and offered her his hand. Luca led her to the dark tiled en suite, where he spun her shoulders and they both gazed at the new addition in the mirror.

The simple band separated her neck from her chest and she raised her hand to touch it.

"You are exquisite. And you continue to make me more and more proud." Luca brushed her hair away and laid a long, lingering kiss below her ear. He wanted to keep going, to taste more of her, but he withdrew.

"Now," he said as he found her eyes in the mirror, "the final element before you wander these savage halls." He trailed his hands down her arms and back up. "To the bed, bent over, panties at your ankles. Eyes down."

Luca's ego allowed him to believe she'd gulped.

Luca's Lessons

She obeyed, because she was a good *sotto*. A splendid one, actually.

He crossed the room, admiring the sight of her, and opened a drawer. He found the untouched package, along with the bottle he needed, and broke the seal on both.

"*Sotto*, I have been reviewing your limits."

Every day since you sent them.

He walked back to the bed and stood behind her, the even-toned cream ass on full display in its understated glory. He set the packages on the bedside table and ran a hand over her cool cheeks.

A quiet purr released from her throat.

Why had he bought this club? Staying in the suite and playing with the divine specimen in front of him would have been enough to fulfill him for weeks.

He dipped a finger between her folds and spread her readiness in a wide circumference around her clit.

"So pleased, *sotto*. I am so pleased with you."

"Thank you, Sir," she whispered.

With a crook of his finger, he gathered the slick and trailed it between her ass cheeks.

"Tell your Master, *sotto*. When you had anal sex before, did you enjoy it?"

Her rim flinched, and he circled it in light brushes.

"No, Sir," she said as she moaned.

"I shall remind you of your words of yellow and red, sotto." After a little more teasing, Luca pressed his finger harder and broke through the tight seal. With his other hand, he massaged the lovely flesh along her hips. "Tonight, as you walk through the halls of my club, you will know who your Master is, not only because he is by your side and will not leave you but because he will be thinking of being inside you the entire time."

Luca removed his finger from her ass and reached for the lube and small plug he'd set out. After squirting the clear jelly into his hand, he warmed it and coated her sinfully tight hole. He teased the opening with the dull bullet-headed plug. Claire's muffled whimpers made his cock throb against his tight pants and he once again cursed his responsibilities.

"Push out a little and relax, my sotto. The sting will be over quickly — or so I've been told."

Without much fuss the plug was in place, its jewel-studded end shining between her cheeks. Luca begged his memory for any reason to flush the round skin and drew a blank. She had been too good. He wiped away the excess lube and told her to stay put as he quickly washed his hands then came back to her. Bless her uncaptured heart, she was in the same position as he'd left her.

The temptation to touch her again was too much and he massaged her lower back and ass one more time.

"My *sotto*, once again, you exceed all expectations." He bent down and slid her white lace back over her rear. "You may stand and turn around."

Claire moved slowly and faced her Master. He kissed her forehead, left cheek and soft mouth. "*Cara*, you've done so well. I feel you deserve a reward. So, before we leave this room, I will grant you whatever you wish…within reason."

Chapter Twenty

Claire

Whatever I wish?

Claire rolled the words around in her brain. What she wanted was just further proof of the Luca-induced metamorphosis she was learning to embrace and not fear.

Before his illness, her sex life with Liam had been...special. He'd been soft and tender. He had teased and satisfied her in any number of ways and she had always been happy to return the favor.

But Luca was fire and ice. Shocking her. Enflaming her. She didn't simply want to repay Luca for the immeasurable satisfaction he'd given her. She had an overwhelming urge to kneel before him in a very different way.

And make sure he was thoroughly satiated before he entered the scene on the floor below. *Jealousy?* She gave her head a small shake and stuffed the unfamiliar emotion down. It wasn't possible. This was temporary. That was the agreement.

"Anything I wish, Sir?"

His chocolate gaze held a hint of trepidation at her response and she fought the urge to grin. "Within reason, *sotto*, within reason."

She thought about ordering him to sit on the couch and nearly laughed out loud at the very idea of trying to top the Dom. Instead, she took his hand and led him across the room. Only hesitating a moment and remembering to keep her voice strong, she lifted her gaze to meet his again. "Please sit, Sir."

Luca did as commanded, an amused smile tugging at his lips. "*Si, sotto*."

Claire resisted rolling her eyes heavenward, but fuck, that man was even more sexy when he lapsed into Italian. He'd never know the effect his pet names had on her. She dropped to her knees and gently pressed her hands on the inside of his thighs, urging them apart.

He trailed the tips of his fingers along her jaw. "I wanted to reward you, *sotto*."

She smiled and made quick work of releasing his belt clasp and pulling it free. "Tasting you is my reward, Sir."

A soft string of Italian met her reply but Claire was too focused on her goal, sliding the zipper down and freeing him from the two layers of material. She lifted her eyes to his once more as her hand closed around the base of his shaft. She licked her lips with deliberate slowness before she planted soft kisses on every inch of his thick cock.

Just holding him excited her, spurred her to be as creative as she could. From day one, he'd played her body likely a finely tuned instrument that he'd had years of experience with. She was certain she could offer him the same.

She ran her tongue the entire length of him over and over as she dove her hand inside his pants and began stroking the soft skin she found there. The leg on her left gave an involuntary jerk and she smiled. Perhaps Luca wasn't impervious to surprises after all.

The muted moans and sharp intakes of breath that escaped Luca's mouth as she danced her lips, her tongue and her hand across his warm flesh caused an immediate flare of heat between her legs in response. The plug moved slightly inside her as she shifted her weight from one knee to the other. An involuntary groan rumbled in the back of her throat.

"*Madre mia.*" He stroked the top of her head, his breathing becoming more labored.

She caved, giving them both what they were panting for as she closed her mouth around the head and took him deep into her throat until her lips met her hand. With every rise, she swept her tongue across the tip, and with every descent, she wrapped it around his shaft.

Claire met his heated stare as she sucked on the head and pumped her hand up and down his slickened length. Within the space of a breath, his grip in her hair tightened as his own fell against the back of the couch. A guttural roar akin to a wild animal ripped from his mouth as hers was filled with hot liquid. She licked every drop, her head spinning from the knowledge she had brought pleasure to her Dom.

She massaged him as his breathing slowly returned to normal. He lifted his head and opened his mouth but Claire stuck an index finger in the air. She rose to her feet and disappeared into the small bathroom, collecting the washcloth, towel and basin he always used on her.

She knelt before him again, running the soft cloth across his skin and drying him before covering him and securing his pants.

As she stood to store the items away, he closed his hand around her wrist. "Drop them."

Obediently she set the carefully folded material and basin on the floor seconds before he tugged her onto his lap. He crashed his mouth into hers with a ferocity that surprised her. Her subsequent gasp gave his tongue the open access it demanded as it tangled with hers.

Countless minutes later, he released her lips. "That was *your* reward?"

A wide, admittedly proud, smile spread across her face. Even though she was in her sub role, she couldn't help it. The knowledge she had evoked such a primal reaction from Luca Bernardi was headier than any drink she'd known. "Yes, Sir."

Luca pressed his forehead against hers with a light chuckle. "*Cosa dovrei fare con te, sotto?*"

Claire lifted one slim shoulder helplessly. "I'm impossibly slow with Italian."

His lips brushed across her temple. "I said clean up. We need to go downstairs."

Rusty though her command of the language was, Claire was certain that hadn't been what he'd said, but she simply stood and nodded before collecting the items from the floor. "As you wish."

His voice stopped her when she reached the bathroom door. "You are magnificent, *sotto*."

* * * *

Luca made small circles with his thumb on the back of the hand firmly clasped in his. Without breaking his stride, he bent down and whispered in Claire's ear. "If there is a scene you want to watch, let me know. Otherwise, eyes down."

She jutted out her lower lip but she dropped her gaze obediently as they entered the club. This wasn't at all what she'd expected for her first official trip to the club under Luca's ownership — *temporary ownership*, she reminded herself — to be like. "Yes, Sir."

He pushed her pout back into place. "Now, now, *sotto*...do we need to go back upstairs so soon and correct your behavior?"

Heat flushed her cheeks. "But, Sir, isn't there a room here for discipline? Public discipline?"

His sharp intake of breath was followed by her back being flattened against the wall and the hard planes of Luca's body pressed to her front. "Eyes, now, *sotto*." His jaw flexed, and his dark stare bored through her with more intensity than she expected. "Do you want that? Do you want me to tie you in one of the public rooms and punish you?" He lifted his hand to her cheek then slid it down her chest before reaching around to cup her ass. "With a crowd watching us? Lusting after every inch of your creamy skin, salivating over the ass I make red with a paddle?"

Oh fuck. Need shot between her legs. The taunting plug moved with Luca's possessive grip. The air left her lungs on a stuttering exhale, but she forced her voice to remain controlled. "As you wish, Sir."

His nostrils flared, but otherwise he didn't move — didn't blink, didn't even appear to breathe. "Soon, *cara*. Soon." Luca intertwined his fingers through hers again. "Tonight, we watch." He brushed his lips against her neck before moving next to her ear, his breath inflaming her flesh. "You will watch the scenes, *sotto*, and I will watch your every reaction."

Luca stepped back and pulled her close to his side again. Claire immediately dropped her gaze, her stomach rolling when his deep chuckle vibrated against her arm.

"Oh, *sotto*, so obedient you are."

They wandered through the wide, open space, separated with half walls or ornate drapes for various scenes and designated play spaces. She fought the mounting irritation at not being able to see what was going on around her. Luca would occasionally bend down and describe scenes, asking if she wanted to watch. Nothing caught her attention until…

"A Mistress has her little sub lined up for inspection."

Hearing the scenes played out through his voice was nearly better than seeing them for herself. *Nearly.*

"And it appears the sub hasn't groomed herself properly." He clicked his tongue.

Her first visit to the club — well, only the bar below because that was all Luca had allowed at the time — flashed in her mind. Three gorgeous girls flirting, kissing, touching…under the watchful eye of a Master. It was the first time she'd seen something so blatantly erotic played out before her eyes and she needed more. "May I watch, Sir? Please?"

Silence. His silence was always so telling. After several nerve-racking beats, he finally responded. "Yes, *sotto*. You may look now."

As desperately as she wanted to witness the scene before her, her eyes went to him first. Always Luca first. "Thank you, Sir."

The corner of his mouth kicked up and he inclined his head before moving to stand behind her, gripping her hips. "Since you requested this, I expect your eyes to stay fixed, *sotto*, no matter what happens around you." His voice dropped to an impossibly low tone. "No matter what I do to you, you may not look away."

Her mouth went dry, her mind racing with the possibilities — until the Domme stepped onto the stage, circling her submissive. All rational thought fled Claire's mind.

The woman — Claire guessed her to be about a decade older than her — clad in a deep red see-through blouse that showcased her dark lacy bra and a tight black leather skirt that barely covered her ass, tapped a riding crop against her calf as she stalked her prey with purpose. The submissive stood still, her hands placed at the back of her head and her legs parted, wavy brunette locks tumbling around her shoulders. She wore nothing other than a dazzling silver, jewel-encrusted collar.

"Did you know your Mistress was bringing you to the club tonight?" The redhead's heels clicked against the floor as she walked, punctuating her clipped questions.

"Yes, Mistress." Her voice was soft, but confident.

A loud crack of the riding crop against the submissive's ass made Claire jump slightly. Or it could have been Luca's hand wandering beneath the plunging neckline of her dress to tease her already hardened nipple. He squeezed and placed his lips against her ear. "Oh, my little *sotto*, do you like watching another submissive being punished?"

Claire licked her lips and swallowed, attempting to wet her parched throat. "Yes, Sir."

"And did you *want* to embarrass your Mistress by not shaving every part of your body?" The Domme on stage continued to interrogate her sub as Luca doggedly tortured his, blowing lightly on her neck as his other hand joined in the play and he twisted both nipples at the same time, making Claire whimper.

"No, Mistress." Her response was met with three strikes in rapid succession.

The Domme snapped her fingers and an older male submissive, wearing only a collar that was identical to the young woman's on stage and a tight red thong, delivered a vibrating wand into her hand before slinking away from the scene. "But you did. You disgraced your Mistress in front of her peers."

She held the wand against her submissive's glistening pussy. The sub stood on her toes at the contact and let out a short yelp.

Luca abandoned the nipples he'd teased until they were aching and Claire moaned at the loss. Then her moan dissolved into a purr of pleasure when his hand reappeared much lower, running along the line of her panties before disappearing beneath the soaking material. "*Sotto*, you are always ready for your Master, aren't you?"

She sucked in a breath. Every part of him was magic. "Yes, Sir."

"Please!" The little submissive's voice was no longer soft and demure, screaming her need instead. "Please let me come, Mistress."

The redhead laughed, taking the wand away. "No, don't be ridiculous." This time the riding crop landed twice against her ass before colliding with the apex between her shaking thighs. The submissive whimpered and Claire couldn't help but echo the sentiment as her own Dom continued to torment her aching core.

"Sir, please." Her voice was hoarse, and she tried to keep her tone low to avoid being heard by the dozens circulating around them.

He skimmed her shoulder with his lips and pumped his fingers in and out of her unhurriedly. "No, *sotto*, you may not come until the little sub on stage does."

Claire swallowed the scream of desperation wanting to escape her lungs. Luca moved his hand to her ass, rotating the plug and causing her to moan.

Three more times the Domme pressed the vibrating toy against her sub, teasing her to the point of tears before pulling away and spanking her again. Finally, the fourth time, she ran her hand down the younger girl's sweat-slickened face. "Yes, my sweet sub, you may come now."

Her screams of ecstasy just before she collapsed on the stage easily covered the shuddering grunts Claire tried to muffle as she reached her own release, falling back against Luca as her muscles spasmed. He smoothed her dress back into place before cradling her against his chest. After a few moments, he turned her within the space of his arms and pressed his lips to her temple.

"Upstairs now, *sotto*."

When they reached his suite, he went into what Claire began calling his Luca Aftercare Mode in her mind. He gently removed the plug the washed her with a warm cloth before he collected her onto his lap on the couch. Softly he whispered the affirmations her soul had come to crave, and all was right with her world.

Until she removed the collar before she exited his room. Despite the smile she offered, a gaping maw formed in her heart at leaving the strip of leather behind.

Chapter Twenty-One

Luca

No. Nein. Non. And No. Luca Bernardi was not cooking dinner for his sub in training, who he had somehow invited, yet again, into his private living space on the pretense of asking her to a social function. This was not a date to ask Claire on a date. It was *not*.

It was simply him checking in with Claire, giving her the liberty to speak her mind without the confines of him in his role as Master, thinking she had to please his every whim. Yes, he reminded himself as he chopped the basil with a chef's precision, the quick taps echoing in his modern kitchen. A mid-training meeting to test the temperature. He wouldn't even kiss her.

No. That would be wrong — and a true shame. He still needed to remain in control, still needed to comfort the delicate side of her that might reel from the implications of what he would ask.

He gathered the dark green herbs, added them to the garlic and pine nuts in his mixer and checked his watch. Plenty of time.

When the buzzer sounded her arrival, the table was set with its clean white flatware, the wine had already been opened and steam rolled off the huge pot on his cooktop.

As soon as she stepped into his apartment, he was at a loss. *Kiss her? How?* He'd been clear on the phone that it would be Luca and Claire, not Master and *sotto*. *But why?* Their roles were so perfectly designed for each other. Why did he insist on this...blur?

But Claire, ever surprising—he should really start to assume she'd know what to do—walked straight over to him and kissed him on his cheek. The oddity made his eyelids flutter, but she passed by and dumped her bag on one barstool as she claimed the other.

"Two things," she said with a little bit of a slumped posture he would have corrected if he hadn't told himself to lay off the Master to get them through the evening. Connecting with Claire was the missing link to their next step.

She continued, "That smells wonderful, and may I please have a glass of wine?" Her fingers separated, and she brought them to her temples. The silk bow from her light blue blouse brushed the granite countertop as she massaged her head.

Luca walked around the island, over to the dark wood table, poured the burgundy wine into the long-stemmed crystal glasses and brought them back to where Claire waited.

"To you," he said, and the clink resonated in the air.

She sipped and softened.

"I take it your day was challenging?"

"Shitty. I had a really shitty day."

His disapproving eyebrow raised as he feathered the fresh pasta into the pot.

"I'm sorry. I know you don't like that language, but you said, 'Claire'." She stared him straight in the eyes then swallowed, perhaps a little less brave. "So I assume I'm not under scrutiny and won't be subject to punishment."

"I never said that."

She smiled. The devious nature of it suited her too well. "In that case, I had a really fucking shitty day." Her eyes flicked to the wine glass and she took a quick sip.

Luca tried not to laugh, but her intentional defiance with its bold claim for wanting punishment was too powerful. But his grin ceased almost as soon as it had hit his face. Her outward obvious display of behavior poked a festering blemish he'd been trying to ignore.

She wanted public discipline and he didn't want to share her with anyone — a truth he'd known the second she'd suggested it and a notion he drank down with another sip of wine.

With dinner served and her venting about how her banking partner was ready to take on a new client who she wanted to investigate more, he sat back to enjoy this Claire, the woman who had — with a husband dying at home — started a private bank. Luca knew it was no small feat. In fact, it was history-making, more impressive than raising a child. She really had been in service to all around her. And while prosperity, success and wealth were rewarding, her melting into him during their times on the floors below were answering a call inside her. A call he'd made. To her. Specifically.

He smiled over at her. She'd eaten everything and dabbed the corners of her lips with her napkin.

"What?" Claire asked. "Why are you looking so smug?"

"Smug?" He chuckled. "Oh, you will pay for that."

She wet her lips and rubbed them together. *A brat.* She was turning into a full-on brat.

"But not tonight." He was careful not to say '*sotto*'. The wine may have loosened them up, but he would never put her welfare at risk.

His phone rang, and with the hour of the evening, he knew he had to answer.

"Excuse me. I need to get this." He rose and, sure enough, his cousin's name appeared on screen with the demand for FaceTime. With another apology to Claire and a swipe to the phone, his goddaughter's stuttered sobs bounced off the walls of his apartment.

Luca embarked on his calming ritual, the one he treasured because he knew he was good at it, and once he'd gotten the little princess to breathe normally, he sang her three rounds of *Ninna Nanna*. From the couch where he held the phone, he watched Claire silently clear the table and wipe it down.

His reward for the song, a simple, "*Ti amo, Cuca*," from the little girl with whom he shared a bond he could not explain but wouldn't trade for anything, was worth the intimate glimpse of his life he'd shared with Claire.

Gianna, her daughter pacified, returned to the phone, thanked him and reminded him to get a date for her event in two weeks.

"I'm working on it," he said before hanging up.

Tasks finished, Claire stood with one arm wrapped around the other, kneading her shoulder.

"My apologies. I can't always take that call, so when I can, I do." He placed the phone on the couch. "Will you come and sit with me?"

With her eyes down, which brought a strange displeasure to Luca, Claire came over to the couch. The teasing brat from before had vanished and her energy read similar to an after-scene drop.

"Are you okay?"

"Yeah," she said, and he detected the lie.

But it was not the time to push her. Damn him and his ridiculous 'Luca and Claire' idea. And now he would have to see it to the finish, hoping they could escape his error without harm.

"I'm sorry if tonight has been confusing for you."

She looked up at him and he relaxed a little. Maybe it was too much to know he had another side that wasn't fully dedicated to her.

"No, it's fine. I mean, if you give me some leftovers for lunch, all will be forgiven." Her tight smile tried to be playful and failed.

"Is there something you need to talk about more than your day, *cara*?"

"No." She let out a breath and shook her head once. "In fact, you invited me here to talk and all you've done is listen. Thank you. It was nice to have a friend tonight."

Friend. Never in the history of amicable declarations had the label pricked more. But he supposed she was right. And, regretfully, he knew it was with a time limit. Any future Dom who claimed Claire would insist on severing all ties with Luca. And after the smarting of being labeled her friend, two more blows hit his gut. The first — the idea of their time coming to an end — was overpowered by the second— his *sotto* with any other Dom.

He ran his fingers through his thick dark hair, scratched his scalp and combed his style back into place. When their eyes met again, Claire only had one open.

"Are *you* okay?"

Closer. He needed to be nearer to her. The zing of their connection would carry him through. He scooted over and took her hands.

"I have something to ask you. At first, I thought nothing of it. Then, as I began to weigh the implications for you, I realized it might be too much. I don't want you to do this to please me. This is not a test. There is no reward, no punishment. No right, no wrong."

"Okay…" Her gaze darted between his hands and face.

"That's why I asked you here as Claire, not my *sotto*."

Her simple nod told him to continue.

"My family has a charity event in two weeks. I'd like for you to go with me."

"Oh," she said and looked away.

"It would be the first time you would be in public with another man. And we can insist we are friends, but people will talk."

"Right."

"If it's too much, you should say no. As Claire, as *sotto*, either way. As I said, there is no wrong answer."

She turned back to him and stared. The energy they were meant to ride like a wave through the conversation stagnated.

"Why?" she asked. "Why are you asking *me*?"

A thousand reasons leaped from his chest. Her poise, status, wit? The fact that she was hands down the most intelligent woman he'd ever known and that made him proud that he could even touch her? The fact that she'd trusted him blindly? Flattered him with choosing him to guide her on her journey of discovery? Not to mention her astounding beauty.

He stroked her cheek and her eyes closed as she pushed into his palm.

In a whisper, one he hoped would cut the thick air, he said, "Because it's you."

Then the lines he was sure he'd already crossed scribbled together and made child's play of his boundaries.

Luca leaned in and brushed his lips against Claire's. Without a rejection, he kissed her again then paused. He tempted fate and did it again. A faded whimper encouraged him and lit the desire beneath his skin.

He claimed her mouth and tugged her hair until her back was against the leather couch. Unleashed, he kissed deeper. She returned the kiss, and he rubbed his erection into the crook of her leg and hip.

Luca nipped down her jaw, swirled her ear once with his tongue and begged, "Tell me to stop."

She moved her head so his mouth covered hers again. He twisted his fingers into hers, and his grind intensified.

It was wrong. It was all wrong. His couch, the lack of control, so foreign. The rush and confusion of his helpless state had him drunk and adrift. She must stop him. She had the power.

She arched below him, pushing her breasts into his chest.

He moved his mouth again to her ear, clenched his jaw and pleaded, "Please... Claire... Tell me to stop."

Was it the brat in her or did she share the need? He hoped it was the latter. Either way, she remained mute and his purgatorial torture continued.

With his left hand, he secured her wrists against the side of the couch and he made quick business of unbuttoning her gray fitted pants with the other. When he found dark lace below, more lines crossed, as if she'd worn the color on purpose or he was never supposed to find them.

The question was quickly forgotten and replaced by the urge to watch her climax. He wasted no time, again out of character and out of body, and went straight for her clit.

"Fuuuuck." Her curse, another beautiful transgression to be remembered at a different time.

"Come for me, *cara*." The throaty command shocked him back to the moment.

The glorious pinch of her forehead and the stiffening of her muscles was all he needed.

With her body in tremors, he slid back to the present and his own need crashed aside.

What have I done?

He flowered her neck and chin with gentle kisses and released her arms from over her head. He lifted his traitorous hand from her underwear and hung his head over her shoulder.

They stayed like that until her breath had completely settled.

He berated himself for losing control. It was everything he hated. His only saving grace was that he hadn't taken it farther. God forbid he'd taken her to his bed.

After a few more sweet kisses in the crux of her neck, he said. "I'm sorry. You should have stopped me."

She giggled.

Giggled?

"There was no chance of me stopping you," she said. "That was basically a free orgasm. No way I was going to pass that up."

Brat.

She was an official brat. He would never let her call him Luca again. Master needed to get back from his vacation and spank the giddy little blonde beneath him.

"Besides" —Claire pushed Luca off her chest. He offered her his hand and pulled her up to eye level — "I knew you would stop yourself."

Her adorable confidence came with a wry grin.

"Oh really? How can you be so sure?" he challenged with lifted eyebrows.

She climbed into his lap and he didn't know which end was up. Were they in her aftercare? On a date? Or maybe just generally confused?

Her eyelids fell, and she traced his beard with her soft fingers.

"I can be sure" —she licked her lips— "because it's you."

With that, her head met his chest and the weight of her words penetrated his skin and sank into his heart.

Chapter Twenty-Two

Claire

Claire arched a single eyebrow at the gray-haired man seated across from her. Thoughts of Luca evoking the exact same expression made her lips twitch with a repressed grin and briefly clouded her mind with confusion. Too often thoughts of Luca were seeping into her daily life and it was…disconcerting. *Sex*. This was simply sex and exploration.

She cleared her throat and folded her hands on her desk. "I'm sorry, Mr. Hauser. Your credentials are unverifiable at best, your references are vague and your history has some large holes in it."

His face turned a mottled shade of red that bordered on purple. "Are you calling me a liar, Ms. Favre?"

"I don't believe I said that word." She inclined her head to her partner, seated beside him, choosing to not acknowledge the flushed cheeks that damned David for not being as thorough as he should have been. "I understand my partner is excited at the prospect of your business, but Steinmetz and Favre is my...baby. I need to do my due diligence to protect it."

That word. That stupid, stupid word nearly didn't make it past her throat. And seeing Luca last week... The memory was a vise around her neck, choking her. His entire countenance had transformed at the sight of the wee one sobbing on his phone's screen. Unabashed love had coated every word he'd spoken—and had sung, for fuck's sake—as he'd soothed the child from some undetermined distance.

She tried to focus on the sputtering imbecile on the opposite side of her desk, but lingering questions that had kept her up far into the night about who the stunning woman and undeniably adorable toddler were to Luca tugged at her brain. *Family.* These were obviously family members, because there couldn't possibly be friends close enough to seek help with wailing children late in the evening. *Sister? Cousin?* She swallowed. *Ex-wife?*

'*Ti amo, Cuca.*'

No, if it were his child, they would surely not use his first name. But the mispronunciation tugged at her heart almost as much as the radiant smile that had damn near split his face in half.

With a brief shake of her head, she packaged every thought of the mystery child into a small box and shoved it into the corner of her mind. Excising the rambling Mr. Hauser from her office was more important, for the moment. Claire rose to her feet, pressing her shoulder blades together as she'd learned in the various poses Luca had taught her, adding to her height, her strength and her confidence. "I appreciate your time and patience." She barely spoke the words without laughing. "Either Mr. Steinmetz or I will get back to you as soon as we are satisfied with what our researchers find."

Arik Hauser flexed his jaw and Claire merely blinked in response. The man really should spend time with Luca if he was looking to affect an air of dominance.

"I suggest you have your researchers work quickly, Ms. Favre. There are plenty of banks in Zurich that would love to have my business."

'You are a representative of me.' Luca's voice echoed in her mind and stopped the disrespectful, albeit warranted, snort from escaping her mouth. *'You will show the world a version of Claire Favre that you never knew existed, and you will take their breath away.'*

His words lent authenticity to the serene smile she offered Mr. Hauser. "That would be a decision well within your right to make and I would be sorry to see our business interactions end before they began." She called herself every kind of liar because never seeing this man's face again would simply be too soon. "However, I will not cave to threats, veiled or otherwise. If all checks out and you are still interested in us, I look forward to working with you. If not, I wish you the very best on your future endeavors, Mr. Hauser."

A chagrined David Steinmetz stood and held an arm out, indicating the other man should exit ahead of him, an offer he took with a huff as he stormed out. David spun around, walking backward as he left and mouthing an apology. Claire nodded before resuming her seat, pulling open the drawer to her left and letting her fingers walk across the manila folders, seeking the one she would need for her next appointment.

She opened it, scanning the documents inside for the third time today, just as she had on Monday and again on Tuesday. She knew every line was perfect and every detail was in order, but she needed to be sure. It was why she had prepared the file herself. Normally, she would pawn off something like this to Julien. He would roll his eyes and bitch about breaking a nail with all the typing she expected of him then have all the documents on her desk within half an hour.

Not this time. Not *this* account.

The numbers made her smile. It wasn't her largest return, but the investments were sound and turning a steady profit. The money was safe. Secure. Stable. It would continue to produce a tidy sum on a regular basis and —

Three taps on her open door snapped her attention to where the holder of said account stood, looking effortlessly sexy in another dark suit, offset by a crisp white shirt. She jumped to her feet and involuntarily licked her lips. "Luca, you're early."

He waved a hand for her to retake her seat as he strolled into her office. "I wanted to have lunch with you and was assured you would have no additional appointments, although it appears your last one ran a bit late, *cara*."

Julien shrugged from the open doorway, mouthing an apology while shooting an unrepentant smile before closing the door. *Rat.* He was a dirty, sneaky rat who gave Luca every drop of information he wanted — and she adored him for it. She turned her attention to the plates Luca was setting before them on her desk. If he'd brought food, did that mean...? The thought of disappointing him bothered her far more than she cared to admit. "I packed lunch. I was getting ready to eat."

He looked up from the antipasto salad he was dividing between their dishes and smiled. "*Si*. Yes, I know. My *sotto* has been incredibly obedient and follows all her rules. This is why I had to be early. I did not want to risk losing my opportunity to dine with you."

She released her breath on a slow exhale. "I don't like disappointing you." She covered her mouth with her fingers as soon as the soft confession escaped her lips. *What is wrong with me?*

He added a sandwich to each plate and pushed one of the dishes closer to her. "You have no concerns there, *cara*. You have exceeded my every expectation." He threw her that stupid fucking wink that made her knees wobbly. "And they were rather high."

Luca unbuttoned his jacket, smoothing a hand down his tie as he took the seat across from her. He speared an olive and lifted it to his mouth. Claire couldn't help but be mesmerized by his every move. And she really couldn't help the avalanche of thoughts caused by looking at his lips, his hands, his fingers…remembering their talent.

"Eat, *cara*." A knowing grin spread across his face. "Later tonight we will explore all the other thoughts causing that attractive pink to creep up your neck."

Claire cleared her throat and lifted the sandwich to her lips, nibbling a small corner. *Damn him.* He noticed everything. As much as she wanted to be annoyed or irritated, the only response she could find within herself was the blossoming warmth in her chest and the aching need between her legs that happened within moments of being in Luca's presence. "Do you want to start looking through the file I prepared while you eat?"

He shook his head, regarding her thoughtfully as he chewed. "No. Tell me. How was your day so far, *cara*?"

She methodically ate her meal. Despite the rich and delicious blending of flavors and spices, she barely tasted the food. Her mind was completely fixated on what his reaction would be to the work she'd done on his account. She battled between wanting to show him all the documents now and hoping he would be called away before they could review anything. And the prospect of talking—just talking as Luca and Claire— once again should not feel this good.

"Stressful. Irritating." She popped the last bite of feta cheese into her mouth and leaned back in her chair, folding her hands across her pleasantly full abdomen. Words began to spill out of her mouth unhindered, words she hadn't planned on allowing to escape her brain. Words she'd never spoken to anyone, not even Julien. But with Luca...they begged to be spoken. "I built this with David from nothing. I put my heart, my soul, my *everything* into this company. I dedicated myself to it while the love of my life lay dying in a bed at home. And it's paid off." She drew her eyebrows together, frowned and the anger she'd managed to bank when in the presence of her partner and his new prospective client rose in her chest again. "But then these fucking snakes slither in here thinking they can... I don't even know. Charm me? Con me? Because I'm a woman, there is no possible way I can be as clever or intelligent as them and—"

She covered her lips with her hands then slid them to cover her eyes before dropping her head. She understood the honesty attached to their...other relationship, but why did she insist on revealing her every thought and problem to Luca?

The chair across from her scraped against the floor and rhythmic footsteps rounded her desk, ending beside her. "Eyes."

Claire faced him, peeking out from between her fingers. He peeled her hands away and held them in his as he rested his backside against the wooden slab.

"Stand."

She rose to her feet, her body under his command, as always, whether he was Luca or Master. He simply was, and she simply was his. Temporarily.

"I heard you." Three words. They meant nothing and everything. The corner of his mouth kicked up. The deep pools that enchanted her seemed to darken. He dropped her hands and cupped either side of her face. "I heard you conduct yourself with integrity and confidence. I heard you handle a less-than-ideal situation knowing your worth. And you were even more breathtaking than I predicted. I am incredibly proud of you, Claire."

Her traitorous heart responded to his praise with far more enthusiasm than Claire liked. She chose to satisfy the plaintive cries of her needy body instead, a much easier voice to obey. "Since we are just Luca and Claire, does that mean I can touch you?"

Luca's eyes widened infinitesimally. He lowered his hands to her hips, pulling her between his slightly open thighs. "You wish to touch me, *cara*?"

She nodded slowly and let the fingers that had itched to make contact from the second his presence had engulfed her office creep around his waist. "Yes, Sir." She smirked at him. Teasing Luca Bernardi was quickly becoming her favorite hobby.

Her smile disappeared the second his lips crashed against hers. He grabbed her ass and pulled her tightly against him. The breath escaped her lungs on a gasp as she came in contact with proof that Luca was equally needy. She fisted the soft cotton of his shirt, desperate to anchor herself.

But they were in her office.

He is my client.

She couldn't strip her clothes and kneel before her Master the way she wanted. She slid her hand up the front of his shirt, stroking his beard lightly before she finally found the strength to pull away. She gave him a small smile, reveling in the feel of his embrace for a few lingering moments. "Do you want to see your first official report, Mr. Bernardi?"

Instead of retaking her seat, she grabbed the file from her desk and lowered herself into the chair beside his, crossing her legs at the ankle. Once he was seated, she slid the thin folder over to him, clasping her hands together in her lap. She refused to bite her lip, fidget with her fingers or show any other outward sign of the nerves raging through her. Luca had said he was proud of her.

He flipped through the papers once. Twice. By the third time, she wanted to crawl out of her skin. What was wrong? She was certain every digit, comma and decimal point lined up.

"Claire...are you certain these numbers are correct?"

Ice trickled down her spine. "Yes, I am. I prepared these reports myself and checked them multiple times to verify."

His gaze lifted to hold hers for a beat before returning to the papers in his hand. "*Madre mia.*" His voice dropped to a whisper and Claire strained to hear the words, slightly irritated when she realized he'd lapsed into Italian again and she could do little more than order food in his native tongue. "*Mia cara, il mio sotto è più brillante di quanto mi aspettassi. Come potrei essere così cieco?*"

She wanted to jump in and argue that while it wasn't her best return, it was a strong start and would be a reliable and continued profit. She wanted to offer to run the numbers again and pray for a better outcome. She wanted —

Claire shook her head slightly. *No.* She would stay still. She would draw on the patience Luca had shown her the beauty of.

"*Cara*... Claire...this is astounding." His gaze stayed focused on the documents in his hands as he spoke. "Any return on investments this early would have been impressive, and I prepared myself for impressive." He held the paper up between them, capturing her eyes and stealing her ability to breathe. "This is spectacular."

Joy bloomed in her chest and heat began to creep up her neck again. She dropped her eyelids, searching her brain for words. Clients had praised her before, and often, but coming from Luca, it meant so much more.

He hooked his finger under her chin. "Eyes." She obediently met his, humbled at the pride radiating from them. "My *sotto*... She just cannot help but outshine every other star."

Luca had a way of telling her everything she never knew she needed to hear, but she needed to address her other reason for making the appointment before she lost her nerve. "I'm so glad that you're pleased, but I... I also wanted to tell you —"

"Confidence, Claire. You've displayed incredible capability and immense strength of character today. Own your confidence, *cara*."

She squared her shoulders and smiled, now more certain of the decision she'd wrestled with for the past five days. "I'd love to go to your charity event with you, Luca."

Chapter Twenty-Three

Luca

Luca placed the phone face down on his empty countertop. Bruno's sudden turn in health, while not shocking, was still unwelcome. Losing the only close friend who truly understood all aspects of Luca's very private life reminded him of the solitude he'd imposed on himself.

Yes, he was a family man and present at all important functions. That was innately Italian. But even his cousin Gianna, who for all intents and purposes was more of a sister than anything else, did not know the extent of Luca's relationship preferences. It was one thing to think a relative was an eternal bachelor, picky about his women. It was quite another to accept the D/s lifestyle in the world of vanilla.

Ten years prior, when he'd met Bruno, a light had flipped on inside Luca — control and service, striving to be his best and bring out the best in every sub who'd crossed his path. It had filled a deep well inside him. And now, with time, each transient sub who had passed through his suite on her knees seemed to replenish his soul less and less.

Because it had been no mistake that Luca had fallen into training subs. Master of all, keeper of none. But none of that mattered. He shook away the murky thoughts and ran his fingers through his hair. Claire waited for him downstairs and he had a commitment to her to honor.

And yet, all of it mattered.

As he rode the elevator, he couldn't think of one single reason to punish the beauty. His *sotto* had indeed blossomed. The fidgeting had ceased. She beamed confidence. She understood the expectations and technicalities of being a submissive. He hadn't caught her late for anything and, thank the heavens, the woman had started to properly nourish her lovely little body. Their time was drawing to an end.

Sure, he could invent bogus reasons to drag out their sessions, but he was starting to realize they were all selfish. *He* wanted Claire, *cara*, *sotto*—all of them equally. He knew it. And he'd known it from the start.

When the door clicked its release and he pushed it open, the sentiment was confirmed.

There she was, her presentation flawless. The display stopped his heart, aroused him, pleased him. Then it nipped at something else, the internal clock, ticking away.

"Good evening, *sotto*. You are lovely as always. Such a welcome sight."

With her eyes down and a timid grin, she said, "Thank you, Sir."

Luca crossed to her and trailed a finger along her defined cheekbone. The connection of skin to skin, even though soft and seemingly meaningless, was anything but.

"You have been superb, *sotto*. Exemplary." Touching more of her was necessary. Imperative. For whom, he couldn't tell anymore. "Stand."

With her breasts at a much more acceptable level and the light rose nipples already pebbled, Luca cupped them before twisting their centers.

"You have your Master at a bit of a loss, *sotto*. Was that your intention?"

Her eyes flickered but her voice remained steady. "No, Sir."

Luca pulled her back into his stomach with his forearm while he held one nipple tight. He palmed down her flat stomach and reached into the flimsy white lace. The erection in his pants screamed for her ass and he allowed himself a full rub as he dipped a finger inside her warm folds. She let out a muted whimper.

"Always ready. Too pleasing," he whispered through a clenched jaw. "You give me no choice but to worship you as the goddess that you are, *sotto*."

He spun her around. "Eyes."

Her blue-gray pools met his regard without hesitation. The finger that had been between her legs met her soft lips.

"Suck."

She twirled the digit once with her tongue while keeping her gaze locked on him. She pulled it into her mouth and the glorious suction began.

"See how lovely you taste, my sweet *sotto*?"

She intensified her work.

"How can your Master resist you?"

Luca removed his finger and instinct commanded over duty. He closed his eyes, as if not wanting to witness the momentary loss of control, and his mouth met Claire's. She accepted him freely and kissed back just as hard.

Madonna mia.

What was happening to him? Never, ever in his life could he remember wanting to kiss a woman, even a sub, this much. And indeed, the residual taste of her own arousal made him starved for more.

Her. I need to be there for her.

Luca tugged his head back and broke off the embrace. "Undress me."

The command was met with a sexy smirk and she said, "With pleasure, Sir."

Claire circled around him and slid her hands into his suit jacket. He shrugged it off and watched her hips sway as she walked to the closet to hang it up.

The small grin stayed on her face as she unbuttoned his shirt and repeated her journey. He sat on the bed, and she knelt before him to remove his shoes and socks. Again, she aligned it all in the closet exactly the way he liked — *needed* — and came back.

He half expected her to be cheeky with his belt, because she was a mischievous little *sotto* from time to time, but once again, she handled herself with nothing but perfection.

With his pants hung and only his boxers left, Claire rubbed her lips together as her delicate fingers slipped into the waistband.

"Is there something in there you'd like, *sotto*?"

"Yes, Sir. Very much."

As tempting as her mouth on him was, it wasn't in his plan. *Pity.*

His remaining piece of clothing fell to the floor and he stepped out of them, his erection full and free. She bent down, picked up the underwear, folded it three times and laid it on the bedside table.

"Get naked. Then, get onto the bed on your stomach. Arms up. Legs spread. Close your eyes and keep them closed."

As she obeyed, he walked over to the wooden dresser where he stored his toys. He opened the larger plug, because his *sotto* was ready for more, and two vibrators — one double-eared for her clit and the second a long cylinder for inside. His *sotto* would be fully pleased.

He placed his loot on the side of the bed. As he fastened down her limbs, he reminded her how proud he was of her, how she was indeed the perfect representation of him. He rubbed her glorious ass one more time and mourned the absence of a need to slap it.

"Lift your hips, sotto."

Luca slid the smaller toy between her legs and secured it around her lips. With a press of the button, the torturous hum commenced.

"Who tells you when to come?"

"You do, Sir."

"Correct."

Without need for lube, the second vibrator slipped inside her pussy with ease. He rocked it back and forth as she moaned then turned on its lowest setting. After warming the lube in one hand, he pushed one, then two fingers into her ass.

"Fuck…"

Finally, she'd given him cause for correction. He smacked the flesh of her meaty cheek once with his free palm and his cock ached with desire.

"Language, *sotto*."

With her eyes tightly closed and her quiet cries stroking his ego, he grinned. He plunged his fingers deeper inside her, and he intensified the speed of each vibrator. Her body trembled and her bottom lip quivered. Such an honor, such pride seeing his *sotto's* hedonism and knowing he was the source.

"Please..." she begged.

"Please, what?" To let her come or not, such a happy decision. Either way, she would need to add the 'Sir' to get permission.

"Please fuck me in the ass, Sir."

If he hadn't been so stunned, he might have laughed. And had he been less experienced, he may have stopped teasing her. Every single expectation exceeded. *Every one.*

"Ah, my sweet *sotto*." He scissored his fingers once more in her ass, confirming his suspicion. "I hate to disappoint you but you aren't quite ready." He took the plug from the side of the bed and teased its tip in and out. Once again, her body responded with openness, and when it smoothed into place, he reached for the condom.

Vibrator out and his cock inside his *sotto*, he rocked his hips with increasing speed. If her appetite was half of his own, their scene was a success. She filled the room with her sounds of pleasure and desperation, and he turned the clit vibrator to its highest setting.

Her echoes were replaced with small burst of air that released from her lungs with every thrust.

"You may come, *sotto*."

A slow scream rose from within her and its crescendo rang out. With the walls of her pussy squeezing his cock, he pumped even harder. He counted to three and growled his own release.

With a quick move from his hand, he batted away the vibrator from between her legs, then hovered over her still-shaking body. He kissed her neck — her sweet neck — and assured her, "You were sublime. You *are* sublime." He stayed on top of her, using his arm strength to avoid putting all his weight down, and continued the small kisses.

With a gentle movement, he untied her arms and massaged the one he could. Regretfully, he backed up and freed her legs.

Her body bent in its release to freedom. He rubbed a hand over her bare ass. After a little wiggle of the plug he asked, "Ready?"

She nodded.

He twirled it a couple more times and pulled it out as she winced, definitely not ready for what she'd asked for. He gathered the toys, wrapped *cara* in the duvet, gave her another kiss and headed to the bathroom. With the toys in the sink, he pulled the stopper on the massive tub and turned the water on full blast.

Steam filled the bathroom as he made quick but thorough work of cleaning the accessories and he headed back to Claire.

He crawled into the bed and put his arm around her.

After a lingering kiss on her temple, he asked, "You okay?"

"Yeah…" She blinked several times. "That was a thunderous orgasm. I didn't even know those existed."

Luca stretched his legs and pulled her closer. "You deserved it, *cara*."

She spun from her side to her back and looked up at him. A sweet but subtle smile graced her cheeks. And the pull from Luca's eyes brought his own smile to match.

"Thank you," she said, more serious.

Manners should have kicked in and he should have said, "You're welcome." Or, "My pleasure." The words were there, in the back of his head somewhere, but his heart was louder.

Luca dipped his head, and he brushed his lips against hers. He closed his eyes and repeated the movement — and again.

Claire smoothed her hand around his neck and played with the hair behind his ear. Luca pulled back only to find her smile had faded. She licked her lips and squinted as if she'd understood a secret.

Luca's heart raced as he contemplated his next move, as if his body would give him a choice. He leaned down again, pecked her lips then searched her eyes once more.

He kissed her yet again, but this time the gentleness abandoned him, and he added his tongue and a grind into her hips. She met his pace and ferocity. Christ, if his cock wasn't waking up and ready for a round two.

With the cool duvet as protection, he continued. When his lips unlocked from hers, she strong-armed him away and caught her breath.

"Luca." She panted.

"I'm sorry." He pulled back and shook his head. This woman, her mouth, their kissing. It was ruining him.

"No. It's the water. Were you running a bath?"

His eyes popped and he hopped up from the bed. When he arrived in the bathroom, the water was at a perfect level. He turned off the faucets and grinned.

He leaned out of the doorway and found Claire propped up on the bed.

"Leave it to you to know the perfect moment to say 'stop'. Come on, little *sotto*. Let's have a soak and you can tell me about all the money you made for your clients this week."

She smiled and climbed out of her duvet cocoon.

"That..." she said as she walked to him in her naked glory. When she was in front of him she continued, "Sounds fucking fantastic."

He swatted her ass as she walked by. "Brat."

"Yep. I'm beginning to think so myself."

Luca fought his grin and met her at the edge of the tub. He extended his hand for her to steady her own, and she dipped a toe in the hot water.

"Scalding. Just how I like it."

"Me too."

They sank into the steaming water, her back against his chest. Instead of the chatter he'd proposed, a comforting silence fell between them.

The wet strands of her hair stuck against her neck and he kissed between them. Their breathing synced, and Luca wondered if he might sleep. The stress of the short timetables of two important relationships floated away in the water as it turned from hot to warm to almost cold.

He gave her one more kiss on the top of her head and said, "Come on, beautiful. I'll drive you home."

Chapter Twenty-Four

Claire

"Blue would show off your eyes."

"But it has to be white — or as close to it as I can get without looking like a virginal bride." Claire snickered in her head at the word 'virginal'. From the moment Luca had walked into her life, there had been nothing about her mind or body that could be considered pure. And she couldn't wait to see what he would teach her next.

Julien and Claire stood locked in a standoff for several minutes. Finally, he threw his hands in the air with a dramatic gesture that was impressive, even for him. "Fine, *cara.*"

Claire narrowed her eyes into slits, feeling the overwhelming sense of possession of the word she did every time her friend mocked her with it — as well as confusion. The same utter confusion that had been haunting her for days centered solely on the only person she wanted to hear speak the nickname. "Just be a good little diva and dress me up in something pretty, okay?"

He flipped his hand dismissively and turned to bark orders at the already-harried boutique employee. Claire only partially listened, too consumed with thoughts of Luca. How had this man come to mean so much to her in such a short period of time? Liam had been part of her daily life for nearly a year before she'd experienced anything on par with…

No. She was *not* falling in love with Luca. That was one of the ground rules, his only hard no. She reached up to her bare neck. Every night upon arrival at the club, the thin, white strip of leather was affixed around her neck, either by her own hand or his, if he was waiting on her. And each time she removed it before departing, the ache deepened a little more.

Luca had explained that the symbolic accessory was as transient as their relationship, only there for training purposes and nothing more. Pain sliced through the left side of her chest. But if it was so temporary, so inconsequential, why was it engraved for her? Why was it the color he insisted upon seeing her in daily? If this was something he used on every other sub he had trained, why was it so uniquely Claire?

A crow from across the room snapped her back into the present as Julien practically skipped over, carrying a frothy confection in his arms, shoving it at her before she had a chance to really see it. "This. You. Dressing room. *Now*."

The phrase 'yes, sir' danced through her mind, something she would have easily said to Julien six months ago without a second thought. Something that now and forever would be reserved for one man.

"You're lucky I adore you." She faked a snarl in his direction but couldn't help the smile that accompanied it.

As Claire shimmied her hips to bring the fitted material over her body, she made a mental note to send Julien for a spa day. He deserved it for being her confidant, for drying her tears and for pushing her squarely into the path of Luca Bernardi when she'd wanted to flee.

The breath left her body on a sharp exhale just as the zipper joined the last teeth together. She stared at the mirror, mesmerized by her own reflection for countless moments before petulant banging on the door broke the spell.

"That skinny ass better be out here in the next five seconds. I need to have enough time to revel in my sheer brilliance."

She smirked at her reflection once more before flipping the lock, agreeing with his assertion of brilliance. Yes, Julien deserved a reward. She stepped out of the room and onto the platform surrounded by mirrors on three sides. She turned and posed to murmured compliments from the store assistant.

And complete silence from Julien.

Just as she was about to crack a joke about finally making him speechless, he blinked and locked his glistening eyes on hers. "Damn, sometimes I even impress myself." He stepped in front of her and cradled her face. "He brought you back...even better than before. Don't let him go."

She waited for the fear, the nerves, the complete dismissal of the suggestion she could even consider making room in her life and her heart for anyone other than Liam. But the only thing that happened was a sense of peace descending upon her and the silent acknowledgment that Julien was, as always, right.

Claire grinned and hugged her friend close. "Now, help me get out of this dress quickly. It's nearly one o'clock and I have a lunch date."

Julien frowned, his brows pulling together in confusion. "I cleared your schedule for the day. You don't — " Understanding flitted across his face. "Yes, we must not keep that sexy hunk of manliness waiting."

"Despite popular opinion, the best things do not always come to those who wait...especially when those who are waiting are named Luca Bernardi."

Julien rolled his eyes, but wisely held his tongue as she quoted her beloved Nanny again. An ache pierced Claire's heart, followed by a bittersweet smile. Nanny Helen would have loved Luca.

She was still smiling thirty minutes later as she walked down the hall where she was told she'd find Luca's office. Mild shock and relief mixed when she called on her way in and his secretary had not only told her he was currently free, but that he had left instructions long ago that Ms. Claire Favre was welcome any time without necessitating approval. She tapped his door three times and was met with a gruff, "Come in."

His dark head was bent, his long tan fingers gripping a pen as he marked the paper before him with slashes and circles. She groaned and clenched her legs together as memories of all the various ways those talented digits had tortured and pleased her body trickled through her mind. The man made paperwork look sexy.

"What is it?"

She smiled at his low, controlled tone. He was annoyed at being interrupted but was trying not to show it. Claire knew her Dom as well as he knew her. "I wanted to have lunch with you." She tried not to laugh when his head snapped up at the first word she'd spoken. "And I was assured you didn't have any more appointments."

He was standing in front of her before she finished speaking. Thankfully, the haunted look she'd seen in his eyes the previous evening was gone. It had kept her up far into the night, wishing she'd been brave enough to ask why.

His molten chocolate gaze swept over her and a wide grin spread across his face when it reached the brown paper bag dangling by its handles from her fingers. "You brought me lunch, *cara*."

Her cheeks warmed and she lifted one shoulder. "You've taken such good care of me. It made me wonder who takes care of you."

His jaw dropped and remained slack for several moments. With a small shake of his head, he blinked several times in rapid succession. He took the bag from her with one hand, lacing the fingers of his other through hers, then led her to the small leather sofa along the wall to their right. He stayed silent as they took their seats, portioned their food and began eating.

Claire's stomach churned with worry as she nibbled the fruit salad on her plate. She swallowed and was just about to apologize when he gripped the back of her head.

"My *sotto*, my *cara*, you never cease to amaze." He claimed her mouth in the softest of kisses that turned into desperate, heady possession.

Claire hummed her appreciation against his lips. *Not a mistake after all.*

* * * *

She closed her eyes and counted to three in her head when the doorbell rang, rather than sprinting down the hall the way she wanted. Luca was early, but she had been ready for ages, not wanting to forget anything and not wanting to disappoint him. She took one more deep breath before pulling the door open...and had every molecule of oxygen stolen from her body.

Luca in a tuxedo was a sight beyond words. Heat crept up her neck, knowing she was gawking at him but helpless to stop herself. Every line of the black material hugged his well-defined frame to perfection. Her tongue darted out to dampen her suddenly parched lips as her gaze swept over him again. How was she supposed to refrain from dragging him to the nearest cloakroom and —

"Good evening, *cara*."

The voice. The voice completed the package to perfection and managed to rumble through her scorching veins without her even touching him. She lifted her chin and somehow managed to meet the intense dark stare devouring her with some semblance of self-control. "Good evening, Luca. Would you like to come in?"

He pulled her hand to his lips, dropping a soft kiss across her knuckles. "More than anything in the world, *cara*, but we are expected at the gala in thirty minutes." The dark orbs melted into liquid desire. "And we both know thirty minutes would not be nearly enough time."

A litany of curses ran through her head and need pooled between her legs. This was going to be an incredibly long night. She swallowed back an offer to donate an obscene amount of money to the charity if they could simply skip the event. "Just let me get my coat."

Somehow, despite the violent shaking of her hands, she managed to button the wrap around her shoulders and collect the small ivory clutch purse. She slid her fingers into the crook of his proffered elbow. They rounded the front of his sleek, black sports car and Luca opened her door for her as always, but this time, just before she lowered herself into the seat, he gripped her upper arm.

"*Proprio quando penso che non si può forse essere più bella, quando penso che non si può superare le mie aspettative...*" His voice trailed off and he shook his head.

Claire laughed lightly. "I'm beginning to believe you speak in Italian around me intentionally, knowing full well I can't follow along."

He trailed an index finger down her jawline, stopping to grasp her chin. "I speak in Italian because it is the only language I know with words worthy of you, *cara*." He bent slightly to brush his lips across hers in the lightest of caresses.

Her heart stopped beating then raced to keep up. This was so many kinds of wrong, but every kind of right. She snaked her hand around his neck, pulling him closer, needing more contact. His lips curved against hers in a smile as he acquiesced to her unspoken request and deepened the kiss.

Luca groaned and pulled his mouth from hers. "*Madonna mia*, we are never going to make it there if you continue with this kind of behavior."

She grinned at him, smoothing a hand down the back of her dress as she took her seat. "Would that be a punishable offense...Sir?"

He stared at her for several seconds before letting loose with a stream of Italian she was certain included profanities and prayers for patience, despite her ignorance of the language. Claire laughed in response as he closed her door and rounded the hood, shaking his head.

Within minutes they were standing at the entrance to an elaborately decorated ballroom swarming with more faces Claire recognized than she cared to acknowledge and a specific one that made her stomach clench—the raven-haired beauty that had appeared on Luca's cell phone with the wailing child.

After Luca and the woman exchanged hugs and kisses on the cheek, he turned to her with a smile beaming with pride. "Claire, I'd like you to meet my cousin Gianna."

Cousin. The relief racing through her was confusing and welcome. "It is lovely to meet you. Thank you for allowing me the honor of attending."

Eyes the same warm shade of dark brown as Luca's hopped between the two of them as the other woman took Claire's hand in both of hers. "We cannot be happier to see our 'Cuca', as my three-year-old calls him, with a date as beautiful as you." Gianna's lips lifted into a knowing smile. "Has he told you about his goddaughter, Claire? My Ilaria adores her Cuca. She will be devastated when he marries and has children of his own and is no longer at her beck and call."

Still. Claire held every limb, every muscle, every cell of her body perfectly still, her wide, gracious, practiced smile firmly in place. She barely registered the hushed Italian racing back and forth between Luca and his cousin, but one word stood out — one of the handful she knew as well as her own name.

Bambino.

Chapter Twenty-Five

Luca

In the middle of Gianna's rant about her 'right' to say anything to Luca's date because she was the only female family member present, Claire turned away from them to the crowd in the massive museum's grand hall.

Her white dress, with its crimson floral embroidery that trailed off just after her pleasing curves, must have been made for her. And the view from the back was equally enticing as the one from the front. The fact that it only had one strap almost gave Luca pause that she was showing too much skin for the cranky fundraiser types. But he beamed having her by his side, which she currently was not—an oversight in need of rectification.

Luca swatted Gianna away, telling her they would discuss her big mouth at a later date. She'd never won any argument with him, and he wasn't going to wave his white flag of surrender in her pushy direction anytime soon. But deep down he loved her attention. So, before stepping away, he kissed his cousin's rouged-up cheek and rolled his eyes. She and her pint-sized pestering had gotten him through dark days as a child. Maybe she did have some kind of right to blabber at his date.

Date. In the weeks leading up to their first Saturday night away from the club, Luca had come to terms with their formal evening being just that. And he hoped Claire accepting his invitation away from all their lessons and physical intensity meant she had too.

But there she stood — stiff, uncomfortable and, at the same time, radiant. A waiter passed by with a silver tray of champagne and she refused the drink with a quick and polite shake of her blonde and elegantly styled head.

From behind him, Gianna's husband boomed a laugh and Luca realized Claire's unease.

Husband.

It was as he'd feared from the moment he'd thought of asking her to come. What would this mean to her and the memory of the man she'd referred to as the love of her life?

He stepped to her, placed his palm on the small of her back but stayed at a socially acceptable distance. Her gaze reached for his and he tried to reassure her with his smile. She softened a little — not enough for his liking — and looked back into the crowd.

"See some people you know?" he asked.

"A few. No one I loathe, so that's always a good start."

"Low expectations for your first..." *First what?* He was an ass. "Sorry."

Claire turned to him with big eyes and a smile he'd have liked to kiss off her stunning face. "An apology and at a loss for words. My, my, and here I thought you'd be more formal in your tux, which suits you well, by the way."

And she'd done it yet again. This timing, this knowing of how to answer, how to be... He hated to say it. *Comfortable.* To somehow make them comfortable. The word had previously held so much weight with him. Thinking his preferences were wrong. Knowing he could never participate in chatter about how men treated their women. But now, it fit. And it gave him a glimmer of hope that maybe all the stars could line up.

Luca leaned into Claire. "Don't think your cheeky lines will be forgotten, *sotto*. In fact, I encourage you to keep them up. That red on your dress is quite inspiring. I do seem to remember you liking the spanking part."

She stared at him for a moment with mischief dancing in her eyes and said, just as quiet as his own words, "If you hadn't taught me better, I would so be rolling my eyes at you right now."

He grinned and led her deeper into the crowd, mindful of the stares. It was hard to know if they were for him, the elusive bachelor, or the stunning widow at his side.

"Well, once again you are exceptional. I'm going to assume my rewards are better than my punishments," he said on the way.

They reached the center of the party on the edge of the dance floor and to the left of the string section, who was playing a waltz. Perhaps it was bold and it was surely fueled with pride, but Luca's next words were out of his mouth before he could grasp their repercussions.

"Dance with me, *cara*."

"I'd love to."

He took her hand in his and gave her a gentle spin. Because that woman, in that dress, doing not only the honor of accompanying him when he needed to be at his best for his family, but also showing all the socialites of Zurich that they were together... It all deserved a spin.

With eyes following them around the dance floor, Luca tried to occupy Claire from noticing by keeping his own gaze directly into hers. The rigid position from before seemed to disappear with every step they took.

"My apologies for Gianna. She likes to think she's my mother and sister."

Claire tilted her head. "Why would she think she's either of those things?"

Luca's eyes narrowed but his lips flinched a smile. "An excellent question."

He studied the room from over Claire's bare shoulder. Gianna had once again done a remarkable job hustling the old money of the city for their family's philanthropy. Thanks to her hard work, drug addicts on the streets would have an easier start at a new life. Luca blinked away the memories of why the foundation had been started and lost himself in guiding the movements of his captivating *cara*.

Claire cleared her throat. The music had stopped. Luca smiled tightly, hiding in the ghosts of the past and, in a move that brought him more comfort than it ever had before, he clasped Claire's hand in his to lead her to the table where Gianna held court.

When he caught his cousin's eye, she shooed away her current flock of fashionable guests, leaving the high-backed cushioned seats open for Luca and Claire at her left. Luca pulled out the chair farthest away.

"Oh, no no no," Gianna said, with a shake of her finger. "Claire sits next to me." The jewel-clad hand pointed to the empty chair closest to his cousin.

"I'd be honored." Claire's simple nod and gentle smile were just as soft as the beautiful glow shining from beneath her skin. *Flawless.* His *cara* was immaculate in every way.

With his date in good hands, he excused himself to make the obligatory rounds of the boring family friends. There was no way he would feed them nuggets of gossip about one of Zurich's most famous bankers. Claire was too good for them.

Throughout dinner, and with a conversation Luca could have done entirely without — one which involved him walking the length of their Italian village without pants — Gianna and Claire giggled like school girls. And for all the embarrassment his cousin heaped on his plate, he couldn't be upset.

Seeing Claire laugh and enjoy herself touched a part of him that had nothing to do with being her Dom. And as he hung his head while Gianna blasted yet another story — this one about an unfortunate mishap of his dark thick hair attempting to be lightened and ultimately shaved off by their *nonna* — he knew the flare of happiness touched the same part of his being that understood he and Claire were on a date.

As the party wound down, Luca even allowed himself to think it was a successful evening. The more time he spent with Claire outside his suite, the more he understood what a privilege it was to have her behind that door and on her knees.

They said goodbye to Gianna and her husband, with his cousin teasing him about finally liking a girl, and walked to the car with smiles from the evening still painted on their faces.

On the ride home, the energy settled between them and Luca cursed Claire's big red 'no' of spending the night. Conceding that he and Claire were on an actual date had opened the safe where he kept all his other confessions.

He liked *her*, not just *sotto*. *Her*. His *cara*. Claire Favre. And lately, with the stress of the club and that lingering cloud of Bruno's health, he'd found solace in her presence. She'd brought him lunch. No sub he'd ever trained had dared to be so bold.

Sure, the others had cared about him, some perhaps too much. But none had cared *for* him. It must just be a part of her magic and would need to be forgotten.

Because if there was one thing on which they had both been abundantly clear, it was that he was training her. And that came with the understanding the relationship would not have an afterlife. He would be gone, like the love of her life.

He pulled into her driveway and killed the engine. Luca was about to get out of the car when her hand stopped him.

"Where'd you go there?" she asked.

"Sorry, *cara*." He tried a smile. "Was thinking about the club."

Claire looked out of the window at her house then back at him with piercing eyes. "That's a lie."

It was. *On all accounts.*

She continued, "Trust, right? Honesty?" Her jaw set as she waited for his reply.

But Luca wasn't sure which question he was meant to answer, so he rubbed his lips together instead of speaking.

"You realize this reading of the other person goes both ways, right? I see you, Luca, better than you see me."

Better than he saw her? What the hell did that mean? His mind raced as to what he was missing. What stone had he left unturned?

"I read the program while you were chatting up the suits. I take it your mother was Sophia," she said with sympathetic smile.

Luca pushed the base of his palm into his beard and wiped his forehead with his fingers. *Clever Claire.* He should really start to anticipate her intelligence.

"Is that why Gianna is like a mother and a sister to you? Because your mom died?"

"I guess." He shook his head. Why the hell were they talking about him?

"You *guess*? You fucking *guess*?" She blinked hard then opened her eyes wide.

He raised an eyebrow at her profanity.

"Oh yeah, I'm saying 'fuck'. That's what happens when I call bullshit." Had she been standing, her hands would likely have been propped on her hips. Instead, she did some kind of head weave she must have learned from her assistant. The gesture was so unlike Claire that it almost made him laugh. But her tone was serious. Was it possible he'd given her too much confidence?

Perhaps the night had been a grave error. Maybe being seen with a new man in the old social circles was more overwhelming than he'd understood it to be. There had been that initial moment of the night where she'd seemed thrown, something the confident Claire would have brushed off had she been by herself. Something was wrong. It was unlike her to be so aggressive.

It was him. He'd pushed too far, backed her against the ropes. Insisted on the damn date, valued his desires over her needs.

Her rant continued but the volume shifted way down and she spoke in an eerie, pissed-off voice. "And that's what I'm doing, Luca Bernardi. I'm calling bullshit. I ask you a question and you don't answer. Where's the trust there? Where's *your* fucking honesty?"

Let her get it out. He could take it. Hell, if slapping him in the face would make her feel better, he'd gladly be on the receiving end. Because all roads to her line of questioning led to nothing—nothing he wanted to think about and nothing he wanted to share.

And yet he refused to look away. As much as her stare seared a hole in his armor, the other hole she'd unintendedly burned was bigger. Fresher. Endlessly deep and far more damaging.

The love of her life.

It would not be him. That seat had been taken. The familiar smoke of rejection filled his lungs and made it hard to breathe.

He finally broke the lock of their eyes and scanned over the dashboard into the dark night. "My mother died. Gianna is my rock. Happy?"

She scoffed lightly. "Why would that make me happy? And just so you know, that's a sad excuse for honesty. I tell you everything. *Everything.*"

He wished he could blame his next words on the lateness of the hour or even the pushiness of her tantrum. But even when he formed them, he knew they were wholly selfish.

"You don't tell me everything, Claire," he whispered, but refused to look at her. The shame of putting himself first bore too much judgement. "You don't tell me what you do on Fridays."

His indignant proclamation hung in the air until an almost inaudible "Red" escaped from Claire's caught throat.

Luca whipped his head around to find a tear-stained face flushed with disgust.

"What?" he asked, as the blinks of his eyes begged the clock to rewind.

"Red," she said, so calm, so simple. She reached for the handle, bunched her skirt and got out of the car.

Slowly—which made it worse—she moved up her front steps and through her door, never looking back.

Chapter Twenty-Six

Claire

She circled her living room for the sixth time since she had sent the desperate plea to Julien for emergency advice and wine. She ran her fingers down the length of her hair and gripped the ends over her right shoulder.

The slam of the front door was quickly followed by a breathless Julien propped against the entryway leading into the living room. "You didn't specify red or white, so I grabbed one of each. We really need to have a better stock for when crises—" His gaze swept over her. "Oh, honey."

The tears she'd barely allowed to subside began in earnest again. Her friend had just enough time to set the bottles down before she launched herself into his arms, sobbing against his shoulder.

The oversized clock above her fireplace ticked away the seconds as she released the pain she'd bottled for more than twelve hours. From Gianna's hint of Luca wanting children to his quiet reminder that she too held secrets, the infractions had unknowingly creating black marks in an otherwise-idyllic night.

Capped off by the darkest moment of them all. The one that had occurred when she was curled beneath her blankets at three o'clock in the morning, sleep eluding her.

The realization that she loved Luca.

Finally, she pushed away from Julien, tucking herself into the corner of her couch, hugging her knees to her chest. He sat gently beside her, laying his hands on top of hers, making small circles with his thumbs. They sat in silence as her tears dried and her hiccups subsided.

"Are we talking or are we ignoring?"

A mirthless smile curved her lips. For all his drama, for all his catty comments, for all his bitching, Julien was her rock. They spoke in their own language, understood each other and were there for each other uncompromisingly. She so needed him right now.

"Talking." She took a deep breath and searched her brain for a place to start. "It was magical, like a fairy tale. I met some of his family and they are as charming as he is. The food, the wine, the music..." Her voice trailed off, remembering the feel of being held in his arms as they'd spun around the dance floor. "It was all so fucking perfect."

Julien nodded along with each point. "So, if it was so fantastic...why are we day drinking on a Sunday afternoon?"

She'd battled the words all night, barely willing to acknowledge them to herself, not at all capable of speaking them out loud, even just into the void of her darkened bedroom. *This wasn't the agreement. This wasn't the plan. This was never, ever meant to happen.* "Because I fell in love with him."

Julien frowned. "Right…and…he doesn't love you back? You met his secret wife who is normally chained in the basement?" His eyes lit up. "He's gay? Oh, Claire, if you love me, please tell me he confessed to being gay."

She smacked his lean biceps with one hand. "I make an earth-shattering revelation to you and you turn it around to try to figure out a way to fuck my boyfriend?"

Julien chuckled and ran a hand down her cheek. "Sweetheart, I've watched you both for the past four months. He challenged you and frustrated you, but he also nurtured you and cared for you. He brought the light back to those baby blues that has been missing for over a year. Hell, I'm pretty sure they've never shone this bright. I'd be more shocked if you told me you didn't love him."

She rested her elbows on her knees and cradled her head in her hand. "But he doesn't know. And he needs to know. His cousin went on and on and on about how much her daughter loves her Cuca and how he dotes on her and…" She swallowed back fresh tears as the image of Luca singing in Italian to the little girl on his phone danced through her head yet again. "I can't even hint that I feel anything more toward him until he knows."

Julien tapped her leg softly before standing, collecting the wine and crossing into the kitchen. "Yes, you can." The release of the cork punctuated his words. Within minutes, he was pressing the cold glass stem into her palm and settling back in beside her. "And don't assume you know what his reaction will be."

"Gianna made it clear, Julien—"

He held his hand up. "Honey, I have called that man a whole host of names in my head, but Gianna was never one of them. Talk to *Luca*, not Gianna."

They each took a long draw from their glasses, silence descending upon them as Claire formulated a speech in her head, one that would not end with her declaration of love because he would be uninterested as soon as she confessed.

The sharp ringing of her phone pierced the air and she groaned. Julien's eyes darted between her and the device before rolling toward the ceiling. "How many times?"

"That's the third this morning...plus two text messages."

Julien shook his head. "All the best private schools, Oxford University, advanced degrees in business and your *secretary* holds all the knowledge."

She grabbed his hand as the phone quieted. "Not just my assistant...my very best friend."

* * * *

One word. When she'd finally been brave enough to send Luca a text requesting he meet her in his suite at the club, his response had only been one word, although it had come in record time, within seconds of her hitting Send.

Yes.

So, as the clock hand crept closer and closer to the six, indicating it was nearly half past their scheduled meeting time, her stomach seized. He wasn't coming. A stream of worries raced through her head, but she dismissed them with a shake. There was no accident. There was no emergency. Luca was fine. Gianna was fine. The precious little angel who FaceTimed her Cuca in tears was fine.

Likely the only thing that had happened was he'd had enough time to replay her words from that night and realize he'd dodged a bitch-shaped bullet. She tried to summon some irritation at the prompt Mr. Bernardi leaving her high and dry, but she couldn't. It had really only been a matter of time, hadn't it?

She sat on the sofa and ran her fingers over the soft material. For the three days since the gala, she had agonized over her emotions. She'd wanted simple, hot, uncomplicated sex. Adding in her newly recognized affinity for a kinkier lifestyle had been merely a bonus. Falling in love was a snag she had never prepared for.

Swallowing back the knot in her throat, she was grateful he hadn't shown. If she could finally trust him enough to reveal the secret she'd held closer than her Friday night ritual as well as her true feelings for him and he rejected her, that would hurt far worse than him simply abandoning her now.

Rejection. Distance. The familiar ache renewed in her chest. Empty seats at her recitals and special dinners to honor her various achievements flashed in front of her eyes. She drank in her solitary surroundings. Just another form of forgotten...

When they'd first begun this journey, seemingly eons ago, he had shown her that housed within the small dresser there were a notepad and pens. She pulled them out and began writing. Yes, she nodded to herself through her tears, this would be far better than telling him directly. She wouldn't have to look into those dark eyes that promised so many things or listen to the deep, rumbly voice that soothed her in so many ways or smell the bergamot and lime cologne that lingered for far too short a time after their contact ended.

Luca,

My deepest apologies that our relationship must end this way. Thank you for all the time and energy you have invested in teaching me all the things I needed to know. They have helped far beyond our encounters here and have made me more confident and effective in all areas of my life.

You will see I am leaving the key card with this note. In the morning, I will be instructing my partner, David Steinmetz, to take control of your account. Most things are in place and he will simply need to monitor them, but if you have any questions, he will be more than happy to be of assistance.

Once again, I cannot thank you enough. The past four months have meant more to me than you will ever know. I wish nothing but the best for you and all the happiness in life you deserve.

Best regards,
Claire

She laid the sheet of paper and the card on the pillow, certain he would see them there. She swiped the moisture from beneath her eyes. She sniffed and squared her shoulders. Yes, this was better.

With one hand on the knob, she paused, staring at the thin strip of leather that meant more than it should. She traced the letters that were burned into the smooth material. *Sotto*. Not allowing herself the time to truly consider what she was doing, she gripped it tightly and left Luca's suite for the last time.

She descended the stairs quickly, still focused on the collar in her hand. No matter what happened from this point on, this would be something she would treasure as deeply as the memories of what she'd shared with Luca.

Her mind a fog of pain and confusion, she didn't realize anyone was waiting at the base until she slammed into them from behind, both of them nearly toppling to the ground. "Oh, I am so sorry!" Claire quickly gathered her bearings and reached out an arm to help the younger woman regain her balance.

The petite brunette smiled softly. "It's okay." Her dark eyes landed on Claire's hand, then back to her face. "I'm sorry to ask, but...are you Luca's?"

Claire studied her for a moment. She couldn't have been more than twenty-five, several inches shorter than herself with lush curves and a dimpled smile. Her words sank in. Was she Luca's? "Yes, well, no, well, I mean..." Not even a week out of his presence and she was stumbling over her words. "No, I'm not Luca's." Saying that out loud cut through her with more precision than a freshly sharpened blade.

Confusion was written across the other woman's face. "Really? But that's his collar." She pointed to the white band Claire still held tightly. "Although I've never seen white before."

Fiery ice began at the crown of her head and covered her body. "His collar?"

She bobbed her brown head rapidly. "Yes, Luca always buys his submissives those collars. Each girl gets a color specific to them. I've seen lots of shades of pink and blue and purple, but never a white before."

Each girl. Lots. The record in Claire's head was broken on repeat. This was not special. *She* was not special. He bought every submissive that entrusted their training to him the exact same thing with only the tiniest variation.

She closed her eyes for the briefest of moments. She was Claire Favre. She was in public. She would not—could not—acknowledge the fact her heart was shredded and her soul void. The practiced smile slipped into place with slightly more effort than she'd ever needed before. "It was my favorite color. I'm sure that is the only reason. Have a good day."

Claire forced her legs to carry her from the building with the poise she had learned while still in grade school. She slipped the valet a tip before taking her seat, fastening her belt and driving home. The entire time the damned words echoed in her mind. She was no more special to Luca than she had been to her parents or to any friend who had flitted in and out of her life.

The only people who ever had or ever would find her special were her beloved Nanny Helen, Liam and Julien. And two out of the three were gone.

She crossed the threshold of her home, shut and locked the door behind her before falling to her knees, emptiness consuming her. All of the trust and love she'd given to Luca—a deeper trust than she'd even shared with Liam—had been thrown back in her face.

She couldn't even manage to cry anymore.

Chapter Twenty-Seven

Luca

Luca pushed Adrian's sobbing head deeper into his shoulder and clutched him harder. He could do this. He could honor Bruno's last wish of being there for the man his friend had wanted to spend the rest of his gone-too-soon life with. He could be strong. He could be stable — or at least give a convincing performance of the two.

With the haze of the clouded hospital glass separating him from his deceased and improbable mentor, Luca choked back his own tears.

No.

Adrian. Luca owed it to the love of Bruno's life to be less selfish.

Besides, the last time he'd put himself first, he'd almost lost Claire. Claire, who would understand why he was late and worry when he was more than a minute overdue. Before the disastrous calling of 'red', she'd said it herself. She knew him. She saw him. That statement had kept him at home on Saturday night and his blood pressure normal-ish on Sunday when she hadn't answered his calls or texts.

And it would have to be enough to get him through the next day until Adrian's brother would arrive to take care of him for the weekend.

Luca squeezed Adrian's neck muscle a few times then said, "Come on. Let's go home." Adrian wailed again, and Luca couldn't blame him. Home was the hardest place to be after a loss — too many reminders, too many moments of forgetting the person was gone.

Adrian shrunk under Luca's strong arm and hunched in his sorrow all the way to the parking garage. As he waited in line to pay, finally with phone reception, he shot off a quick text to Claire asking to push their meeting to Saturday. She would certainly understand, he reassured himself again.

After getting Adrian settled on the couch, Luca sprawled out in the leather chair facing him and kicked off his dress shoes. He bent down, tidied them together and asked, "Do you think you could eat?"

Adrian flashed him eyes that would have brought a correction from Bruno.

"God no, but I could drink."

Luca pushed into his knees and stood. "What's your poison?"

"Grappa," Adrian said with pursed lips.

For the first time in twelve hours, Luca laughed. "You must be kidding."

"Don't look so surprised," he said as he tucked his feet deeper under the beige throw blanket. "I've been pulling off your private stock for years. It's in the freezer." Adrian waved in the direction of the open kitchen, where Luca found everything required for the prefect drink.

Back in the living room, Adrian said, "Thank you," and took a sip with closed eyes. They drank to Bruno, and Luca let the iced, sweet fire burn down his throat. One drink turned to two and well, two would have to be three.

The unlikely duo clinked their shot glasses again.

"You know, I never thought he would do it." Adrian said, as he studied the remaining clear liquid.

"Die?" Luca blinked. *Everyone dies. Everyone.*

"No. I mean, choose me. Of all the scenes I watched that man direct, after all the asses he paddled and fucked, I never thought mine was good enough for him."

"He adored you, Adrian, even from the start." Luca's memory pulled up a slide of him teasing the balding Bruno about going too easy on the young and impressionable Adrian.

"I know. And I worshipped him. It took me a long time to understand we weren't imbalanced. That as much as I wanted to impress him, he was trying a hundred times harder to keep his shit together for me."

Luca sneered and poured himself another drink. He slammed it, hoping it would keep down his familiar ghost. But grief knew when to rise and the alcohol could only numb his body. The transparent phantom that kept him from relationships was ready to dance the night away at the loss of the one man Luca had let into his life.

"You're not driving home after that. Bruno…" Adrian cleared his throat. "Anyway, you're staying here. But I get the couch. I can't sleep in our bed."

Luca checked his phone one last time, now sure it was too late to call Claire and more worried that she hadn't replied.

But she would understand.

The words became a warped mantra as he fought to sleep in Bruno's guest room. *She* would understand. She *would* understand. She would *understand*. He decided that the first way was the best. His *cara*. His Claire. They would move past the muddied line he'd crossed. He wouldn't wait until he was old and ailing like Bruno. He would take a chance with Claire.

Because losing her would be too much. He would ask to be her boyfriend, to try dating. He could do that. He had to.

* * * *

As much as Luca wanted to stand by Adrian and honor his friend, he needed to get out of Bruno's apartment. Indeed, being in his personal space without his boisterous laugh was proving to be more trying than Luca had bargained for.

There was the ridiculous cane in the umbrella stand that Bruno had stolen from a restaurant and threatened to use, but never had, on one of his more rebellious subs. The fragrance of the citrus hand soap in the bathroom that Bruno had sworn by for fighting germs. And the list continued. Every sighting brought a story and each story a slap in the face that there would be no more.

And, per strict orders, there would be no funeral—no long goodbye, no chance for a send-off. Bruno had been clear about that. *'Burn me and urn me.'* His crude words left no room for error.

It wasn't until late afternoon, after Adrian's brother had showed up and Luca found himself in the quiet privacy of his car on the way back to Zurich that it fully hit him. His mentor, father figure, brother by oath and only genuine friend was gone. There would be no more laughs, no camaraderie and absolutely no more guidance.

His throat swelled and tears blurred the road. *Claire*, he thought. Claire would make this better...because she would understand.

He coughed a few times to rid his lungs of the emotions that seemed to want to linger there, sniffed and wiped away the tears with the palm of his hand.

Claire. He needed Claire. He tapped the voice control and dialed the bank.

From over the speaker phone a chipper voice rang out, "Thank you for calling Steinmetz and Favre. Claire Favre's office, how may I help you?"

"It's Luca for Claire."

"Oh, I'm sorry, *siiir*..." Her assistant drew out the word 'sir' as if he were sucking lemons. "Ms. Favre is unavailable."

She told him.

Merda.

There was no hiding 'red'. Luca let out a long breath. Explorers climbed mountains. He could find a way to talk to his *cara*.

"Is she there?" Luca needed a shower and a change of clothes, but his window before her next red cut-off was closing in. He would drive straight to her if he had to.

"I'm sorry. That's not information I can give you. Can I direct your call to Mr. Steinmetz's office?"

What? Luca checked his mirrors and pressed his foot into the gas. What the hell had happened in Zurich in the forty-eight hours he'd been away?

"Is she there? In her office?"

"Mr. Bernardi, I do many things. Many. I can assure you, stuttering is not one of them. Ms. Favre is no longer available...to you. Would you care for a transfer?"

Luca ended the call without saying goodbye. Nothing made sense—except driving fast, getting his ass back to Zurich and seeing the one woman who would know how to put him back together.

Friday night traffic and an accident brought out Luca's normally dormant temper. He swore at Porsches and Audis, all the while the clock ticked away his timeline.

Knowing she'd no longer be at the bank by the time he'd reached the city, he reluctantly drove home. The continued lack of messages and calls from Claire, combined with the horrid exchange with her assistant, gnawed deeper at Luca's heart.

He showered, changed into a black turtleneck and black pants and made himself a coffee. Eating would have been better, he scolded himself as he rinsed the cup, but he had no appetite. He paced around the kitchen until deciding the distraction of the club would be his only chance of getting through the next few hours before he could contact her again.

He grabbed his jacket and headed down the elevator. When he reached for the button to the ground floor where he would find his security team and the bar, he switched to the level of private suites and jabbed the number three.

His shoes echoed in the barren halls and Luca reached for his keycard. The empty room in front of him was in perfect order...except the bed. His gaze jumped to the pillow. He gaped and his skin flushed from fire to ice.

The letter, whatever it said, was pointless. She'd left.

Thoughts reeled and twisted over his head but they all ended in the same conclusion. He'd failed her.

Luca dropped to the bed and slumped over as the letter sat taunting him to his right. Slowly, he reached for it and raced through her formal and maddening words. He read it again, searching for hidden meaning. After a final time, he still found none.

He folded the paper and laid it back on the pillow next to the keycard.

His bottom lip twitched. This wasn't right. This was not how things were done. His *cara* would never have left him for not showing up. He hadn't pressed on about the Friday night. There was something else. She claimed to tell him everything, but he was missing something. As things stood, they did not add up.

He rose and walked to exit. He passed the threshold and paused. After one step back, his gaze darted to the hook. *Her collar is gone.*

Against his better judgment, he found himself driving to her house — on a Friday night, when he should have been anywhere but there.

But Claire would understand. If she would *see* him, as she said she could. Whatever her issue was, they could work through it.

He killed the engine, ran up the steps and banged on her door. After five minutes and with only darkness behind her windows, he deduced that either she'd known he was coming or simply was not there.

Back in his car, and almost relieved he'd not been caught for officially crossing her line, he vowed to try again the next day. He backed out of her driveway and drove down her street.

Normally, the cemetery across the road never gave him pause. All the villages on the outskirts of Zurich had their own small plots. But with Bruno fresh on his mind and nowhere to mourn his friend, he pulled into the church parking lot next to it.

He looked up to the clock tower of the church when its ominous bell chimed to mark the half-hour.

Movement between the tombstones grabbed his attention. *Blonde movement. Claire movement.* Wrapped in a multi-colored blanket that hung over her shoulders, she sat on the ground next to a tombstone. Her shoulders shook and she wiped her nose with the back of her hand.

Her husband. She spends every Friday night with him.

Luca sank deeper into his car seat but still watched Claire. He had no right to be a part of her Friday night. There was no place for him here, no place for him in her heart. And based on her sunken posture and shaking body, he'd done her more harm than good.

To further avoid discovery — and perhaps to fully witness the damage he'd done to a woman like no other — he stayed hunched down until she finally stood.

Claire kissed the top of the light stone, wiped her cheeks and walked away. There would be no understanding for Luca.

Chapter Twenty-Eight

Claire

"He wants to talk to you."

Claire dragged her eyes from the headache-inducing papers in front of her. "No, he really doesn't." The collar taunted her from her purse. She knew it wasn't special. She knew *she* wasn't special, but keeping it close soothed her somehow.

Julien pushed off the frame then closed the door softly behind him. "You can't hold him accountable for his cousin's big mouth." He sat in the chair across from her. "It's been a week. Don't you think you've given him the silent treatment long enough?"

She tossed her pen down and pressed her thumb and middle finger into the corners of her eyes. "It's not a silent treatment. This isn't some proverbial standoff. Whatever you want to call the thing we had…it's over. We both knew it was temporary from the beginning. It isn't like this is a huge shock." The crushing realization that he hadn't found her worthy of showing up to talk still weighed heavily on her chest. "It's better this way. If you don't have anything nice to say and all that."

In an uncharacteristic display of anger, Julien leaped to his feet and slapped his palm against her desk. "Better for who, Claire? Better for you so that you can continue to exile yourself from love and relationships because you had grade-A assholes for parents and because Liam had the audacity to get cancer and die?"

Her mouth dropped open, her eyes widened, but her reliable, consistent, rock-solid advocate continued his chastising tirade. "Better for Luca because you *think* based on a five-minute conversation — with his cousin, I might add, not even from talking to him — that he has his heart set on being a father to a litter of kids? Or are you somehow trying to salvage all of humanity because the kind of power couple that would result from a mixture of Claire Favre and Luca Bernardi would undoubtedly lead to world domination?"

A single tear tracked down her cheek. "Better for everyone, because love is his only hard no — and even if it wasn't, I am physically incapable of being what he wants."

"You. Don't. Know. That." Julien struck the solid surface with his fist to punctuate each word. "All you know is that you pulled that same fucking bitchy Claire card you've played since high school to keep everyone at arm's length. And when you finally pulled your head out of your skinny, gorgeous ass, Luca was nowhere to be found." He paused long enough to suck air into his lungs. "Those are the *only* things you know."

She sat back against her chair, pulling her bottom lip between her teeth. "I hate it when you're right." She didn't say that her stomach had been tied in such tight knots for the past seven days that she had barely been able to keep food down—wondering, worrying, fearing where Luca was and what he was doing. "I fucked this up and I don't think I can fix it."

The steel eyes that had cut impassioned daggers through her during his outburst softened. "You are Claire Favre. You can fix anything." He gestured toward the papers spread out in front of her. "You made Arik Hauser your bitch. He had every document you requested couriered over within a few days."

Her jaw worked back and forth. Work—something she understood, something she could handle. She would focus on work and untangling the puzzle Arik Hauser's account presented, answering the mounting questions that came with each new piece of information.

Then she would approach Luca—with a clear head and a trepidatious heart.

"You haven't eaten a decent meal since the gala."

Julien's soft words seeped into her consciousness, pulling her back to their conversation. Her mind conjured all the images she'd been fighting against since she'd left the club for the last time—Luca cooking for her, bringing her lunch, glaring at her with blatant disapproval when she failed to follow instructions.

They were quickly followed by the more painful memories—his dark brown eyes glowing with pride at her obedience and simmering with need that matched her own, his constant affirmations during aftercare and when they were just being Luca and Claire, his ability to be aware of what she was doing and what she needed from him without suffocating her and his constant reminders that she held the ultimate power in their relationship...and over him.

Her gaze landed on the clock on her computer. "You're right." She stood and collected the stacks of papers then filed them neatly in her briefcase. "It's already four. I'm just going to work on this at home." She held up her index finger to silence Julien's protestations. "After I stop and pick up a plethora of Chinese takeout."

She rounded her desk and dropped a kiss on Julien's cheek. He pulled her close for a tight embrace.

"He's special, Claire. I know this started as a fun and sexy adventure for you, but it became so much more. You don't love easily or lightly. Don't let it end this way."

"I need to get Arik Hauser handled first." She shook her head, frowning at her friend. "I can't lose my boyfriend and my company at the same time."

Julien smirked. "That's the second time you've called him your boyfriend."

Claire rolled her eyes, hiking her purse strap onto one shoulder while gripping her briefcase on the opposite side. "Fucking queen."

He affected a pseudo-innocent expression, holding his hands up, palms facing her. "All I'm saying is perhaps you need to unblock his number before you call him your boyfriend again."

* * * *

"No. No, no, no, no." She spoke the words to her empty living room in a voice that was barely above a whisper. She'd been looking at the piles of papers for so long that her eyes burned and the numbers swirled together. She shook her head and blinked, certain she was misreading something. But after checking three more times, everything was still the same.

That fucking snake.

She jumped to her feet, pacing the length of her living room, an avalanche of options racing through her mind. She had known from the second her partner had set the proposal before her that there was something off with Arik Hauser's plan—and now it was clear.

It wasn't his fucking plan. He was just a pawn for a far slimier foe. But his guilt was evident. *'If you lie down with dogs, you will get up with fleas.'* Isn't that the saying? Well, Arik Hauser was infested.

Unfortunately for him, he'd landed in the path of Claire Fucking Favre. Her nostrils flared as she gathered the five most damning of all the documents and read through them once more. The clock above her fireplace ticked and the alarm on her phone rang out with one name flashing across the screen. *Liam.*

She would deal with this first thing Monday morning. He didn't know who he was messing with and sure as hell didn't realize that he was threatening the two things that mattered the most to her in this world in one fell swoop. If he did and he was trying to pull this anyway? Then he was a bigger damn fool than she'd originally thought.

Claire fumed the entire walk to the cemetery. She had numbers and worries running through her brain and she would need to check the account as soon as she got home—lock it down, make sure nothing happened to send it into the red.

Her body walked straight to the familiar headstone with little input from her brain. She spread the patchy rainbow-colored blanket on the frozen ground before sitting and wrapping the other, a more sedate one, around her shoulders. "I am not in a good mood today, Liam."

Her gaze wandered over the etched letters she had memorized. Shortly after he'd died, Claire had begun coming here every day, sobbing her pain to the cold, unforgiving stone. Gradually she had weaned to less and less frequent visits, but Friday nights were non-negotiable. They always had been and always would be their date night, since their awkward first encounter while they had still been at university.

Until now. Until Luca. Until love.

Claire shook her head. "But it isn't anything I can't handle. And...it's not why I'm here anyway."

With a sigh, she leaned forward and brushed dust off the granite. "Liam...I'm in love." Despite the icy air hitting her skin, warmth radiated through her. "I never thought it was possible to be in love again. I thought my heart died with you."

Luca's smirky smile and twinkling eyes danced in front of her vision and, despite the deep ache at everything that had gone wrong, she smiled. "That pushy, domineering Italian made me fall in love with him." She lifted one shoulder helplessly, dislodging the blanket. "It's different, this love I feel for him. I can't really explain it. It isn't better or worse, just...different."

She picked at the brittle, dead grass. "I trust him, Liam. Implicitly. And I am going to tell him everything and hope I haven't fucked things up so badly that he can't forgive me." Claire made a face. "Yes, yes, I played the bitchy blame game card again. I know... Julien already lectured me about it."

The tears she had expected finally arrived, filling the corners of her eyes and clogging her throat. "I wanted you to know, Liam. I needed you to know because…it's all because of you. You taught me what love looks like and how to give it." She smiled again. "And he taught me how to trust."

She sat for several moments in silence, allowing the fat drops to roll down her cheeks unchecked. Then she stood, collected the blanket from the ground and held it close to her chest. She bent down to brush her lips across the granite. "A part of me will love you forever, Liam. I hope you know that. But regardless of what happens with Luca, I think I won't be coming quite as often." She ran one hand across the width of the stone top. "You gave me the strength to fall in love again and Luca gave me the strength to move on. I don't know what I have ever possibly done in my life to deserve two amazing men like you both, but I am forever grateful."

Claire straightened her posture into a tall, confident pose that would have made Luca proud, and she firmed her jaw. "And now I need to go save him before that slimy snake tries to ruin him." She narrowed her eyes into slits and settled her mouth into a thin line. "I am going to make that bastard wish he'd never messed with my fucking boyfriend."

Chapter Twenty-Nine

Luca

The black-and-white closed-circuit images of the club faded in and out as Luca's eyelids closed and bounced back open. Being out on the floor, mingling with members and guests, had proven to be overwhelming. Plus, as Gwendelyn and Max had pointed out with the subtly of elephants, he was a bit 'testy'.

So, once again, on a Friday night when the rooms were packed and he had no inclination of partaking in the fun, he sat in the dark cool office and monitored from afar.

But falling asleep on the job would have been grounds for firing. He stood up, slapped his cheeks a few times and threaded his arms through the jacket he'd freed from the back of the chair.

"I'm going to grab a coffee. Keep an eye on camera six. The sub is gagged, and I happen to know his Dom likes it rough. It could go wrong quickly," he said to the muscled man who flanked the door.

"You got it, boss."

Luca buttoned his coat and smoothed it as he walked down the hall. It was still relatively early — despite the intense scene on the third floor — and the ground floor bar buzzed with chatter.

A group of women he referred to as 'The Geneva Convention' was in town for a monthly visit and the single Doms had crawled out of the woodwork. The ladies were all a bit older but their years brought experience, and they had a reputation as being down for more than the average sub. If a Dom wanted to flex his Master muscles or test his own limits, this was definitely the bunch with whom one should mingle.

He went over to their table, pasted a grin on his face and welcomed them to his club. Luca caught Max's eye from behind the bar, signaled for a coffee and the liquid battery was in front of him before he'd made the rounds of kissing all their rosy and lifted cheeks.

They tag-team flirted with him, and six months prior, he would have taken three of them upstairs and publicly bound and adored every inch of their used flesh. And while he respected their jovial united spirit, it no longer suited his needs, much less his desires.

As he excused himself and reminded them to ask for him should they need anything, the novice caught his eye in the corner of the room.

Noah Paulick was hunched over the armrest of his black leather chair and was monopolizing Elias' ear while Gwendelyn waited patiently at their feet. What Luca wouldn't give to hear what the sleazeball must be proposing. *A business deal on a Friday night.* Luca grumbled as he walked out of the bar. His club was meant to be an escape.

Escape. Ha.

Then why was it harder to breathe every minute he spent inside? Even his apartment above offered no solace. She was nowhere and she was everywhere. She was under his skin and remained untouchable.

Being angry with Claire would have been easy, and it might have even been gratifying. But Luca *knew* in the depths of his being that something else was going on with her. Some nerve had been hit and the pang had hurt her beyond what she had been ready for.

He'd retraced his steps countless times. It had to have been something at the gala that had thrown her — beyond the stress, beyond the gawking. And yet, she had been impeccable, until his comment had been the drop of water in the pool that had drowned her.

He swiped his all-access card to the security room and the guard rose from the black-wheeled chair in front of the screens. Luca reclaimed the seat and resumed managing his club at a bearable distance.

Distance. Maybe that was what she needed. Maybe that was what he needed.

In the wee hours of the morning, with the out-of-town guests ushered into luxury cars to be dropped at their high-end hotels, Luca resolved to finally go to bed. He called the elevator — knowing that despite his fatigue, sleep would evade him — and waited.

When the doors opened, Gwendelyn's mascara-stained cheeks and red puffy eyes looked up to him in horror.

"Are you okay?" Luca's instinct was to touch her, but she was a claimed sub and off limits.

She closed her eyes and he pushed his hand against the door to keep it from closing.

"I'm fine." She let out a breath. "I'm not hurt, if that's what you're wondering."

"Do you want to talk about it?" Where the hell was Elias? Where was his aftercare, letting his most valuable possession wander away in this state?

She took slow steps forward, caught his eyes for a brief moment, said, "I can't," and walked down the hall to the front entrance where the guards opened for her and she left.

* * * *

Gravel crunched under the tires of his Maserati as Luca drove down the long driveway of his family's Italian estate. The hot fall sun beamed through the olive trees, contradicting the cool exterior air.

It was no mistake he'd searched out his *nonna* to console him. While Gianna had been a shoulder to lean on, *Nonna* could take one look at her grandson and understand his internal woes.

Before exiting the car, he tried yet another futile call to Claire. Her willpower was astonishing — and incredibly discouraging. There was no getting through the wall of her assistant at work and there had not even been a reply to his first text from over a week ago.

Anybody else and they would have at least had a conversation. Anybody else and he would have stopped trying after one unreturned call. Hell, anybody else and he probably wouldn't have cared.

He hung up, tossed the phone onto the passenger seat and scrubbed his face after the long drive. With his eyes closed, the haunting image of Claire next to her husband's grave reappeared in his mind, just as it had multiple times a day since he'd invaded her privacy and witnessed it. The cold dead body had more to offer her than he did.

A massive groan filled the car. His self-pity had really escalated to an all-time high.

Luca climbed out, grabbed his overnight bag from the trunk, swung it over his shoulder and headed into the stone-walled manor. Leaving his affairs in the foyer, he knew just where to find his *nonna*.

The windowed room basked in warmth and she sat at her easel, looking down her nose at the half-finished canvas in front of her. Even in her studio, every brush, tube and work-in-progress was tidy. Here, among the order that typified *Nonna*, he let out a long breath.

Still focused on her painting, she said, "I wasn't expecting you. According to Gianna, you met Cinderella and took her to a ball."

Gianna and her flapping jaws. She'd probably rented out a billboard at the other end of the village, the same one she'd threatened to post his dating profile on.

"The clock struck midnight," he said and turned to the windows.

"And yet you remain a prince."

He tilted his head over his shoulder to find the deep brown eyes that had saved him so many times. Luca longed to be the young boy who could curl up in her arms while she hugged him close and played with his tiny, most likely dusty, toes.

"I'm not sure about that, *Nonna*."

She squinted at her art, added a final stroke of green then wiped the brush. "Are you insinuating that I'm wrong?" Her barely visible eyebrow arched, not unlike his own would have done, and he couldn't help but smile. The gesture tapped on the door of the tension he'd been holding in for too long.

"I would never."

His *nonna* crossed the room and her knobby knuckles brushed against his high cheekbone. "What have I always told you?"

"That I can make my own happiness. That death is the reason to live."

After a pause and with a gleam in his grandmother's eyes that Luca swore mended his soul, she tapped the cheek she still caressed and said, "Good boy. Now go make me lunch."

There was no need to guess where knives, cutting boards and condiments resided. Luca had modeled his own kitchen after the one in which he stood. His *nonna* sat opposite him at the bar and studied his work, no doubt ready to correct any minor mishap.

She stole a cherry tomato and popped it into her mouth with a grin. "So… What's the other thing?"

Luca set down the knife and wiped his hands on the starched dishtowel. There was no point in lying or skirting around it. *Nonna* knew all. He and Gianna had long contemplated the real chances of her being a witch — a very well organized, shorter than most, witch who'd painted pictures of her backyard every day since he could remember.

"I lost a trusted friend." He wiped a small drop of water from the counter. "And when I came back, I'd lost her too."

"And you're hiding here because everything happens in threes?"

Luca rubbed his facial hair and let his chin rest in his hands. *Yes. Everything happened in threes. Good, bad, indifferent.* And if he could tally up the good and indifferent, maybe one day they would outweigh the bad.

He went back to cooking as *Nonna* set the table in the glass-paned winter garden off the kitchen. They spoke of mindless topics during the meal, but when the coffee was served, they boomeranged back to where they'd begun.

"You're not like Gianna, Luca. Don't confuse her idea of happiness with your own."

Luca stirred the sugar into his small cup. He tapped the spoon three times out of habit and *Nonna* cleared her throat.

"You know," she said and sat back deeper into her wrought-iron chair, "I didn't want children."

Luca stopped mid-sip and blinked.

"I wanted to be a painter, to live a life of freedom. Don't look at me like that." She shot him playful eyes. "It's true."

The last drips of coffee popped back up his throat when Luca coughed to cover his laugh.

"And being the warped artist that I am, I fell madly in love with a winemaker…who *wanted* children. I had to make a sacrifice — keep him for me or share him with someone else."

"Well, thank you, *Nonna*. Without your selflessness, none of us would exist and that makes me feel better. I've known for a long time that I don't want children."

"That's a relief."

Luca turned to his *nonna* and his face dropped. "What's that supposed to mean?"

She waved off his objection. "You would be a hopeless father. You spoil Ilaria rotten. You lack the backbone for discipline."

Before he could object, or even ask if she was joking, *Nonna* stood and cleared their cups.

"Grab your coat. Let's take your walk of shame through the village. There's a stray dog I want to feed."

When they returned with wind-whipped faces, Luca went to light a fire in the living room. *Nonna* joined him, her latest mystery book in hand.

"You know," she said as she settled into her worn leather chair, the same one where Luca had spent so many days cuddled on her lap as she read to him as a child. "According to this book, not having kids is a good thing. The earth is over-populated. Think of it as environmental protection."

His phone dinged from the hall and he shook his head on his way to fetch it. Only his *Nonna* would be the one to encourage him not to have children.

I need to see you.

Chapter Thirty

Claire

Claire's gaze darted to the clock for the third time and she knotted her fingers together as she paced the area between the kitchen and living room in Luca's apartment. Stupid Luca and his stupid training that now made her habitually early.

The mechanism of the front door opening made her hands fall to her side. Luca strode in confidently, stopping a few feet in front of her. His jaw flexed beneath his beard and Claire fought the urge to reach out and stroke the length of it. Stupid Luca, indeed. Had it really only been a little over two weeks since he had spun her in his arms around the dance floor?

"Claire." His voice was strong but measured. His gaze washed over her, his mouth thinning as he zeroed in on her undeniably leaner waistline before returning to look into her eyes.

She held up a hand, certain he would begin lecturing her on eating properly. "Later. We have a lot to talk about, but later." And that would certainly include a discussion about the dark circles rimming his eyes. "There is something much more important I need to show you."

Claire turned to the long dining table where she'd already spread out all the documents, certain he would follow her. "I was reviewing all the papers on Arik Hauser's proposal and it never sat right with me. I knew something was off." She shook her head and picked up the first stack, handing them to Luca. "And then I discovered why... It isn't his. He is running a dummy corporation as a front for someone else."

Her breathing shallowed as the same anger that had consumed her when she'd connected the dots washed over her afresh. The anger that had turned into seething rage with the revelation that so much more than the good name of her bank was at stake. She recognized the moment Luca zeroed in on a familiar name and he looked from the paper to her face.

"This is incredibly unethical, and I not only understand your irritation but also share it. However, what does this have to do with me?" He turned toward her, taking two steps to stand right in front of her, nearly touching. "Why did you reach out to me, *cara*?"

She swallowed, wanting nothing more at that moment than to beg for the fulfillment of all the clandestine promises hiding in the deep brown pools that held her gaze — and so many other parts of her — hostage. She moistened her suddenly parched lips and reached blindly beside her for the second, far more damning stack.

"I'm not irritated, Luca. I am fucking pissed and you will be too." She couldn't help but smirk at the arch of his eyebrow she'd known would follow her epithet. *Later*, she reminded her easily distracted libido. "You have a target on your back. This snake is trying to use a cover and my fucking bank to ruin you. And the asshole almost succeeded, thanks to my apparently gullible partner." She rolled her eyes for good measure. She couldn't resist.

His entire energy shifted the more he read. With each paper he flipped through, another part of his body stiffened. His movements precise and wooden, he laid the stack on the table softly and gripped the back of one of the chairs, his knuckles whitening under the pressure.

"I trusted him."

Her heart ached at the quiet declaration she knew meant so much and she itched to touch him. Luca didn't trust easily. "I know."

A long stream of Italian burst from his lips. She didn't have to ask for a translation. Claire knew they were extremely colorful expletives.

Then he barked out a mirthless laugh. "*She's* involved too. She's in charge of all the dues. I would never have suspected anything was amiss if she hadn't inadvertently alerted me. She has been faithful and honest for so long—or so it seemed."

Claire was at a loss for what to say to comfort the man who had no idea he cradled her heart in his palms.

His tan face paled and turned to her. "How far in the red am I, Claire? I can transfer funds from another account first thing in the morning, but I need to know how bad it is first."

"Not in the red at all. I caught the problem before any negative charges were incurred and transferred enough into the account to more than keep things functional until we straighten this out."

He nodded. "*Si.* Yes. Very good idea. The investments were brilliant, but you will reinvest once this is stable and —"

"I didn't cash out your investments, Luca. They are too new and gaining far too much return to make a decision like that with long-term repercussions for a short-term problem."

His chest heaved as he pushed off the chair and spun on his heel to face her. "You are brilliant and astoundingly clever. You exceeded every expectation I have ever had for you in every area...but even you aren't magic. How did you do this?"

Claire fisted her hands at her sides to stop her disobedient fingers from making trails all over Luca's body. "There is no magic involved. I merely transferred the necessary funds and a little extra for a cushion to cover the bills for Sopra for the next two months to give us time to iron out any wrinkles they created."

He took a single step toward her then another. If he moved a millimeter closer, barely more than a breath, their bodies would be touching. And she cursed him silently for stopping short. "You do not have access to any of my accounts at any other bank. How, *cara*? How did you move my money into this account?"

She held her breath for a moment, hoping he would understand what she was about to say. "It was quite simple. I didn't transfer your money, Luca. I used mine."

His mahogany eyes darkened. One hand gripped the back of her neck and the other landed on her left hip before his mouth descended on hers, greedily devouring her lips. With a groan, she gave in to the pleas of her body and reached up to his shoulders, needing to anchor herself.

Unbidden, silent tears tracked down her cheeks. She was home. For the first time in over a year, she had found her sanctuary...in Luca's arms. Her brain managed to overpower her heart and she broke their kiss, pushing gently against him.

He leaned his forehead against hers and they stayed locked in that position until both their breathing had finally regulated. Claire pulled her head back, an ache in her soul at the confusion spreading across his gorgeous face. "We have to take care of this first, Luca. I need you to get this shit locked down."

He drew his thick eyebrows together, a deep V settling between them. "None of that matters if you are not by my side, *cara*."

She rocked her hips forward, pressing against his. "It does if I need my Dom to have a clear head and handle punishment accordingly when he learns I've broken his rule."

He held her at arm's length. "Are you asking me to be your Dom again, *cara*?"

Fighting the urge to bite her lip, she summoned the extra measure of confidence Luca had awakened in her. She dropped her hands from his shoulders and pulled his from her body, cradling them in her grasp. Silently, she led him to the couch, sitting close enough that their knees bumped. With a deep breath, she launched into the speech she had spent the previous evening preparing—one that was far more difficult to utter than telling him his business was in jeopardy.

"Friday nights were date nights for Liam and me. It was something I clung to after losing him." His fingers tightened around hers. "Every week I would watch a rerun of a BBC show he loved, eat nauseating amounts of Chinese takeout and go to the cemetery to visit him."

"I saw you." The words were little more than a whisper, but they were enough to bring her head up from its previously downcast position. "I wasn't trying to intrude, *cara*. After Bruno died, I was looking for a measure of comfort, and when I couldn't find you at your house, I parked beside the church, hoping for a miracle."

The need to touch him overwhelmed her. She climbed into his lap, running her fingers through the short hairs at the back of his neck. "Bruno died? I had no idea that he..." A lightbulb flickered in her mind. "When?"

He frowned. "Wednesday. I texted you as soon as I had a signal outside the hospital that night."

Claire winced, heat creeping up her neck. "When you didn't show up at the club, I... I wrote you the note and" —she sighed and squeezed her eyes shut—"I blocked your number."

When she finally found the courage to open her lids, the hurt reflected back at her stole every molecule of oxygen from her lungs.

"I thought you trusted me," he whispered.

She held his face between her hands. "I did. I do. I... I was hurt and stupid. The gala... Well, your cousin... Sh-she didn't know, and obviously, you didn't know —"

He hooked a finger beneath her chin, forcing her to meet his intense stare. "Confidence, Claire. Remember your confidence."

In spite of the admission she was about to make, she smiled. The absence of his quiet reassurances and reminders had left a hole in her world. "Gianna spent much of the evening talking about how amazing you are with her daughter and how you will make a wonderful father. And I think she's absolutely right. But that revelation came at the same time as another contradictory one." She straightened her shoulders. "Luca, I want more from you than just having you as a trainer, but I had an accident as a child and I can't have children. I can't be what you need."

A myriad of expressions danced across his face, beginning with shock and ending with warmth. "One thing I expect you to remember from this point on, with the understanding it is a wholly punishable offense to disobey this, is that you are never, ever, under any circumstances allowed to listen to Gianna again." He brushed his lips against hers and smiled. "*Cara*, I want more than to be your trainer. So much more. And, yes, I will bow to every whim of Ilaria's perfect little heart, but simply because I adore my goddaughter does not mean I want a brood of my own. In fact, that is completely the opposite of my true desires."

She buried her face in his neck. "I'm sorry, Luca. I promise I will never keep another secret from you. If I had just been honest—"

"No. *Non*." He shifted her on his lap. "You keep any secrets you want, as long as they don't hurt you, as long as you are not suffering." He tucked a strand of hair behind her ear and smiled. "You are mine, but you are not a robot."

Claire swiped a tear from her eye before it had the chance to fall. "There is one more thing you need to know. Luca, I violated your only hard no." Despite the overwhelming desire to look out of the window or at the kitchen or, really, anywhere other than facing the sexy Italian holding her in his arms, she forced her gaze to meet his. "I'm in love with you."

Before she'd finished speaking the words, Luca flipped her onto her back and settled himself between her legs, nuzzling his face into the column of her neck, his beard tickling the sensitive flesh. "*Grazie, Dio.*" He worked his mouth up to her ear, nipping the lobe. "I adore seeing your pert little ass red, but not for this, *cara*, because I have somehow fallen in love with you too."

She whimpered beneath his touch, wondering how she had lasted so long without it. Completely consumed with Luca and all the delicious sensations from his mouth and hands, the sharp rap on his front door made her jump against him.

He lifted his head long enough to bark out, "Go away." But the rapping continued, heedless of his warning. With a snarl he lifted himself off a giggling Claire. He barely had the door open before Adrian and the pushy asshole who had hit on her repeatedly at the club came charging into the room. Claire stood, adjusting her clothes.

Adrian's knowing gaze swept over her before returning to Luca. "I promise we won't keep you, Luca, but Noah has something you really need to hear."

Chapter Thirty-One

Luca

A snide grin slid across the novice's smug face as he passed by Luca. From the moment Luca had met Noah Paulick, something had been off. After hearing that he'd put a sub's health in danger, Luca had gone back and watched the security footage. Many times.

Too many times. Luca shook his head as he escorted Adrian and Noah into his living room. But from what Luca had be able to see of Noah and the sub's scene, apart from the blatant inexperience of the Dom, there had been no infraction. The sub had never used a safeword and the camera hadn't caught any removal of a condom.

That had left Luca with the option to do nothing, as he'd had no proof. But it didn't translate to Luca wanting the young blond man on his couch, checking out his girlfriend.

Girlfriend. Luca blinked. What the hell had just happened? Had he and Claire 'made up'? Was that what people did? And the realization that he loved Claire back hit him in the chest like a truck.

He smiled over to her and she pointed to herself, wondering if this conversation should include her. One glance at Adrian's face and the fact that he was even in the building he'd vowed never to return to told Luca she should. Bad news— which Luca was sure always came in threes — seemed to be on its way.

Luca sat next to Adrian and tapped his knee. "How are you?" he asked with a tilt of his head.

"Miserable." Adrian rolled his eyes and Bruno frowned from the afterlife. Adrian let out a huge sigh and continued, "But that doesn't matter. Not right now." He shook his head and shivered.

Luca glanced to Claire then back to Adrian.

"So, I have a confession to make before I give you some really bad news." Adrian interlaced his fingers in his lap, pointed his palms to the ceiling and sat up straighter against the leather sofa. "Before the sale of the club was complete, I heard some...rumblings. We subs can be chatty bitches in our little circles." He winced.

Luca worked his jaw in silence, still wondering why Noah was sitting to his left and what had been so important that Adrian had come back to Zurich.

"Well, I was busy with Bruno but I was worried. And, selfishly, I didn't want to come back here and get to the bottom of it. I thought it might jeopardize the sale, and well, I was torn."

It was wrong for Luca to mentally scream for him to get to the point. Fortunately, he had years of practicing patience.

Adrian's light eyes darted to Noah, who cleared his throat. He looked back to Luca and said, "So I didn't want to be here, and honestly couldn't. But I also couldn't let Bruno's club go to shit. So I arranged for Noah, who used to date my sister and I knew had some *tendencies*, to become a member—and my internal eyes."

Bruno's former sub shrugged. "I knew I had to place him as someone you wouldn't like so he could find a way to endear himself to the other side."

"The other side?" Luca asked. Every word Adrian spoke worried Luca and yet made him happy for Bruno. He'd taught his lover well. Making Noah a pain in his ass was a stroke of Adrian's genius, if he'd truly been a spy. And based on his discussion with Claire, he'd never been more sure he'd needed one.

"Gwendelyn." Adrian's fallen face matched the pit in Luca's stomach. "She's been begging Elias to buy her the club for a while, and she was really pissed when she wasn't even mentioned as a potential owner."

Noah pivoted toward Luca. "I'm afraid they've been telling everyone not to pay their dues. She's started rumors you're not really interested in the management and that she's bearing the brunt of the work around here." Noah blinked several times. "Your last trip to Italy only fueled her fire."

Luca exhaled through his mouth and dropped his head back. He'd seen the proof a half hour ago in Claire's paperwork, but hearing about the betrayal out loud added a gunshot to the stab wound.

"I'm so sorry, Luca. I hated keeping this from you, but I had to be sure. Bruno's time was almost up, and I didn't want to raise any red flags to stall the sale," Adrian said with a sympathetic frown.

Trust. It boiled down to trust, a lesson he tried to teach every sub he'd ever met. He could almost laugh at himself for falling victim to giving his to the wrong people.

Except Claire.

Claire, who had tracked Luca's wellbeing on her radar, even when they'd been apart. Luca rolled his shoulders back.

"You are a true friend, Adrian. And this explains everything about you, Mr. Paulick." Luca shot a side-eye to Noah for good measure. "And fortunately for me, Claire is as clever as Bruno's greatest love. She has just presented to me the financial proof."

When he searched her eyes, he found no pride. In fact, he was quite sure there was more concern than anything else — another reason to love her. He could hardly believe he was willing to admit it. But the confession was liberating, even with all the complications surrounding it.

"What now?" Noah asked.

Luca was ready for Adrian and Noah to leave, but there was one piece of the puzzle he needed before seeing them to his door, so he could feed the unacceptably thin frame of his *cara*.

"Is there any reason to believe that Max is in on it?" Luca asked Noah.

Noah scratched his blond head. "I wondered that myself, but as far as I could tell, no. I don't think so."

At least there was that. Luca should probably give Max a raise and promote him to manager, because there had been some truth in Gwendelyn's words. While ensuring a safe haven for the community was a priority for Luca, buying the club had been more of a favor to Bruno than a passion for him. During his time with his *sotto*, he'd not so much as wondered what else went on outside the door of his suite. And without her...it had been worse.

Luca and Adrian hugged tight as they said goodbye, and he promised to lighten up on Noah. After all, he had helped save the club. He walked back over to Claire, who was staring out of the window at the river below. The city's lights reflected off the water, creating a shiny blur as a backdrop.

He wrapped his arms around her and pulled her back into his chest. She leaned in, and supporting someone for the first time in the day allowed him to relax deeper.

"What about us, Luca?" Claire asked in a soft whisper. "What's next for us?"

Luca skimmed her neck with his lips. If she thought he was unclear about his plans for his *cara*, she was mistaken. "First, my little popcorn-eating genius, I feed you."

"Then?" she asked with mischief.

"Then you prove to me you love me."

Claire spun slowly to face him. She uncrossed her arms and brought them around Luca's neck. "I do love you — and I am very ready to prove it."

He arched a brow, more out of instinct than doubt. "What I'm going to ask you to do may not be easy."

"I trust you."

And he didn't want to abuse her trust, especially after the hard lesson of his day, but there was one thing Luca needed from Claire that she might not be able to do, that she may not *want* to do.

"Spend the night with me. Here. In my bed."

Claire rubbed her lips together and he wondered if he'd gone too far, wondered if he was asking the one thing she wouldn't give.

"As you wish."

Their lips met with a gentle kiss and they held it. Luca ran his hands down Claire's ribs and landed on her bony hips, reminding him of his duties before their celebration.

Reluctantly, he broke their embrace and pushed his forehead into hers. "Time to eat. Your diet missed me."

She smirked. "Shall we discuss the bags under your eyes?"

Luca scrunched his nose. *A brat.* He'd fallen in love with a brat disguised as blonde financial superhero.

"I don't think we shall, *cara.*"

They shared a bottle of wine at dinner, offering more proof to Luca that they would be entering his bedroom—a sight previously unseen to anyone but his maid—as Luca and Claire. Master and *sotto* would be back soon enough. Luca already had plans for correcting her eating habits and language.

But for him, he needed to be Luca. He had to be sure that she was there for him, not the man he was when she wore the collar—a collar that would need to be replaced with one far more superior and suitable for the likes of Claire Favre.

She stacked the plates in the dishwasher and he dried the final pot from their pasta. With it secure in the drawer with the other pans and all tasks finished, Luca was finally able to turn his attention to worshiping the woman he loved.

He slid in behind her and pushed his hips into her ass, pinning her between the counter and his hungry body. He slipped his hand into her blouse as she let out a small moan and dropped her head into his shoulder.

"One night only, *cara*." He found her nipple and pinched hard. She whimpered, and he pushed his erection into her ass. "One night, no permission needed to come. But then" — he pinched again — "they're all mine again. Always."

"Fuck…" Her curse was both a plead and an admission.

"Naughty, naughty." He nipped her neck. The urgency building inside tempted him to take her right there in the kitchen. But that contradicted, and was immediately swallowed by, the desire to make sure she knew how much he cherished her.

And not just her body or her brilliant mind. The woman had offered him her heart, the one part of her they had both been sure was off limits.

"You are divine, Claire Favre," he whispered in her ear as he kissed the spot that made her shiver. He lowered his hand to meet hers. Luca grasped it and tugged. He led her out of the kitchen and down the hall.

At the base of his large wooden-framed bed, he stroked her cheek. "Thank you for coming back to me. Thank you for saving the club."

"Thank you for saving me."

The words were barely out of her mouth when he covered her lips. Kissing her had always been the best part of their time together, and now he understood why.

He unbuttoned her blouse and she made fast work of his shirt. The intensity of their kiss grew with every article of clothing left wrinkled on his floor. Luca wrapped an arm around her back and pushed Claire to the bed.

His cock ached for her, but it would have to wait until his mouth had been satisfied. He pecked, sucked and nibbled his way down between her legs. With a gentle push, he spread her thighs apart and took a long lick of her sleek folds. He twirled his tongue around her clit before he kissed and pulled it toward him. In a slow, deliberate rhythm, he repeated his path. As her moans deepened, he added more suction and slid two fingers inside her.

Claire's breath caught, her walls clenched and a blissful scream echoed in his bedroom.

He let her settle and went back to work. This time, he added a finger in the ass he longed for and watched her shake and wiggle under the skill of his quick movements.

She came again, much harder, and he kissed her gently as she recovered.

"So help me, but I do love you," he said, once she'd finally opened her eyes.

The tip of Luca's cock flinched as skin touched skin for the first time. As if sensing his need for permission, she nodded once, and he pushed through into her warm velvet depths. The foreign sensation bathed him in rapture.

Claire stretched her arms overhead and he gripped her wrists as his lazy rock continued. Too soon, but what could have been a lifetime later, the mounting need tore him from the utopia of her eyes. His balls tightened and his cock stretched to its limit as he came.

The release—of so much, perhaps everything—left him longing for more intimacy. At some point, he moved from being on top of her to his back and she cuddled in.

And she stayed. With him.

Chapter Thirty-Two

Claire

"You have been there a million times. You aren't allowed to have a fashion crisis over this anymore."

Claire made a face at the phone sitting on her dresser blasting Julien's voice on speaker. "This time is different. We are more. He's mine as much as I'm his."

"Yes, yes, yes. You are wonderful. He is wonderful. You're just so fucking wonderful together and neither one of you ever think about the poor, lonely, single Julien who so wisely nudged you toward your multiple orgasmic bliss." His mini tirade ended on a huff followed by a string of expletives at Claire's answering laugh.

Her gaze landed on the black, backless dress she'd worn the very first time she'd gone to the club with Luca and she grinned as she pulled it from the closet. "Oh, this will be perfect! And I promise, my pretentious little queen, that I will find you someone worthy of your catty bitchiness soon. It is at the top of my to-do list."

Julien snorted. "I thought Luca was the only thing on your to-do list."

She wiggled her hips as she slid the satiny material over the new white-lace thong she had bought to surprise Luca tonight. "First thing tomorrow." The doorbell rang and fire immediately shot through her, knowing only one person would be here at eight o'clock on a Friday night. "Monday. Make that Monday. Yes, first thing Monday we will start the search for someone I deem good enough for you."

Groaning, Julien bade her farewell and clicked off the line. She stepped into the black shoes lined up beside her bed and raced down the stairs as fast as she dared on the spindly five-inch heels. The complete lack of oxygen when she opened her door had nothing to do with her pace and everything to do with the sexy Italian waiting on the other side, looking more than delicious in a fitted gray turtleneck sweater and black leather coat.

"Good evening, *cara*." His dark gaze swept over her and a smile immediately curled his lips. "You are looking stunning, as always."

The knowledge that this man loved her was still too new to not inspire intense awe. "Good evening, Luca." She stepped to the side, matching his pretense of manners and etiquette. Knowing that so very soon all the polite words would be stripped away when she presented to her Master. "Won't you please come in?"

He hesitated barely more than a moment before crossing the threshold but enough to make her heart ache with understanding. His respect for her didn't end when they stepped out of their roles, when they were simply Luca and Claire. That made her love for him grow.

He arched his eyebrows as he walked slowly between the rooms. She tried to see them through his eyes, comparing his monochromatic world to her eclectic and colorful one. Her nerves suddenly settled and she gripped her hands tightly together in front of her.

"This is…quite different from your office, Cara."

Quite different was an understatement. Her office had been designed for very specific intentions and personality played no factor there. But her home housed every little mismatched and imperfect item she'd collected along the path of her life — the tchotchkes she'd used to hide in a box beneath her bed for her parents never to find, the chipped and cracked cups and saucers, the handmade quilts spread across the back of her couch.

Often each piece had a little story attached that the seller would solicitously share and she'd tuck into the back corners of her mind. When they didn't, she'd craft her own tale of happy homes and loving families.

Luca turned back to where she waited anxiously for rebuke or derision. So few were aware of this side of Claire Favre and none had ever truly understood it. Julien, as precious to her as he was, merely indulged her little idiosyncrasies, the same as Liam had.

Slowly he shook his head as he ambled to her. He gripped her hip firmly and cupped her cheek. "I cannot wait to hear what each piece means to you." He schooled his features into a stern expression. "But first we have something to discuss, my *sotto*."

At the use of her submissive title, she dropped her eyes. "Yes, Sir?"

"No. *Non*. I need you to look at me, *sotto*." When she lifted her gaze, he gave a brief, approving nod. "I believe you took something from my suite, something that you are not allowed to enter the club without wearing."

Her eyes widened, mouth falling slack. "Oh! Yes, Sir. My collar. It's upstairs, I'll—"

Luca held up one hand. "No, *sotto*, no need. That is not the collar you were ever intended to wear anyway. That was my desperate attempt to deny that you were different from everyone else—a stupid and futile move." He winked. "Even Doms make mistakes...although it is quite rare."

A smile tugged at her lips, despite the pang in her chest at his words. Even after she'd known it was the same as every girl's who had come before her, it still meant so much to her and she wanted to put it on.

"Although, even in my misguided attempt at lying to myself, I still managed to add details unique to my *sotto*. Thoughts that had never occurred to me before." He cleared his throat and reached into his pants pocket, pulling out a red box and lifting the lid. "I ordered this the same day as the other, for reasons I wasn't yet ready to admit."

Claire struggled to get a clear picture of the necklace lying on the crushed velvet lining. The thin silver chain held a delicate heart-shaped lock, accented with diamonds that caught every ray of light in her living room. "Cartier makes collars now?"

He smiled as he pulled the jewelry from the box and held it up. "They do when I speak with the designer. Now, *sotto*, remember everything I told you about the training collar? How it was temporary? How it would claim you as mine publicly at the club for your protection and nothing more?"

Her eyes darted from the item to Luca and back again. She nodded vigorously. "Yes, Sir."

"Forget it all." He reached behind her to lock the collar in place. "This is for my *sotto*, my *cara*, my Claire. This is a piece for you to wear every day — work, home or club." He ran his lips along her cheek. "This is a symbol of my commitment to put you first and make all decisions with your best interest in mind. *Cara*, this is a symbol of my love, protection and promise."

She ran her fingers across the cool metal. "I love it." Their lines eternally blurred past the point of caring about allowances, she leaned forward and kissed her Dom. Her Luca. Hers. He belonged to her as much as she belonged to him. She pulled back slightly and smiled. "Are we ready to go play, Sir?"

* * * *

Entering the main floor of the club brought newfound nerves for Claire. No longer did she worry about what she would see, but now she worried about what Luca saw. The membership had waned slightly in the wake of his expulsion of Elias and Gwendelyn. Several subs who had aligned themselves with them had left as well — and a small handful of Doms. Although, he was entrusting more and more of the day-to-day operation to the ever-capable Max, who was flourishing under his newfound power.

But Claire knew the club's success went far beyond financial for Luca. He couldn't care less about the money, but Bruno's memory — as well as honoring the promise he'd made to his dear friend to keep the safe haven running — was of preeminent importance. And for that reason alone, Claire worried.

She tugged on his arm as soon as they'd entered the main floor, while they were still simply Luca and Claire. She pulled him toward a dark corner close to the cloakroom.

Luca grinned down at her, pushing her against the wall and pressing his knee into the apex of her thighs. "My little *sotto* can't wait?"

Claire gasped as he ground against her. She reached for his face seconds before his mouth claimed hers. She moaned against his lips, reveling in the passionate kiss for a moment before pushing him back slightly.

"No." She shook her head. "I mean yes, but no. Luca, are you okay? This is the first time we've been on the second level in two weeks, the first time we've watched any of the playtime." She rubbed herself on the length of his thigh. "The first time we will play."

"*Madre mia.*" He groaned. He left feather-light touches along the length of her spine before finding her ass with a tight grip.

She frowned. "There will be empty places. There will be familiar faces you will no longer see. Are you okay?"

His body stilled and his eyes softened. "My *sotto* is protecting her Dom?"

She smiled, toying with the short hairs on the back of his neck. "Subs can be possessive too, especially when they are in love with their Doms." She pulled him close, whispering against his lips, "And I do love you."

Their mouths joined again, softer than before. When he finally pulled back, he had to clear his throat three times before his Dom affect was securely in place.

"Now, I believe my *sotto* said something about public play."

He gave her a moment to readjust the tight dress before lacing his fingers through hers and leading her toward the stairs. She dropped her eyes as they climbed, intent on not embarrassing Luca by being disrespectful. "Yes, Sir."

"And have you thought about where to start, *sotto*?"

"Yes, Sir. I was thinking the public shower. If you allow."

Luca let loose with a string of colorful expletives and Claire was gratified she'd instructed her newly acquired — and very bewildered — Italian tutor to start by teaching her what the curse words were in her beloved's native tongue.

Gaze still fixed on the lush red carpet, she grinned. "Yes, Sir. I do think it's a 'fucking good idea'."

"Eyes." He barked the single word with a hoarse voice. "You may choose a stall and begin whenever you are ready." He brushed his lips along her jawline up to her ear. "You have ten minutes to tempt every man and several women here, *cara*. Then we will go to my suite, you will explain your sudden knowledge of Italian, then I will paddle that gorgeous ass red for your language."

She smirked, stepping away from his side and reaching up behind her neck to release the top of her dress, walking backward toward the center stall. "As you wish, Sir."

Epilogue

One year later
Claire

"Care!"

A flurry of pale pink streaked toward Claire and the small body launched into Claire's arms, confident she wouldn't falter. Claire held the little girl close, nuzzling her nose against the baby-soft cheek. "Oh, Ilaria, I missed you too, even if it has only been two days."

A loud huff sounded behind her and Claire turned to grin at the pseudo-irritation plastered on Luca's face, his twinkling eyes and twitching lips giving away his true emotions. "I have been so easily replaced."

Claire leaned close to Ilaria's ear. "I think your Cuca is feeling a little sad that you aren't paying attention to him." With a conspiratorial giggle, the little girl leaped from Claire's arms to Luca's waiting grasp, planting a kiss on his bearded cheek. Claire patted his shoulder and dropped her voice to a whisper only the three could hear and only two would understand. "Wouldn't want to damage the fragile ego of a Dom, now would we?"

"Brat," he growled the single word to her retreating back.

The intimate—by Gianna's definition—gathering was already well underway, thanks to Luca's complete lack of control when he'd seen the flimsy white bra and panty set she'd purchased especially for this occasion—and especially to tempt him. She located the other woman easily in the crowd and linked arms with her. "Gianna, this is stunning. Completely unnecessary, but stunning."

She inclined her raven head, kissing Claire three times on her cheeks. "My cousin finally found a woman able to tame him and he actually had the good sense to propose to her. My darling Claire, if this isn't a cause for celebration, I don't know what would be!"

Claire laughed, snagging a glass of Luca's family's prized Barolo wine as the tray passed. She had largely stepped back from planning and allowed Gianna free rein, but she had insisted on one thing—white. Every flower and accent needed to be white. Her eyes roamed from the gardenia centerpieces to the crystals hanging from the ceiling and her heart sighed contentedly. It truly was perfect.

Then her all-too-intuitive gaze zeroed in on the one face in the crowd not celebrating and only sporting fleeting, fake smiles. With Gianna reveling in her hosting duties, Claire slipped away from her side. "Adrian?"

He lifted his anguished eyes from the drink he had been twirling between his fingers. He frowned in an all-too-familiar fashion and pain lanced through Claire's heart. She knew exactly how he felt. "This party is beautiful. I am so happy for you and Luca."

She wrapped him in a firm embrace. Finally pulling back, she held his hand in hers. "It will get better. I promise you, Adrian, that you will find love and happiness again. I never believed it was possible either, but it is."

"I still miss him. It's been a year, but I still miss him like it was yesterday." He drained his glass and made a scoffing sound in the back of his throat. "Trite and cliché as that sounds, it's true."

She tilted her head to one side, regarding him silently for a moment. "Do you trust me?"

He eyed her warily, his gaze roaming from her head to her feet and back again. "I feel like this is a trap, but...yes?"

"Good. Very good. Wait right here." Giving him no choice, she spun on her heel and quickly crossed the room to where the only person who mattered as much to her as Luca stood, regaling a small group with some random tale of a college faux pas.

When he finally paused to allow his public to lavish him with laughter and praise, Claire unceremoniously tugged his arm. "Please excuse Julien. He is needed by the bride-to-be."

"Listen, gorgeous, just because today is all about you doesn't mean your beloved Julien doesn't deserve just a little attention too." He launched into a typical tirade as soon as they had cleared the crowd. "Your so-called search for my perfect man has been fruitless — pun completely intended — and I at least need to get a little adoration from a group of random strangers."

She stopped a few feet shy of where Adrian stood and turned to face Julien. "Do you trust me?"

"That isn't even up for debate."

She cradled his face. "And do you believe I love you and want nothing but the very best for you in every part of your life?"

He gave her a suspicious look, as Adrian had, and she suppressed the giggle that bubbled up. "Yes…although I feel as though I may regret that now."

Claire dropped her hands from his cheeks and she crooked a finger at the frowning blond. "Adrian? Come here." She pretended to ignore the sharp intake of breath from the man beside her. "Adrian, I would like you to meet my very best friend in the world, Julien." She hooked one finger under Julien's slackened jaw, pushing it back into place. "Julien, my darling, this is Adrian. Please enjoy some more of the Barolo, yes?"

With that, she stood as inconspicuously as possible a few feet away, her heart warming as she saw their awkward small talk develop into passionate discussion.

Arms wound around her waist. "Did you do that, *cara*?"

She turned her head, smiling at Luca over her shoulder. "No, my love, you did."

He spun her in his arms, leaning down to press his forehead to hers. "I am very, very good, but I don't believe I understand how *I* did this."

She linked her arms around his neck. "You taught me how to trust. You reminded me I could love. I simply passed along your lessons."

Want to see more like this?
Here's a taster for you to enjoy!

Love Repaired
Deana Birch

Excerpt

I parked the loaner SUV in line next to the other shiny overpriced automobiles, did a final check for personal belongings in the seat next to me — no need to learn the same lesson twice, my cell phone had spent the day in my car — and headed into the office. With the sun set, the cool evening air hit my cheeks and I perked up as I walked. My Cayenne sat in front of the large metal garage doors, a sparkle reflecting its recent wash. At least luxury came with attention to detail.

When I reached the glass door, I tugged it toward me only to find it locked. *Jesus.* I'd even failed at picking up my car. I stood on my tiptoes and rapped my knuckles against the glass. On the other side, the room was dark and the half-circular reception desk was abandoned, a black office chair pushed into its place. But from the hall behind it, a light peeked out — my ray of hope.

I knocked again and pressed my lips together while readjusting my shoulder bag. I shifted my body weight from side to side and banged louder.

Florescent beams flooded the showroom and I blinked. My skin flushed, and my mouth went dry. A legal aide at the firm had once said something about man candy, but I thought that was like a unicorn — not real, a legend in a forest I would never visit. But Man Candy had a warm smile, combed-back dirty blond hair and a build that screamed heaven through a tight, black, untucked work shirt. The last few buttons were open and matching pants hung low on his waist. He was also headed right toward me, tapping a wrench in his hand.

With dimples in his smile, he slipped the tool into his back pocket and unlocked the door. His sea-blue eyes must have been designed for skinny dipping.

"Mrs. Benton, I presume." The low, scratchy voice matched the light stubble on his cheeks. His dimples deepened, and the warm showroom air hit my already-heated body.

"Ms." I couldn't resist the urge to brush against him, and as I did, the perfect blend of motor oil and earthy spice came with me.

Testosterone, how I've missed thee.

I walked over to reception and placed the key fob on the desk.

He followed and squinted down at the neat paper piles next to the flat computer screen and keyboard. He picked up my keys from the tail of the stuffed squirrel that held them and dangled it like a time piece.

"Nice keychain." After a quick arch of his eyebrow, the damn dimples reappeared with his tight-lipped smile.

"Thanks" — I glanced at his chest — "Ben." I took the stuffed animal from his grease-stained hands and slid the other key toward him.

"Did you fill it up?" he asked.

"Uh…no." Add one more failure to my day.

Ben shook his head and grabbed the fob before popping it into a drawer. "No one ever fills it up. You know it costs double, right?" He peered up with one eye closed.

"Well, it was either fill it up or make you wait longer."

"Either way, it's my time. I'll have to do it Monday." He rubbed his face with both hands and a tattoo poked out from the tight sleeve around his bicep. His very full bicep.

I cringed and lifted a shoulder. "Sorry. Anyway, I only drove it to my office and back."

Ben walked out from behind the desk and over to the door. Holding it open for me again, he motioned for me to leave.

I'm too young to suffer hot flashes, right? And I was not dreaming of ways to sabotage my brakes or engine. That would be silly — and a further inconvenience that my schedule would not allow.

"You had a failed fuel pump. It's a pretty common problem. That was what was causing the stalling."

Note to self — Get another failed fuel pump.

When we stood in front of my car, he pulled up on the handle, swung the door open, and I froze. A big white pastry box sat on the passenger seat.

"Fuck me."

"Pardon?" he asked with an airy chuckle.

I brought my hands to my face and pulled them down slowly, probably ruining the effects of the anti-aging cream I'd put on that morning. "Fuck. Fuck. Fuck."

"Are you okay?" Ben leaned in closer.

"I forgot the fucking cupcakes. Fuck me. *Fuck.*" I let my bag fall off my shoulder and dragged my feet over to the steel garage. My back met the cool wall and I slid down to the rough concrete. I stomped my sensible beige heel before slumping into a ball and whimpering into my hands. My entire day, week, month… They had all been colossal fails.

The motor oil and musk were back, now touching my wrist and seated on the ground next to me.

"Shitty day?" He draped his defined forearms over his knees with his fingers interlaced.

"I wish I could say it was the shittiest, but it just seems to be par for the course. *Fuck*." I stomped again.

"You have quite the potty mouth for a lady."

"Did you just call me a lady? Oh my God, now I'm really going to cry." Forgetting Shae's cupcakes was the cherry on top of my botched-Mom sundae. But being one step away from a 'ma'am' was the rainbow sprinkles. Asshole-expensive face cream… It obviously wasn't working. And I wasn't even forty.

"You wanna talk about it? I'm a pretty good listener."

If that were true, then Man Candy truly was a unicorn and I *was* in an enchanted forest. But the words flew out before I could stop them.

"My client lied to me and made me look like a fool in a deposition. I forgot my phone in the car this morning, which means my older daughter has probably called it three hundred times. And because I was behind closed doors with said lying client, I couldn't call her.

"It was my little one's last day at dance camp and I was supposed to bring the cupcakes. Which, as you can see, I did not do. Oh, and their father is in prison for vehicular manslaughter. Sorry you asked?"

He frowned and shook his head. "Where are they now? Your girls?"

"My sister takes care of them so I can keep working."
I wrapped the hem of my skirt around my legs.

"Who takes care of you?" The smile and dimples
were gone, but the warmth stayed in his eyes.

"Me, I guess." I shrugged and tried to recall any
moment my ex, Pete, had ever really taken care of me,
and I drew a blank.

He narrowed his blue eyes. "Is that enough?"

The beautiful stranger next to me had gotten as far
as my walls would let him. Although, I had to admit,
someone being concerned about me might have made
a tiny crack.

"That and the half-bottle of Chardonnay waiting in
the door of my fridge."

"That's depressing," he said, getting up. He offered
me his strong, rough hand and I clasped it. With a
gentle yank, I was on my feet. "You ready for me to add
insult to injury then?" He wet his lips and tilted his
head.

"Oh, God. I don't even care about the bill. Just tell
them to send it to me." I smoothed the front of my skirt
and dusted off my rear.

"It's not that." Ben cleared his throat.

I scanned my car for a scratch or dent.

He continued, "I'm really sorry, but I ate one of the
cupcakes."

I darted my eyes back to him and he hunched as if
waiting to be smacked.

"You eat cupcakes?" I leaned back a little. Whatever
moment sugar had spent on his lips, it was not
spending a lifetime on his hips. *Bastard.*

"It's my cheat day. And those damn things were
next to me in the car all day. Staring at me. Taunting
me. Like, *'Ben, you know you want me.'*" He wiggled his
fingers. "Then you were late, and, well…I made some

kind of weird justification that I could have one. I'm really sorry."

"You ate one of my daughter's pink frosted cupcakes?" I planted my hands on my hips.

Ben nodded with a clenched jaw.

"You're a fucking unicorn." I picked up my bag, tossed it in the back and climbed into the car.

With the seat belt fastened, I reached for the door, but he held on to it stopping me from closing.

He blinked hard. "Did you and your potty mouth just call me a unicorn?"

"We did." I smiled at the mythical man candy creature, shut the door and drove out of the enchanted forest.

* * * *

"Want a cupcake?" I slid the box onto the center island of my spotless kitchen. My older sister, Jude, sat on a barstool at the other end with her ankles crossed and feet dangling over the white granite countertop. She swiped her phone a couple more times and looked up at me with gray-blue eyes that matched my own.

"Epic fail on the mom front today." The grin shifted from smug to sympathetic in a flash.

"Who's more pissed, Carly or Shae?" I opened the box and let my finger dip into the melted pink frosting. *Irresistible.*

Jude set the phone down on the counter and locked her fingers behind her neck. She leaned into the back of the stool and said, "Carly is reading that book again and the ballerina mob boss is tending to Lasagna."

Shae had random names for her many, many — most likely too many — dolls. Lasagna had been christened the night Pete had brought the brown-eyed baby home—the same night we'd told the girls we were getting divorced. 'Lasagna' had initially seemed like a joke, a way for Shae to rebel against her parents splitting up, but the name had stuck. I had to admit, she was my personal favorite doll.

I licked the frosting from my finger and closed the lid. "She wasn't too disappointed?"

Jude yawned and stood, planting her hands on the gleaming counter. "It's fucking weird." She scratched her short hair that was adorable no matter what she did to it. "She practically made a grown man cry for putting the wrong topping on her frozen yogurt yesterday. But when it comes to you, it's almost like she knows how hard you're trying. She told her friends your car broke down and you were waiting for a tow. Did you eat?"

I shook my head as Jude reached for the handle of the fridge. Everything she had said about my baby girl was true. Shae defended me above all else. But that didn't change the fact that I would need to tread lightly with her older sister.

With my hand on the banister, I climbed the stairs. Colorful paper flowers and butterflies plastered Shae's door, a summer project she and Jude had adopted. I pushed it open and my baby girl was busy, as always. Her blonde hair was still in place from ballet, a perfect bun with only the thinnest locks having escaped at the base of her neck. But instead of her tutu, she wore a purple T-shirt, a yellow-and-black bumblebee skirt and red ladybug rain boots.

"Is Lasagna sick again?" I walked over to the bed, sat down on the floor next to her and kicked off my heels.

"She's afraid she's a cannibal. I fed her spaghetti." She cradled the doll and stroked her plastic head.

"Did Jude teach you that word?"

She ignored the question, but the mature vocabulary pulled at something deeper inside me. My six-year old had grown up too fast already and there was no going back.

Initially, Pete and I had been on the same page about exposing the girls to life. There were no nicknames for body parts, and we were honest about current events — no matter how brutal. Pete and I shared our matter-of-fact views on science and religion. But when their daddy had become the news on television by driving drunk and killing another father, I'd wished for drapes and shutters on our glass house of reality.

I'd had no idea how to protect them from the truth and therefore didn't do it. After I'd told them Pete would go to prison, Carly had stared at me like it was my fault — and maybe it was. I had asked for the separation. I had been unhappy. I'd broken up our family. At least our divorce had been final before his accident. But even that seemingly made me selfish somehow.

But it was Pete who'd spiraled into drinking more. His art had never taken off, so he'd busied himself with distractions, the biggest being golf. *Fucking golf.* My free-spirited painter had hung out at the clubhouse and drank with the retired businessmen, pretending he belonged. Wanting to belong. But he couldn't — and he didn't — which made it all the worse. To be fair, he'd never fit in as an artist either. With his Oxford shirts and clean-cut style, he was more in line with what his fellow painters were moving against.

Shae, with her hazel eyes the same shape and color as her daddy's, tucked Lasagna into a toy crib. She gave her a butterfly kiss on her cheek — just as Pete would have done for her and Carly when he'd said good night to them. The months of anger were over and my heart broke for my girls every time they held on to their father's memories and the good times.

A single tear fell down my cheek. I held my arms open for my sweet girl and said, "I'm sorry about your cupcakes."

She climbed into my lap, legs straddled around my waist, and laid her head on my shoulder. Shae rested there for a moment before pulling back and saying, "It's okay. You have more jobs than anyone I know. You're a lawyer, a mommy and a daddy. You're a grandma to all my babies and you're planning the Fall Festival for our school." She wiped a tear away from my face and added, "Don't cry, Mommy. We all make mistakes or forget."

I brought her head to my shoulder again and inhaled that sweet, busy-little-girl scent. "You want me to read to you?" I kissed her head next to the bun.

She popped up and went to her book case. "No, it's okay. Jude said if I can read this whole book, she'll buy me a new baby and I can name her Fortune Feimster." She kicked off her boots, slid into bed and Jude appeared in the doorway. Maybe she'd been there a while. There was no sign of snark in her eyes.

"Carly's waiting." Jude came into the room and sat on the edge of Shae's frilly bed.

With a kiss on Shae's forehead and a battle of who loved who more, I said goodnight to Shae. I snatched my shoes on the way out and went to my own room to change.

In my pajamas, and with the stupid night cream that promised to hide my wrinkles rubbed into my tired face, I headed down the hall. Behind my soon-to-be nine-year-old's door, a single light shone from her bedside table. She continued reading her book as I walked over and lifted the covers. My cold feet found her warm little legs and I nuzzled into one of my favorite spots on earth.

"I'm mad at you," she finally said before tapping my head with her paperback. She frowned, but it lacked conviction.

"I'm trying, Carly. I really am." I plead my case with sincere eyes, but the guilt of never being enough soured inside me.

She shifted onto her side, set the book on the table and turned off the light. Facing the wall, she said, "I want to go and see daddy for my birthday. That's all I want, not even a cake." Her quiet confession tore at what I was sure was my last layer of strength.

I snuggled her tight and moved my fingers to her hair. I twirled and gently tugged, as was our ritual since she had stopped being a bald baby and turned into a toddler with thin, silky locks.

"Whatever you need, bunny."

"I need you to never forget your phone again." She interlaced her sweet fingers into mine and moved our hands under her chin.

"I'm sorry." I was. I truly was.

She nuzzled her cheek into my forearm. "Those words don't help."

Not much did. Jude was right. I was an epic fail.

Home of Erotic Romance

Sign up for our newsletter and find out about all our romance book releases, eBook sales and promotions, sneak peeks and FREE romance books!

About the Authors

Deana Birch

Deana Birch was named after her father's first love, who just so happened not to be her mother. Born and raised in the Midwest, she made stops in Los Angeles and New York before settling in Europe, where she lives with her own blue-eyed Happily Ever After. Her days are spent teaching yoga, playing tennis, ruining her children's French homework, cleaning up dog vomit, writing her next book or reading someone else's.

Amelia Foster

Books, coffee, and chocolate make up both the heart and body mass that is better known as Amelia Foster. She has been a lifelong lover of the written word, both as a reader and an author, and completed her first manuscript at the ripe old age of five, complete with illustrations. Sadly, her art was a medium that never improved over time, although thankfully her writing has.

From sweet to salacious, the only requirement Amelia has in books she reads – and definitely in the ones she crafts – is an excessively satisfying happily ever after… and then a little bit more.

Deana and Amelia love to hear from readers. You can find their contact information, website details and author profile page at https://www.totallybound.com